"Pyles makes it look easy. His characters come instantly alive with the cocksure verve and swagger of rock stars."
—Daniel Knauf, creator of HBO's "Carnivale," Executive Producer/Writer, NBC's "The Blacklist."

"Pyles exhibits an eagerness to explore the darkest corners of his mind and crafts effective tales that will leave you in wonder."
—Kenneth W. Cain, author of Fresh Cut Tales and United States of the Dead

"Nelson W. Pyles' collection is a brilliant exploration of the nature of evil...leaves the reader rooting for the hero and aching for the villain. Most disarming of all, is the sense of what small weight might tip the scale of the reader's own pain and yearning toward the evil lurking beneath."—Chelsea Cefalu, Stunt Poet

"Everything Here is a Nightmare serves up a great collection of pieces from a talented voice in short horror today."
—Jessica McHugh, author of Rabbits in the Garden, The Green Kangaroos and the Darla Decker Series

"Pyles shows off his stylistic range, his trademark humor, his unique and witty voice and of course his disturbing storytelling in this cool as a cucumber collection. This book will keep you hanging on like you're hanging onto that little landing rail on a helicopter."
—Jon Towers, Artist/Writer/Podcaster and Indie Comic Book Icon

"The word "showmanship" sums up the fiction of Nelson W. Pyles quite nicely. While reading Everything Here Is a Nightmare, I forgot that I was reading. At no point did I stop and check how close I'd come to finishing the book; I simply read and got lost in the stories and came away feeling very impressed."
— Lindsey Goddard, author of The Tooth Collector and Other Tales of Terror

"Delightfully disturbing and grotesquely witty, Pyles knows exactly how to hit you right in the feels in one way or another, but rarely in the way you expect. With characters so vivid that you'll swear you've met them and a keen knack for keeping you in suspense —or mortal terror—each of these stories is guaranteed to leave you with that "HOLY SHIT!" kind of feeling somewhere in its twisting, turning, stomach churning course."
—Mae March, Author

"These stories are indeed nightmares of the very best kind. This fun, dark, and wholly enjoyable collection of character driven tales made me lose sleep, not because they are scary as hell, but also because I was terrified to put the book down."
—Daniel Foytik, host of The Wicked Library

Everything Here Is A Nightmare
Collected Works Vol. 1

NELSON W. PYLES

Burning Bulb
PUBLISHING

Everything Here Is A Nightmare: Collected Works Vol 1
By **Nelson W. Pyles**

Burning Bulb Publishing
P.O. Box 4721
Bridgeport, WV 26330-4721
United States of America
www.BurningBulbPublishing.com

Cover designed by Gary Lee Vincent with the following licensed element from Fotolia.com: Lighthouse (#17803934) © AJE44.

First Edition.

Paperback Edition ISBN: 978-0692519981

Printed in the United States of America

For my sister…

CONTENTS

AUTHOR'S INTRODUCTION

Ever since I was a kid, I have imagined the "Author's Introduction" to my collection of short work, even before I had written a single story. This is not bullshit, I'm totally serious. I had ideas for books. Stories, comic books what have you dating back to the third grade (*or, 1979/80 if you want to make me feel really old.*)

When I began to pursue other interests like theatre and music, the unwritten collection of stories and its amazing introduction lay waiting to be brought into existence.

In other words, all I had to do was write it.

Easy, right?

Actually, yes. Very easy. Easier than I ever thought. When I finally decided it was time to actually write and stop *talking about writing*, the stories poured out in a flood. It's been one hell of a journey and to go from just discussing things to actually doing them is fulfilling. I've had most of these stories published and before I even had realized it, I had a pile of stories…enough for a collection of my very own. Enough for a pompous little collection of short work with a grandiose "Author's Introduction!" I mean, hey, I'm even a novelist for crying out loud and now, I have a collection!

Except, for the life of me, I can't seem to write a stupid introduction to my own work.

Odd, right?

Maybe not.

I guess technically, I'm writing the intro now, but it's not really the same.

I spent hours reading short story collections, but not just the stories, but the introductions. The notes from the author(s), the editors of the thing whether it be an anthology of work from different authors, or a collection of a single author, that's what I wanted to read almost as much as the fictional worlds within. I'm a liner notes kind of guy. The Introduction to BOOK OF THE DEAD edited by John Skipp and Craig Spector remains a favorite. The Intro to NIGHTMARES AND DREAMSCAPES from Stephen King is awesome, as are the after notes about the stories. These introductions are what spoke to the latent author in me. They spoke of how the stories came to be, the why they came to be. The promise of what writing is and what it could be. What I could be.

And here I am with my own collection and my own little introduction, but I'm afraid it's not going to be as cool or as groundbreaking as those other intros were for me. Maybe I'm wrong; it's hard to be objective about your own work after all, but I don't think I'm passing along any kind of desperately important information at this point.

Maybe on the second collection…

And there will be another one. No matter how many other novels I churn out, or however many more songs I have left in me to write, or podcasts there might be lurking around in me.

I'll always have stories.

For now and until the next novel or two comes along, these stories have been assembled together for the very first time all together for ease and comfort and hopefully, your enjoyment.

It's not a very long Author's Introduction, but it's all I got I guess for this first time out. I hope you like it and if not, well, there's a ton of short stories inside you might like a lot better.

Oh, by the way, there are little notes about the stories in here at the end of the book, but I'd honestly read the stories first. (It is however my preference, but it's your book now.)

WORKING IT OUT
FOREWORD BY PAUL MICHAEL ANDERSON

Before we properly begin, can we all take a moment and appreciate the title?

Everything Here Is a Nightmare.

Now, we *shouldn't* judge a book by its cover, or a story by its title, but we all know that's an impossibility, right? If it wasn't, marketing wouldn't exist. Editors and writers and ad men spend hours and money, trying to come up with that...*hook*...which will latch into a consumer's eye or ear and direct them towards the product.

The title here just...*gets me.* It's surreal enough to make the consumer go, "What?" without being completely incomprehensible.

(It could also be a cynical indictment of the day-to-day of being an artist, a less-than-positive assessment of what it is to create but, a, that's a little too pretentious and, b, the people who *would* think that way--that the work is always insufferable--are incredibly obnoxious. Anyway. Onward.)

Let's not bury the lead any more than we already have, shall we?

I rejected Nelson W. Pyles twice.

The first time was for *Torn Realities*, a 2012 Lovecraftian anthology I did for Post Mortem Press (and also, consequently, my first gig at editing). The second time was two years later, when I was, for a time, the Editor-in-Chief for *Jamais Vu - The Journal of the Strange Among the Familiar.*

And now I'm writing the foreword to his first collection of short stories.

Funny old world, ain't it?

Now, to be fair, those two rejections were for the same story--"Buzz". The first time was--and Nelson would agree with this--the story wasn't quite...*ready* yet (I'll come back to this in a moment). The second time, the story was ready, but I had limited space.

Tough old world, ain't it?

As I felt around for something to hang my hat on thematically with this little bit of nothing--I need something to *talk about* without sounding like a commercial or rambling--I kept coming back to "Buzz", which is the second story in this collection. I reread it before beginning to write, mostly to see how--and if--it'd changed since the last time I'd read it (we tend to be relentless tinkerers; I talk to a fair number of writers and most of us can't look at something once it's been in print--we see all the things we *would* change or tweak if possible).

"Buzz" is the perfect example for an assessment of Pyles both as a writer and as a person.

Nelson W. Pyles fits the true definition of a literary journeyman.

Let me unpack this a little, with a little backstory.

I first met Pyles at a small Pittsburgh convention--Horror Realm Con, if you care--in...2011, I believe. He'd recently published his story, in this collection, "Where the Apple Shine Won't Reach" with Post Mortem Press. I had also done some work with PMP by this point. We became fast friends over a love of sarcasm and weird fiction (fiction that doesn't necessarily fit into a single genre but tends to bounce around, which would be a little too loose of a definition for the current iteration of "weird fiction"--paging Jeff Vandermeer).

As you'll see throughout this collection, and I noted quickly when first meeting him, Pyles wants to try *everything*. Different forms, different formats, different genres. Different jokes, too.

At this point, Pyles has published one novel--*Demons, Dolls, and Milkshakes*--and enough short stories "to beat a whale to death with," as he once told me. He's also run the successful podcast *The Wicked Library* for five seasons, which included work by such people as Joe R. Lansdale, Craig Spector and *Cemetery Dance* publisher Richard Chizmar--and pinging me for work four times, as well.

In this collection, you'll find Westerns, straight-weird, crime, horror, teleplays, and radio scripts. He takes tropes and inverts them--as in the title story, "Everything Here Is a Nightmare"--or uses the reader's preconceived notions and shakes them up as in "Spiritus Ex Machina".

And "Buzz".

"Buzz" is a Lovecraftian tale, avoiding the pastiche reworkings that tend to dominate the arena whenever the idea of "Lovecraftian" comes up--trust the editor of a Lovecraftian anthology; a lot of people can't see beyond an actual Elder God--that insinuates itself much like the headaches in the protagonists.

And I rejected it. Twice.

(I told you I was going to come back to this.)

A journeyman is also interested in improving one's skill. That comes from taking criticism and just...well, *working it*. Putting the foot-pounds of pressure, to paraphrase Harlan Ellison, and reams of paper to get better.

When Pyles sent me "Buzz" the first time, it wasn't where it needed to be, and told him so. Like a professional, he didn't argue with the criticism, since it was meant sincerely and cruelly (even if it had been, writers--unless, maybe, you're the aforementioned Ellison--arguing with editors never ends well; acolytes take note), and we remained friends.

When I saw "Buzz" again, I was editing the inaugural issue of the ultimately-short-lived *Jamais Vu* magazine. It was where it needed to be, but, when stacked against limited space, it lost out (another unfortunate truth of publishing; sometimes a story's good, but there's just not enough room).

And now it's here, right after "A Box of Candy" (another story I'll, briefly, discuss). Now, is it the *greatest, most electrifying* story ever put to print? I could wash Pyles in meaningless accolades and praise, "Yes! Yes, Lord! *Yes!*", but I can't and Nelson, as a friend who values honesty, wouldn't want. It's a *good* story, a *workable* story. The story a journeyman in the middle of his travels would make. Five years from now, he might look on it with embarrassment of his construction and unfurling of story, but, for now, it's a fine milestone or monument for Where Nelson Is Now.

All these stories are mileposts on Pyles' travels, even the best of them ("Spiritus Ex Machina," "The Fishing Hole," and "Just Enough Rope", in my opinion). Sometimes I almost think that's the point of collections-- more than just pulling together all the separate pieces and offering them in one place, they serve as like photo albums. Showing you where you were at that time.

This collection, even five years from now, shouldn't be a milepost Pyles is embarrassed at five years from now. It shows where he's come, and where he's going. And, hell, at the end of the day, it's entertaining. And that's the whole point, isn't it? Beyond all the lofty ideas and conceits, our job is to entertain.

And Nelson W. Pyles, regardless of format or genre, is very entertaining.

Paul Michael Anderson
June 2015
Northern Virginia

(Oh yeah--"A Box of Candy". I rejected Nelson twice, accepted him once. "A Box of Candy" was that story, when I served as "Creative Consultant" on the Post Mortem Press anthology Fear the Abyss.*)*

A BOX OF CANDY

Frank Ridgeway winced as the ship violently lurched against the crashing waves. He cursed himself for booking a ship across the Atlantic. He had suggested it as a sort of second Honeymoon; a cruise to the Caribbean would be "romantic" he had said to his wife. He cursed himself again for thinking it was a good idea.

He also thought that taking the cruise three months after her death was a good idea too.

He thought about her as he lay sprawled on his cabin bed, always on the verge of throwing up, but never quite able to do it. The storm had been going on for an hour and wasn't getting any better. Sometimes, the lights flickered on and then off. He couldn't even watch the flat screen TV as a distraction because they had opted out of the closed circuit and satellite networking to save money.

"Why get TV on a ship?" Candace had asked, unsmiling. "We'll be having too much *fun*."

He laughed a little, thinking of that conversation when they were booking the trip.

Then, he started to cry.

They'd been married for ten years and although some patches had been rocky (*like the discovery that he would not be able to father any children*) he'd thought it had been a decent marriage. He had watched in growing horror that all of their friends were getting divorced while they just "kept rocking on" as Candace had put it. There wasn't anything wrong in their little world at all.

The three months since her death however had brought the reality a little more into focus.

Candace was a stunningly beautiful woman; honey blonde hair, a very fit figure and ice cold green eyes. She was a confident, brilliant scientist.

Frank was very average in every way; slender, nearly pale in complexion, balding prematurely and slouched a little. Candace had said he was a milquetoast.

And Candace hated him.

Her accidental death at the pharmaceutical research company though had just about killed him too, or so it felt. The details of the accident were sketchy at best and Frank was considering suing the shit out of them, but the life insurance settlement and the additional financial amount given to him by the company had held him off for the time being.

"It was a freak occurrence," Stephan Bosen, the company's CEO had told him. "As safe as we try to make radiation research, sometimes…" And he just waved his hand dismissively as if to say *"You know what I mean."*

Frank still didn't know what he meant.

All Frank knew were that the last things he'd said to her were in anger as were the last things she'd said to him. He'd never argued with her before (*as much as he'd wanted to,*) but she had always liked to yell at him. He had always been hesitant to argue with her and yes, he knew she pretty much walked all over him, but she was still his wife and that needed to count for something.

And *God,* she was angry that morning. She'd mentioned calling her mother in Ohio and that maybe she was going to move out for a little while.

Maybe for a lot longer.

He tried to block that conversation out, which was easy as the ship lurched to the right. He heard something move in his room and then heard a thud. He pried his head off of his pillow and looked in the direction of the noise. His suitcase has fallen over and spilled out some clothes.

And the box of Candace.

He bolted upright and got out of the bed. The room wobbled and he wobbled with it as he made his way to the suitcase. Dropping to his knees, he picked up the box with Candace's ashes and cradled them like a baby.

He sat on his knees and looked at the little cardboard box. Inside was a sealed plastic bag and in the bag was his wife-all that was left of her; a small pile of ash. He choked a little but didn't start crying again. He was thankful for that at least. He was tempted to open the box, but he didn't want to see her like that again. It was bad enough when he had collected the bag in the first place. He had cried until it hurt and the funeral home had to call a cab to take him home.

The ship rocked again, but the sick feeling had stopped when he held the ashes. He stood up and although the boat still wobbled, he wobbled a little less.

The stateroom was small, but had several places to sit other than the bed. He'd been in the room two days already and had only left for dinner. He decided to take the box over to the little desk in the corner and sit down. He carefully walked over; trying not to fall as the ship still tilted, and rested the box near a small clock radio. He pulled out the chair and sat, turning on the little desk lamp.

The radio was off, but he heard a humming sound. The digital number display was flickering. Puzzled, he moved the box away from the radio to see what was wrong with it. He picked it up and held it to his ear.

Nothing.

He looked again at the number display and it read 5:34PM and it was not flickering. Shrugging, he put the radio back in its spot. He figured it was just the power as the ship negotiated its way through the storm.

He reached for the box (*of Candace*) and slid it in front of him. Almost instantly, the radio began to buzz again. He looked at the radio and the display again was flickering, although softer than before. Frank frowned at how odd this was and without thinking, he slid the box slowly closer to the radio. The closer the box got, the louder the buzz was and the more the display flickered.

He slid the box away from the radio slowly and it adjusted itself once again-quiet and non-flickering.

This was odd, Frank thought, but nothing that unusual either. Most things had some sort of electrical discharge. Candace had taught him that early in their relationship. They were at a carnival, years before getting married-when things were good and happy. She had taken the balloon he had bought for her and rubbed it on her head. Frank had laughed.

"Now, check this out," she said gleefully and held the balloon over her head. Frank laughed harder as her thin brown hair rose up from the static electrical charge. "That's pretty damn wicked, right?"

"No one says wicked, Candy."

"I do," she replied, rubbing the balloon on his head. "All the cool scientist chicks are saying it."

She held the balloon up and Frank's longish black hair had stood up as well. She giggled at the look on his face.

"I only know one scientist chick," he said grinning down at her.

"Yeah, but I am the only one you need to know," she replied and kissed him, letting the balloon go.

If a stupid red balloon could do that, Frank rationalized, then why *not* a box of scientist chick ashes? He chuckled and moved the box back and forth from the radio, hearing it buzz on and off as it neared the radio and then away.

After a few minutes of this, he decided he would leave the room for a while and try to get up to the dining deck. It sounded like the storm was backing off at last and he was feeling a little less nauseated and slightly hungry.

He stood up and left the box on the little desk.

"I'll be back, Candy." He said. He slipped his shoes on and left the room.

When he came back an hour later, the first thing he noticed besides that he'd left the light on, was the buzzing. He closed and locked the door. The storm had indeed ended and the Captain assured the passengers that it would be relatively smooth sailing for the rest of the trip there and possibly on the way back. Frank was half resigned on catching a plane ride back though, but he decided to wait until he got there.

He walked over to the desk and the buzz coming from the radio was louder. The display of the time was worse. Not only did it flicker, but it was displaying the incorrect time. It read 9:43AM.

The box, however, was on the far side of the desk.

He sat down and picked up the radio. It was buzzing, louder than before, but the box was further away. He put the radio down and slowly slid the box closer to the radio. The buzz increased in volume and the display began to flicker once again, but this time the numbers changed.

The display was churning out random numbers. Sometimes it would seem to count down slowly and then quickly. But it was moving the numbers around in no discernable pattern.

Frank slid the box away from the radio and it calmed down, but it did not stop. The clock went back to reading 9:43AM.

Frank leaned back in the chair and rested his chin in his left hand. Candace used to call it his "ponder face" and that what he was doing.

Pondering.

He sat like that for a minute and turned the radio on.

There was a screech of electronic noise; static, but somehow worse. It didn't sound like white noise. It sounded almost like a scream and it was nearly deafening. His head began to pound and he shot a hand out to turn the radio off. The scream sound stopped and the buzz returned. He looked at the radio again and saw the volume knob on the side. He turned it all the way down and turned the radio back on again, this time, ready for the sound.

He could still hear the screaming electronic noise, but the volume control lessened it-even though it was all the way down. Slowly, he turned it up to a comfortable level-as comfortable as the screeching sound could be.

He listened carefully to the sound. It really did sound like a scream, but there seemed to be something else behind it.

He looked at the box (*of Candace*) and slid it closer to the radio. As he did so, the scream seemed to change. Not in intensity, but in pitch.

He slid the box right next to the radio. The digital display again jumped to 9:43AM, but the last number kept flickering to the number 4 and then back to 3.

The scream stopped and a voice came out of the radio.

"*Frank?*" the radio asked.

Frank's face went pale and he felt seasick again. His stomach began to swing.

"*Frank, can you hear me?*" the radio asked.

He opened his mouth to speak, but that was absurd. This was not happening. There's no way it could.

"*Frank, its Candy. Can you hear me?*"

Frank's world went black and he slid off of the chair.

When he came to, he found himself half under the desk in the stateroom. His mouth was dry and it felt like he'd eaten a pair of socks. He pushed himself off of the floor. The ship was rocking again, but he felt a little better.

He pulled himself in the chair by the desk and looked.

The box of ashes (Candy) was still next to the radio. The radio display still read 9:43AM and the radio as far as he could tell was still in the on position, but he couldn't hear anything.

Frank sighed and chuckled.

"My wife is a radio," he said aloud. "That's almost funny."

"*I'm not a radio,*" the radio said. "*Frank, I need your help.*"

Frank stared at the radio.

"I don't believe this," he said. "You're dead."

"*I still am.*" The radio with Candace's voice said. "*At least I think I'm dead. I don't really know for sure what I am.*"

Frank began to weep. He was going crazy, he was sure of it. He was talking to the fucking radio now, on a cruise he was taking with a box of his wife.

"I'm talking to myself," Frank said, almost laughing. "Or, I'm talking to the box of ashes with you in it, but it isn't you."

"*Frank, you need to listen,*" Candace's voice returned. "*I know this is hard to accept, but you are hearing my voice and I need your help.*"

Frank looked around the stateroom and as he thought, he was still all alone.

"Where are you?" he asked.

"*I'm not exactly in the room with you,*' his dead wife said. "*You can't see me and I can't see you.*"

"No," Frank said softly and put his head in his hands. "It's not possible."

"*Frank? I don't want to scare you.*"

Frank, still holding his face in his hands laughed.

"I don't know if it's fear or misery, Candy. I really don't." His laugh turned into a sob. "I don't want you to be dead and I don't want to be crazy."

"*I'm dead. And you aren't crazy. You have to help me.*"

Frank considered this for a moment; his dead wife was talking to him through a radio on a cruise ship headed for what was originally a second honeymoon.

"Some second honeymoon, huh?" he said.

Radio Candy laughed.

Frank stood up and walked away from the desk to clear his head a little.

"*Where are you going?*" the voice sounded worried.

"I'm here," he replied. "Just, walking around a little. Trying to let this sink in, you know?"

"*Okay, thought I lost you. I'm so sorry.*"

"Sorry for what?"

"*I don't know,*" Candace said.

"It does put a damper on this trip, but it's not like it's your fault. I was thinking of suing that goddamn company."

"*You won't win*" Candy said. "*It's not their fault. It was mine. I got stupid. Clumsy.*"

Frank looked at the radio and frowned.

"You aren't clumsy or stupid, Candy. You never were."

Candace on the radio sounded like she sighed.

"*I was. More than you know.*"

Frank walked back to the desk and sat down.

"How are you able to talk to me? You're some kind of ghost, right?"

"*Not exactly,*" she said. "*There was an explosion at work. They told you that much I'm sure.*"

"They did,"

"*Well, the explosion didn't just kill me; it irradiated my body in some terrible way near as I can figure. It killed me, but it kept the molecules intact. Alive and aware somehow. Even when I was cremated. It must have been the new isotope generator we had started using. Experimental. My ashes are nearby the radio I guess.*"

Frank looked at the box and put a hand on it.

"You're right next to the radio."

"*I can feel it. That makes sense,*" the voice said. "*Where have you kept the box? I've been hoping you'd put me near something electronic to test my theory.*"

"Theory? You've been a pile of ash for three months."

"*Yes, and I've been just hovering around. It's been awful-hearing you and not being able to say anything. It's like being in hell.*"

Frank was still reeling from this, but it was starting to sink in a little bit more.

"God, I've missed you so much Candy," he said.

"*Then you need to help me Frankie. You have to free me.*"

"Free you how?"

"*I need you to dump the ashes. You need to separate the ashes and scatter me. I think I can move on if you do that,*"

"Is this another theory?" Frank asked. Although he was getting closer to believing what was happening, he wasn't so sure he wanted it to be over; just hearing her voice made him feel better.

"*It is, but if I was right about the radio, I should be right about this,*"

Frank felt his eyes well up again.

"I don't know that I can do that, baby. I really don't know-"

"*I have to tell you something that may make you change your mind,*" she said.

"What?"

"*I didn't accidentally blow myself up.*"

"I know. Those bastards were careless..."

"*No, Frank. I blew myself up.*"

Frank stared at the radio in disbelief. That didn't make sense.

"Honey, that-"

"*I killed myself.*"

"You're lying," he said. "You were happy. We were happy. You didn't kill yourself."

"*You were happy,*" Candace said. "*You were always happy, Frank. I'm sorry to say that, but you have to know.*"

"You're just saying that to make me dump the ashes," Frank said, but he knew when she was lying. He always did and she wasn't lying now. "Why didn't you say anything?"

"*I tried to, but I couldn't. I knew you'd never divorce me. Not without a fight. I just couldn't...face you after our argument.*"

Frank sat there, looking at the clock. He didn't say anything at all, he just looked. The digital display still read 9:43 and flickered to 44 every few seconds.

Candace had wanted out. And she got out, alright. But that number...what the hell was that all about?

"*Frank?*" Candy asked. "*Are you still walking around?*"

"No, I'm here." He said. "Just pondering I guess."

"*Ponder face,*" she said and gave a small laugh.

Frank wasn't getting something. She couldn't face him about not being happy? She was able to face him about nearly everything else and talked about leaving him. He looked at the clock.

"What happened at 9:43AM, Candy?"

"*What?*"

"The radio your voice is coming through? It's a clock radio. It flickers on and off between 9:43 and 44. What's that all about?"

There was a silence and she responded,

"*I don't really know.*"

"The time of death was 10:32AM, so it's not that. What happened at 9:43?"

Again there was silence.

"I don't...really know. That's odd."

Frank laughed.

She was lying.

"You're a box of ash talking to me through a radio and *that's* odd?" He clapped his hands. "Oh Candace, that's wicked."

"Frank, are you going to scatter my ashes? Are you going to let me go?"

"I want to know what happened at 9:43." Frank said.

He stood up from the desk and walked over to the TV. It was a big widescreen television that was mounted on the wall. In all the time he was in the stateroom, turning it on was never an option. He just wanted to cry, mourn and go on. But now...

"I have a theory, Candace." Frank said and pushed the power button on the TV.

"Frank?" Candy said through the radio and then a large burst of static shot out.

The TV screen was a bright blue that began to break up as soon as the static sound blared over the radio.

Behind the loud white noise he could hear Candace calling for him. It sounded like she was at the bottom of a well, but slowly on the TV, the screen began to clear up; not enough to where he could see anything clearly, but he could make out something.

"I can almost see you Candy," Frank said and sat the edge of the bed. "Are you there?"

"What are you doing?" Her voice was very faint, but he could hear her.

"I turned on the TV." He said. "I have a *theory.*"

"Frank, turn off the TV," she said, still sounding distant, but getting closer.

"Let's see. Show me the explosion," Frank said, and almost instantly, he got a grainy looking point of view looking image on the screen. It was Candace's lab. It was scattered with microscopes and gloves and computers that all flashed by like a continuous wild camera shot. Occasionally, Frank could see Candace's hands come into view and she was moving frantically across the lab. The quick blackouts that happened must have been her blinking, he thought.

"I'm seeing what you saw that day," Frank said. "This is amazing,"

"Frank, stop it! Please-you don't want to see this!"

Frank ignored her and kept watching. He watched Candace walk to a power box filled with fuses and switches. She began to flip random switches and then she ran to a large terminal that had a huge warning sticker above a dial. She grabbed the dial and turned it all the way to the right. She spun around and looked at the power box from across the room. There was a moment and then a blinding explosion. Frank jumped back from where he was sitting and gasped.

He had just watched his wife die from her point of view.

He cried as he heard Candace calling to him.

"*Frank, turn the TV off. Oh God, please...turn that off.*"

Frank let out a big sigh.

"Show me what happened at 9:43," he said.

The TV went to static and then cleared again. It was another point of view from Candace but this time she was typing at a computer. It looked like she was typing an email. Candy looked away from the email and at a picture of her and Frank on her desk. Then she looked at something in front of the picture.

It was a pregnancy test. Frank couldn't make out what brand, but he could see the color pink.

Candace again looked back to the email. She hit the 'send' button and the email sent. Candace looked at the bottom corner of the computer screen and saw the time.

9:43AM

And a split second later, it was 9:44.

Frank turned the TV off.

He sat there.

"*Frank?*"

Frank sat and said nothing.

"*I'm so sorry, Frankie. I don't know what to say.*"

"You couldn't tell me?" he asked. "You could tell me every horrible other thing but that? Who was it?"

"*No one you know,*" the radio said.

"Obviously," Frank said and chuckled. "You cheated on me and then you got pregnant and then killed yourself *and* your unborn child."

Silence.

"How could you?" Frank asked.

"*I'm in hell, Frank. Literally. I'm sorry. You'll never know how sorry I am.*"

Frank laughed.

"What was the email? Was it to him?"

"*Yes,*" Candace said simply. "*He didn't want to pay for an abortion and I wasn't about to tell you. I panicked and told him I was going to kill myself. He wrote back, 'fine.' Can you believe that?*"

Frank just sat there, not saying anything. She sounded so cold. As cold as ever in fact.

"I'm going to go take a walk, Candy. I'd ask you along, but I don't think the cord to the radio is that long,"

"*Frank, wait!*"

Frank got up and stormed out of the stateroom.

He walked around the entire length of the ship twice, which took longer than he thought it would take. He thought about what had just happened.

He had spent three months feeling broken and now, he was broken all over again in a different way.

The question now was what to do.

After an hour, he came back into the room. He didn't hear anything on the radio, but when he slammed the door closed, he heard Candace start to cry.

"*Frank? Oh, baby. Are you back?*"

Frank sat at the desk.

"I'm here, Candy."

"*Are you okay?*"

"Is the baby in there with you?" Frank asked. "I know it wasn't really formed yet I guess, but is it?"

"*Yes,*" Candace replied. "*You can't hear her? She screams all the fucking time.*"

Frank remembered the scream when he turned the radio on earlier.

Frank nodded. "I'd always wanted a daughter, you know."

"*I know,*" Candace said, sadly. "*But you wouldn't have wanted someone else's baby, would you? You would have thrown me out and-*"

"Bullshit, Candy. Just bullshit." Frank said. "You should have known me better than that,"

"*I do know you better than that,*" Candace shot back. "*You never would have let me go. You would have wanted counseling or some such thing. Truth is I just wasn't in love you anymore. Sorry, but it's true.*"

"You're sorry." Frank said flatly to no one in particular.

"*Yes I am and I'll never be able to make that up to you. But please. You have to help me! After the explosion, all I have is this baby screaming and nothing else. There's no light, nothing else but her and her damned screaming and I hate it!*"

Frank looked at the radio and cocked his head to one side.

"You hate your own daughter?" He asked. "Candy, that's *your daughter!*"

"*She was an accident!*" Candace nearly screamed and Frank heard, for the first time, the faint sound of a baby. But he also heard something else, in the back of his head.

She really doesn't love you anymore and probably hasn't for a very long time.

Then another thought.

She killed herself and an unborn baby to get away from *you.*

"You really hated me. Didn't you?"

"*Yes!*" She screamed. "*I fucking did and I'm sorry, but I did. For a long time I did. Now, I just want to move on.*"

"Why didn't you just go to your mother's in Ohio?"

"*Just dump my ashes, Frank. Can you just do that one fucking thing for me please?*"

"Candace, I want to know-"Frank started. But Candace, dead or not, still interrupted him.

"*No, we are not picking up from our last fight!*" Candace said. "*Can you just let it go? For the love of God, can't you just let it go?*"

Frank, heartbroken, said nothing.

"*You're pathetic! I figured you'd at least get a little satisfaction out of dumping my ashes into the god damn sea, but you just want to talk and argue. I wanted you to be a man! You never fought back no matter what I threw at you. Do you see why I-*"

He got up and turned off the radio. He grabbed the cord and yanked it out of the wall. He threw the radio hard on the stateroom floor. He picked up the box of ashes, stormed across the room and put it roughly in the suitcase, then put the suitcase in the little closet.

He walked over to the bed and kicked his shoes off. He felt awfully tired and figured he'd try to go to sleep. Tomorrow or the next day (*he couldn't honestly remember*), he'd be in the Caribbean. Frank fell onto the bed, still in his clothes and fell fast asleep.

In the early afternoon two days later, Frank walked off the ship-the SS Celeste from Happytime Cruise Lines-in a pair of shorts, a t-shirt, some flip flops and a back pack. The air was warm and smelled like sunscreen and tourists. The sky was a deep blue and there wasn't a cloud in the sky. He put on his sunglasses and looked for the nearest beach.

He found a bar instead.

After about an hour, he'd managed to have three Pina Coladas. He was directed by a young islander to a small beach about a mile away from the bar. Somewhere there weren't a lot of people was what he'd wanted and after about 45 minutes of walking, he saw the beach the young man had told him about.

It was perfect.

He walked on the sand about half way to the shore line and took his back pack off. He opened it up and pulled out a very small blue kid's shovel.

Then he pulled out Candace's box of ashes and dropped the back pack.

He dropped to his knees and began to dig a hole. Not a very deep hole, but one just deep enough.

Frank had been tempted to bring a small portable radio so he could hear Candy scream and yell, but he'd decided he'd had enough. He picked up the box and rested it in the hole-it was about two feet deep.

"Bye, Candy." was all he said and covered up the hole. Somewhere in his head, he could almost hear her yelling at him.

He stood up and looked at the small grave. Bending down to grab his bag, Frank stuffed the small blue shovel inside. He turned and walked away. Maybe he'd go back to the bar. The drinks were great and inexpensive.

He thought about Candace one more time and hoped that someone with a radio didn't lay their blanket anywhere near the box.

BUZZ

1

On the day he got the news of his mother's death, Cale got all of his crying done within the first hour. Then, he was fine. At least as fine as he was going to get, he thought. He had never been much of a crier. What would be difficult would be the trip to the lousy coastal town of Ogunquit, Maine where he had lived as a boy. He figured he'd be okay if he managed to get there and get back in a quick 24 to 48 hour period. He would find a small bed and breakfast, to avoid sleeping in the old house and he'd be fine. It was off season after all, and it should be no problem to find decent and cheap lodging.

Of course, he knew better. He headed straight to the house where his two older sisters were waiting for him. It was almost fate, but mostly just pathetic, Cale thought.

By the third hour in the old house, the headaches that had plagued him in his younger days returned. He tried to spend as much time outside of the house as he could, even staying longer than necessary at the funeral home but it really didn't make a difference. The house, which was over two hundred years old (*and not even the oldest house on the coastline*), had always been a source of all things bad for him from the time he was a kid.

It was a huge house, nearly a mansion according to his father, who had committed suicide from the ledge of the top floor balcony when he was only seven years old. He had found the very simple note near the open window in his parent's room and no one had ever figured out what it meant. "It's the only way to let it out," it said, with a brief apology.

That's when the headaches started. They were awful, wicked things that seemed to be constant; backing off only enough to allow him to go to school it seemed. It caused insomnia and a very lousy disposition. His doctors said it was the stress of having a suicidal parent and that he should seek treatment. His mother of course, simply thought it was Cale's way of acting out, so she gave him children's aspirin and later, when he was older, just regular aspirin. He just did the best he could and somehow managed to get through it.

It wasn't until he had left for college that the worst of the headaches all but vanished. At home, he was manic, and downright miserable, but when he left for college, it changed his persona. He was pleasant almost to a fault.

On his first return home during winter break however, the headaches returned with a vengeance. By the time he came home for spring break, he had decided that the house was just too painful to keep returning to, so he stopped. If he went back home, he stayed away from the house at a friend's house, much to the mild chagrin of his family. He was doing so well though, and the memory of how much pain he was in was still so clear, that no one except his mother really blamed him.

He was a different person. He was happier than he had ever been, but halfway through his final year of school, he had been arrested with some friends who had propensities for stolen goods and even though he had nothing to do with it, the New Jersey legal system didn't seem to care. This solitary incident sadly ruined his future potential as a law student and he was kicked out of school.

After a six month house arrest stint, he was free to go about his business and try to carve out some sort of life. It would prove to be hard and he wound up getting a very menial job driving a school bus, making a mere pittance of what he could have been making. He felt ashamed and depressed for quite some time. Eventually though, he'd learned to like the job. He had a small apartment above a pizza shop and although it was murder in summer, the winters were spent being nice and warm. Slowly but surely, he was finding a place for himself. He was still young and the world was open to him in a way he couldn't describe.

And finally, he didn't have those rotten headaches.

Then, his mother had died. She had refused to speak to him, long before the arrest and that made Cale sadder than he would have been, but the dread of the possible return of the headaches made him nervous.

He lasted two days and had to return back to his life in Piscataway, New Jersey. The headache had developed and stayed with him from the moment he set foot in the old house. It refused to leave and he had hoped the trip back would allow it to run its course and be gone. Not only did it stay with him, there was a new feature to the pain.

The buzz.

At first, the buzzing came in small bursts. It increased a tiny bit in bits and pieces throughout the day at first and just felt like one more thing. After two weeks, the buzzing had gotten worse. He tried taking over the counter migraine pills, which only kept him awake. After the first month, the buzzing in his head never seemed to quit. Sometimes, it got softer, but now, it was always there, as if he'd swallowed an electric razor and it somehow stayed on; buzzing constantly and sharply. This was very unlike the million or so headaches he'd had since he was a kid. But now, it followed him, worse than ever.

Late at night, alone in his apartment, he began to hear something inside of the buzz. He wasn't really sure what at first, but there was something making a sound almost underneath the buzz. This began the first week of the second month. By the end of the second week, he clearly heard a single word. Not a word he understood; it sounded like another language, but not any language he'd ever heard before. The word sounded terrible; and somehow *impossible*. A word that sounded like no word ever uttered anywhere and any attempt to actually spell it would be futile.

The word began to turn into two words, and then four until a collection of words formed into some bastard sentence. The words were unnerving on their own, but now a small collection of them made a phrase or something more terrifying. He looked this condition up on the internet and began to think he might be losing his mind.

Cale made an appointment with a psychiatrist through the halfway house that got him his job. He met the man, a Doctor Simkins and spent some time being tested, poked, prodded and questioned. The nice doctor had no easy answers for Cale and told him this as well. There wasn't anything other than mild depression over his mother's passing that appeared to be really wrong with him. There was a small bit of anger at his mother and to some degree, his father as well, which was normal. All perfectly normal. "Frankly," the doctor had said with a slight smile, "There'd be something wrong with you if you *were* totally okay with both of your parents."

The doctor gave Cale his cell number and advised him to call if he needed anything at all; even if he just wanted to talk.

Cale never called the doctor again.

As Cale was getting somewhat used to the buzz that was now melted into the constant headaches, the buzz expanded again. No longer stuck with one phrase of gibberish words, now the buzz had more words and more phrases.

And different voices.

The voices came one at a time at first. After the last week of the second month, all of the voices were speaking at once; in the buzz, below the buzz, above the buzz and the pain was excruciating.

In an act of desperation, he'd bought an MP3 player and tried keeping his headphones on as much as possible, even while working. He spent the better part of an afternoon loading the device with as much music as he could find. He downloaded his favorite CDs and newer music that he found online. The device held a large amount of music and had a long battery life.

The buzz didn't go away while listening to his music, but it did seem to slightly lessen the pain. He hated it when someone needed to talk to him, because he'd have to pull one of the earphones out to hear and even that was a crap shoot, because it was still hard to hear with the buzz *and* whatever he was listening to on the MP3 player. It was becoming more of a struggle to get through the days.

The third month since his mother's funeral brought minor change; the headaches and the buzz became softer, but the strange things the buzz was saying got louder and clearer. Sometimes, it would be a single word said over and over again. Other times, it was like some poem or chant still in that language that wasn't really a language. Although the pain had mercifully decreased, the words became somehow *worse* than the buzz. At least he could *try* to ignore the words in the buzz, but now it seemed like something was trying to tell him something.

Something dark.

With the lessening of the pain, sleep came a little easier until the nightmares started. They were vague dreams about his late father on the day of his suicide. Poor August Boone standing in the house in Ogonquit and Cale being a little boy. His father would always be standing at the window ready to jump and holding out his hand to young Cale. Cale doesn't reach for the hand and watches his father throw himself out of the window. Cale had not actually been in the room when his father killed himself but this was the clearest part of the dream. He had the dreadful feeling that he should have *tried* to take his father's hand to save him. As the dream kept occurring, small changes would happen and Cale was able to actually reach for his father. Little Cale moved closer and closer to his father's hand. At one point, he was able to clearly see his father's face. This was the part that terrified him the most about the dream, because his father didn't look sad, or scared as he had thought. His father's expression was one of angry determination an,d the closer Cale got to his father's hand the more he realized that he isn't reaching out to his son so he can be saved.

He was reaching out to pull Cale out of the window along *with* him. Cale had woken up screaming and the pitch nearly matched the buzz in his head.

During the fourth and final month, he could no longer listen to his MP3 player at work. He had gotten two reprimands and he was told if he got a third, he'd lose his job. Cale was reminded that he was in fact, lucky to have a job in the first place and although he'd been a great employee up until now, there'd be no problem in replacing him. He smiled weakly, nodded and went back to work, near tears.

The voices were getting louder.

Desperate, he tried a series of experiments in his room, late at night. Once he tried yelling at the voice inside of his head; a sort of inner monologue argument.

"Shut up!!" he screamed in his loudest inner scream, but the voice just powered through it, ignoring him in a way he could not ignore *it*. On another night, he tried singing in his head; to get a song stuck in there and block out all other thoughts. It was hard, but he managed to get "Happy Together" by the Turtles running at full tilt in his mind to no avail.

The last experiment was to recite all of the things the voice in his head was saying at the same time. He knew all of the things the voice would say and *when* at this point. There were at least five different configurations, like songs or prayers that rattled on in his head at this point and he had been forced to recognize them and to know them all by heart.

So when he thought along with the words in his head, like some bastard inner sing along, the pressure that always seemed to make him feel that his head would explode began to lessen. The voice itself, so often retaining most if not all of the buzz it originally had, began to sweeten, as if a gentle woman were speaking those words.

After an hour, he began to speak the words aloud.

He had no idea what it meant and he didn't care. Four months of sheer agony were gone. The words still sounded unreal, but hearing them outside of his head brought on a different set of feelings.

Elation.

Peace.

Comfort.

His eyes were closed and his head was thrown back. He stopped speaking, and the voice in his head stopped. His body throbbed as if he'd just woken up for the very first time. He opened his eyes and looked around the room. Everything looked new and alive.

It was four o'clock in the morning. He stood up and walked around his apartment. The air felt humid and electric-like a thunderstorm had just passed though. He was awake and refreshed. He felt like he hadn't felt in months. He took a deep breath and could swear-although impossible, but he could almost smell the sea air of his boyhood home. Cale decided to make himself breakfast and wait to go into work in lieu of trying to sleep.

Cale smiled.

2

By the time the fire department had put the fire out later that morning, the school bus looked like a huge, scorched bumble bee. The fire had been so intense that the tires had melted onto the rocks and dirt. Most of the bodies that had been pulled out were in no better condition.

Some of the witnesses who had seen the bus drive over the embankment said it hadn't seemed to slow down. Like it was actually trying to break the guardrail and go over the side intentionally. Others, who had caught a glimpse inside of the bus, said the children were screaming, but the bus driver was smiling.

The bus and all of its occupants were burned beyond recognition. The only things that had made it through was a six year old girl's lunchbox, which had a half-eaten apple and what was left of a small post it note that said "Mommy Loves You!" that was only slightly charred on the edges. The other item had been the on board video camera which had, for the most part, remained intact. When it was recovered and watched, it was astounding. The bus driver got onto the bus, smiling broadly. He picked up the children and cheerfully talked to them. The children seemed to not regard him much at all, as they often had in the past.

On the tape, the bus driver pulls over and stands, facing the children with his arms spread. He begins to speak to them as a group for almost a full minute. He then sits back down and launches the bus back onto the road. Because the camera is mounted in the very front of the bus, you can't see his face until he turns around, and without sound, what he said to the children is lost. However, when he sits back down to resume driving the bus, the children are all holding their ears and screaming. The looks on their faces are that of sheer terror. The bus driver talks the rest of the time through a large smile. Several attempts have been made to decipher what he is saying, but it seems to be for the most part, gibberish. As if the bus driver had made up his own language. The tape goes on for about five full minutes before the bus hits the guardrail.

Although the driver's words can't be deciphered, some of the children's words can be. Mostly, the words include cries for the driver to stop the bus, and that they wanted their mommy or daddy or both.

In the final seconds of the video, the children bounce and jerk as the bus hits the guardrail and topples down the embankment some seventy feet below. When the bus finally hits the ground below, the video ends, mercifully. The look on the bus driver's face remains the same until the tape abruptly stops.

Nothing in the bus driver's toxicology reports indicated that he was anything but a relatively normal 22 year old man named Cale Dalton Boone with a few relatives out of state and even fewer friends. The police *did* find a note scrawled on a wall in a black marker that read simply, "There's another way to let it out." The family refused to comment on this as the man's father had committed suicide nearly two decades ago. News interviews with his neighbors revealed that he seemed to be suffering from headaches that had begun to plague him for the past few months.

One even made mention that he hadn't seemed the same since his mother died.

In a case that was already odd to begin with, the oddest and only other piece of evidence is the MP3 player that the bus driver listened to almost constantly. After downloading its contents, the lead detective put on a pair of headphones and listened to what was on the player.

What he heard was a buzzing sound played over and over again as if in a loop. The buzz at first seemed to just be noise, but after a while, it seemed to be forming words, but not words he'd ever heard. He thought some of the words sounded like another language, but it was hard really to make out anything through the constant buzzing. The detective found himself listening to the file for over fifteen minutes straight before pulling the headphones out of his ears.

He rubbed his temples and reached into his coat pocket. He pulled out a small bottle of aspirin.

He felt a wicked headache was coming.

DECORATIONS

Riley walked out of her kitchen and into the living room. There was a small tree with lights and tinsel. No ornaments-she hated them in spite of the urgings of her boyfriend to at least have a star on the top.

"It'll just look better, baby." He said that every year. Of course, what he usually said was much worse. Things that were terrible and demeaning. The worst thing he said, next to "You know I love you," was the bigger lie.

"I won't hit you anymore."

That hurt worse than the actual hitting, because she knew it wasn't true. Of *course* she'd get hit again. Worse than the last time. It was always the case. But she never, *ever* bent on the tree. It was the one thing that was hers and hers alone. Once a year she decorated it as she saw fit-lights and tinsel. Period.

But this year *would* be different.

She was wearing an apron and thick black rubber gloves. The floor around the Christmas tree was lined with plastic.

It had been six years since she first met Parker. He was handsome and funny. And, oh *Christ*, he was charming. She had never gone to bed with someone after knowing them only a few hours, but Parker was different. There was a connection-an almost instant attraction that she'd never had before and she knew, he was *it* for her.

Four months in, he had hit her for the first time. Not a slap, but a punch, right in the stomach. She crumpled instantly-she was a very petite girl and Parker was over six foot three. He had played football in college *(a lie, she later discovered)* and had kept his physique. Riley had spilled a glass of wine on his white canvas hi top sneakers and he had gone through the roof.

"Oh Jesus, I'm sorry," she had said as the rich merlot covered his left shoe. Parker's face distorted into a knot of fury and he punched her as she stood up to get a rag to start the cleanup.

"Sorry," he said sarcastically. "There, does *that* make it all better? Look at my fucking *shoe!*"

From that moment on, she told herself that it was a fluke-they *had* been drinking and well, she *needed* to be careful. Every punch since then, she had gone down the list of excuses for him because as much as she feared him, she loved him. She was still attracted to him. Still wanted him. He was the one and only after all.

And then, when enough had been enough, she realized she didn't love him. She hated herself for staying and had told him she was leaving. When she woke up in the hospital a week later and opted to not press charges, she began to formulate her plan.

She had seen him cry after that one.

"Oh baby," he sobbed. "Never *ever* again. You'll see. I love you so much. I don't know why I do it…"

She lay in bed looking at him and found she kind of liked watching him cry. She knew it was the same old lines. The same old bullshit. She knew what she had to do, but needed to wait for a sign, and then, right after Thanksgiving, she knew.

The tree went up the day after. The smell of turkey and baked pie still hung in the air like a cloud. It was eight thirty in the morning when Parker came down stairs and saw the tree as Riley threw on the last bit of tinsel.

"Another boring ass tree huh?" He asked. "Just try a fucking ball or a star. It'll just look better." And then he slumped off into the kitchen. Riley just smiled.

As the month went on, Riley acted exactly how she was expected to act. She was doting, overtly affectionate and worst of all, compliant. It nearly made her nauseous, but she held it together.

And suddenly, it was Christmas Eve. They had blown off all invitations for a surprise Riley said she had for Parker. She'd been working on it all day, so she told him he should go out for a few hours. She smiled at him and he left without a word. She went to work as soon as the car pulled away.

Hours later, Riley turned the tree lights on and waited patiently for Parker to come home. Hopefully, he'd be home before Midnight, and he did not disappoint.

She heard the car door slam and she sprang to life. Darting into the kitchen, she hid behind the door that lead to the basement. Most of the lights were off, and the only lights in the front of the house were the tree lights. She smiled.

The door was flung open and quickly slammed behind him.

"Fuckin' cold," muttered Parker. He was drunk. *Perfect.*

"In here, babe." Riley cooed and coiled herself.

"Got anything to drink?" He asked as he lumbered toward the kitchen. He walked in and turned on the lights. He had a full three seconds to register that everything was covered in plastic-the stove, the counters, the floor-even the little swinging tail cat clock. He was about to speak, when Riley sprung from the basement door and caught Parker behind his right ear with a swing from a pipe wrench. He fell sideways and landed hard on the floor. She looked and saw no blood. He was out. She put the wrench on the plastic covered counter and got to work.

As Parker came around, he experienced several things at once. The first thing he noticed was that his head hurt very badly of course. The next was that "Holly Jolly Christmas" was skipping on the CD player that ran through several speakers all though the house. It was stuck on the "*Somebody waits for you, kiss her once for me*" line of the song, except it was only saying "*Somebody waits for you, kiss…*" over and over.

Then the pain from his hands came next. And, oh *Christ*, his legs. He was still on his back from the fall. He'd have to think about quitting drinking he thought as he tried to stand. He couldn't move. He opened his eyes and looked around. He was still on the floor of the kitchen and the lights were really bright.

"Babe," he croaked, "Baby, I fell. I don't feel…" He turned his head and started to vomit. He opened his eyes and blinked after he'd finished and saw the cabinet under the sink. It had red lines running down both doors.

"What's that?" Riley called from the other room? She padded brightly to the doorway to the kitchen. He moved his head up and saw her there in her apron and rubber gloves. She was holding something wet.

"I think I fell…and I just yacked." He said.

"You did yack and you didn't fall. Just relax for a minute. Kay?" And she went back to whatever it was she was doing.

Parker started getting angry despite the pain. He was going to yell, but he was sweating. He reached up to rub his forehead and saw that there was a thick rubber tube like they have in hospitals tied around his elbow. The rest of his arm was missing. His eyes went wide. He lifted his other arm and saw a similar scene.

"What the…" he started to say and threw up again. He spat and tried to sit up using his legs. He looked down and saw that the same thing had happened to his legs. The world swirled for a moment and began to turn black. His head dropped to the floor.

Somebody waits for you, kiss…

When he came to again, he saw he was in the living room. That made him feel better for about three, maybe four seconds. Then he heard the CD was still skipping in the same spot.

Somebody waits…

"Merry Christmas, Parker." He heard Riley say, pleasantly. "I'm almost done with the tree. Do you like it?"

for you, kiss…

Parker couldn't speak. He turned his head and saw it for the first time. She had put ornaments on the tree.

Somebody waits…

There were eight of his fingers with hooks through them, hanging off of the branches. His two hands hung there as well, and had retained the thumbs. The branches strained, but held. His hands reminded him of the Fonz for some reason.

…for you…

Ten toes were also sporting their places on the tree, although the pinky toes were hard to see. He began to cry. His arms and legs had been cut into chops and hung with wire instead of hooks. The branches were bent nearly down, but the chunks of flesh were cut thin, so the branches held. His feet were nowhere to be seen.

…kiss…

Parker tried to scream, but couldn't. He couldn't do anything but look at the tree and sob. He turned his head and saw Riley. She was smiling and holding an ax.

"You always said it would look better and you were right." She said. She moved next to him and sized up the ax to his neck. He looked straight up.

Somebody waits for you

"Too bad you won't get to see the tree topper," she said, genuinely sounding sad by the prospect. "Merry Christmas."

She swung as hard as she could and the ax found its mark. The last thing Parker registered and heard before it all went silent was the CD finally catching and finishing the line.

…kiss her once for me.

FISHING HOLE

Jeb cast his line out across the lake in the early morning mist. The sun had just begun to peek through the mountains and caught the yellow and red bobber as the line arced in the air. It was a good cast and the bait, bobber and hook landed with a gentle splash about five feet from the large, dead tree half submerged in the water. After a moment, the bobber settled and floated gently on the water. Pleased, Jeb sat down on his tackle box and planted the fishing rod on an angle into the soft, wet dirt of the shore.

It was a beautiful morning and Jeb was alone. He was a little surprised since it was mid-July on a Saturday. The sixth grade loomed in the distance and wasn't only a passing concern this morning. He enjoyed the silence and the solitude. Silence by a fishing hole, his Daddy had told him, wasn't really silent. "You'll never hear things more alive and busy than a Saturday morning at your favorite fishing spot," he'd said once. Of course, he'd said this during the opening day of fishing last year, when the shoreline had been crawling with Dads and their kids, all jockeying for a good spot to throw their lines.

But today, it was just him, and that suited him just fine.

He took a deep breath, anticipating a bit of a wait for any fish to take a swipe at his bait, when he saw the bobber dip. Then, dip again. He went to grab the pole, but hesitated. He didn't want to spook whatever was sniffing around his hook. In near perfect synchronicity, the bobber dove under the water and Jeb grabbed his pole, pulling a decent chunk of the dirt with it. He felt the line being pulled forward, set his feet and pulled back on the pole.

Got him!

He started to reel in what he had caught and was surprised at just how much of a fight he was getting. He reeled, pulled and repeated. This thing felt big. His heart raced and he smiled. He wished his Daddy could see this and this thought darkened his brow slightly. Daddy had been dead only a year now, and fishing was the one simple thing they both loved. It felt odd sometimes fishing without him, but sometimes it felt like it brought him closer to him too somehow. Still it wasn't the same, and it made Jeb sad.

Jeb's Daddy was a long haul trucker. He'd be out on the road sometimes six days a week, sometimes longer, but when he would be done, the first thing he'd do is kiss his Mom for a good long time, pick Jeb up and say, "Grab them poles, boy! Let's go catch us some grub!" And Jeb would run to the shed and grab all the fishing gear and throw it into the back of the battered old green pickup. Jeb and his Daddy would fish for a few hours, sometimes not catching anything at all, but enjoying every single minute of it.

Jeb would fill Daddy in on school, what he'd been doing to help Mom during the week and Daddy would tell Jeb about all the cool stuff he saw on the road.

Like tornadoes.

"You really saw one?" Jeb had asked, the last time he fished with his father. His eyes were as big as saucers.

"Yes sir, I sure did." His Daddy said. "Spookiest thing I ever seen, too. I was on one of them long stretches of highway right smack in the middle of Kansas. 'Course, pretty much any highway in Kansas might as well be smack in the middle. Anyways, all you can see for miles and miles is corn stalks, just like in them postcards I sent last month."

Jeb's Daddy would send him a postcard from wherever he gassed up. He told him he could make a map one day of all the places in the country he'd been.

"So, the sun's just a beatin' down like it does and way off in the distance I seen it. This big son of a you-know-what black cloud just getting bigger and bigger. I'm just thinkin' to myself that it's just a storm with some rain, which woulda been nice seeing as how the sun beats on a man even if he's in a truck."

Jeb listened carefully to every word. His Daddy was one good storyteller.

"Well, in about ten minutes I see the sky turn green. I mean from a really pretty deep blue like your Mom's eyes to an angry dark green. I heard of this before, like when we was watching that show on tornadoes a few months back? So, I get a little spooked and slow down a hair. Then, all of a sudden I seen it start to hail. It's slamming all over the truck like I owed it money or some such thing. And then, I saw *it*!"

Jeb was nearly holding his breath.

"They used to call them things "Fingers of God" 'cause it really did look just like the Big Guy, sticking His almighty finger right into the ground. It was huge, even though it was a few miles away. It was just tearing' through this corn field. All you could see was dust filling this thing up and somehow makin' it bigger. Like it was eating everything that it happened to run over. I stopped the truck, 'cause I wasn't gonna get any closer to this thing than I had to. I reckoned I'd be okay as long as me and that tornado didn't get closer to each other. It kept rolling along and I swear it sounded like a freight train. I seen it come up on this old looking corn silo and it just picked it up and threw it."

His Daddy looked at him and smiled.

"It was pretty spooky, son."

"I can't believe *you* were scared, Daddy." Jeb had said when he was able to breathe again. "You ain't scared of nothing."

His Daddy chuckled a little and put his arm around his son.

"Well Jebediah, I reckon there are only about three things that spook me in this here world. Makin' your Momma mad is one. Not getting home to fish with my boy is the other. And nowadays, tornadoes." He looked his son in the eye. "But I don't know that I'm scared of some wind-finger."

Jeb laughed and hugged his Daddy's torso.

"You just remember one thing, son. Your Mom and your Daddy love you more than anything in this world and the next. You remember that, and you won't be scared of nothing either."

"Why's that?"

"'Cause your Mom and you love *me* and there *a*in't nothing can touch you if you got that."

They pulled in their lines and went home to get some dinner.

Two weeks later, Jeb's Daddy would be killed on the same stretch of highway by an oil truck thrown by a tornado. The crash was so bad, that his remains had been sent to the funeral home in a parcel envelope.

Between the money they got from the trucking company, the oil company and his Daddy's life insurance, Jeb and his Mom were pretty well off. All Jeb had to worry about was going into the sixth grade.

And a life without his best big buddy.

He thought about this the whole time he was reeling in this monster on the other end of his fishing pole and the excitement of it pushed his sadness out of his mind. His arms were starting to ache and it was getting harder to pull on it. He hesitated for a minute, remembering what his Daddy said about difficult fish.

"If he's fightin' you good, let a little line out and let him run a piece. Count to five and start again, hard, but not too hard to snap your line."

He pushed the release on his reel and counted to five. It was a long five count and he heard the line scream as that sucker took off. He spoke the word "Five," and pulled back on the pole and started to reel again. He was making headway again. Still fighting, but he felt renewed strength and he even smiled.

Reel, pull, and repeat. He saw the yellow and red bobber through the water at last as it came closer to the shore. He steadied himself and stood up. Jeb couldn't wait to see what he had caught.

As the bobber came closer, Jeb saw something dark and large in the water. Really large in fact. He worried that his line would snap, and tried to not be as forceful with his reeling. It was about twenty feet from the shore now.

It didn't look like any kind of fish he'd ever seen before. He didn't know what it looked like, but it was big, and he was dragging it through the lake, right to him.

He was getting a little nervous because it was getting easier to reel. That meant one thing. The thing was swimming towards him.

The lack of tension on the line made him stumble backwards and he sat down hard on his tackle box. It hurt more than he thought it would and he nearly dropped the fishing pole.

Ten feet away now and he had stopped reeling. He stood back up and with one hand, opened his tackle box. It was what his Mom had called a hot mess. Lures, hooks, sinkers were strewn all over the inside of the box, and the knife he was looking for was not in sight anywhere. His eyes darted to the lake and he saw it.

Jeb's mouth went dry.

At first, it looked like he'd caught one of those horseshoe crabs he'd seen on a show about sea life. Then as it rose out of the water, it looked like a helmet. Now, as it rose up further, he saw a nearly black moldered weed covered skull, with a hook in its bottom jaw. The skull was still attached to the body, which seemed to be dragging itself up from the lake. The water this close to the shore line was less than a foot deep, and he saw two arms rise up and push down. It was trying to stand up. And it was succeeding.

It stood up about six feet tall and was dripping water and filth from the lake. It looked like it was wearing a suit. Casually, the thing ran its gnarled hands across the front of itself as if to smooth out the rotted cloth suit coat it was wearing. The skull looked to the left and to the right and then right at Jeb, who had fallen back down, still holding his fishing pole and trembling.

The thing stared at Jeb and reached up to its face. It grabbed the fishing line with one hand and followed it to the hook. It took a moment, but the thing managed to work the hook out of its jaw. There was still a chunk of bait on it, which the thing bit into and tossed the hook aside. The thing loudly chewed.

Jeb couldn't breathe. He did not and could not believe his eyes. He had never been so terrified in his entire life.

"You got any more of that fish, boy?" the thing in front of him asked.

Jeb kicked his legs to get away from the thing. The voice had sounded like a rusted steel car door being slowly opened. The thing took a step forward.

"Quit moving around, boy." The thing said. "I'm trying to focus what's left of these eyes."

The thing was still dripping and still chewing the piece of bait. It crossed its arms and cocked its head to one side.

"How 'bout that fish? Got any left?"

Jeb tried to swallow to speak, but couldn't. He nodded his head no, and it was true. He'd only brought the one chunk of fish because he didn't expect to be out that long.

"Shame," the thing said. "It was mighty good. Nothing caught outta this here lake for damn sure."

Jeb just sat there, shaking.

The thing stretched his arms out and seemed to be basking in the sun. It threw its head back and howled. Its arms shot back down to its sides and did what looked like a little dance.

"Boy howdy, that feels so damn *good*!" it beamed. It stuck out its right hand, or what closely resembled a hand.

"They call me Old Gooseberry, but you can just call me Goose. I'm right grateful for the little breakfast you give me this morning!"

The hand stood there in front of Jeb's face for about ten seconds until Goose pulled it back.

"Oh, sorry boy. I guess I look a little...*worn* to those young eyes of yours." Goose said, straightening up. "Hope I ain't scared you too bad. Hell, I was mighty scared when I took a bite outta that hunk of bait you threw in and found myself getting dragged through the lake!" Goose took both arms, wrapped them around himself and laughed like he'd just told the funniest joke in the world.

After Goose's laughter died, he put his hands on his hips.

"Well? You just gonna sit there with your mouth open or are you gonna say hi?"

Jeb slowly closed his mouth. He prayed silently for someone, *anyone*, to come by and save him, but no one did. He swallowed hard and managed to say,

"Hi,"

"Hi yourself," Goose said. "And what's your name young man?"

Jeb blinked.

"Um,...I ain't supposed to really talk to strangers, sir."

"Sir?" Goose chuckled. "Well, we got us a nice, polite Southern boy here!"

Jeb didn't know how to respond to that, but he didn't have to as Goose squatted down on his haunches.

"Your Momma and Poppa done taught you right, boy. Lotsa dangerous people in this world. Lotsa dangerous *things* in this world too."

Jeb nodded and had to agree. He felt like he was looking at one of them right now. Goose must have sensed that very thought because he immediately responded.

"Oh you don't have to worry about Old Goose, boy. How dangerous could an old man in the bottom of a lake be? And if I was dangerous, why would I be talking all *nice* to you?"

"W...why do you live in a lake?" Jeb asked.

"Well, that's a real fair question. 'Fraid can't tell you that, though."

Jeb looked puzzled. Before he could ask why, Goose supplied the answer.

"How can I tell a secret to someone who ain't told me their name?"

Jeb, still afraid, heard some logic in that question. He was hesitant to say anything, much less tell this thing his name, but he didn't get the impression he was going to be leaving anytime soon either. He took a breath.

"Jeb."

Goose stood up and gave the boy a small salute.

"A pleasure to make your acquaintance, young Master Jeb." Goose said. "Can I help you up Jeb? You sure do look uncomfortable sitting there in the dirt."

Jeb looked down and saw he was still sitting in the dirt. He pushed himself up and stood on steadier feet than he thought he had under him. He slapped the back of his cut off shorts, getting the dirt off of him. He looked at Goose who was just simply standing there, like he'd been there all day.

"There you are!" Goose said, looking him up and down. "Gonna be a tall drink of water I'm sure when you're grown."

Jeb looked back at him and saw just how big Goose seemed to be. The sun was directly behind him and Jeb really couldn't see his face, which he considered a good thing.

"Well now, you wanted to know how it is I come to be living in this here lake. And now that we're all *friendly*, I feel much better about telling you all about it."

Goose turned towards the lake and again stretched his arms out as if he were going to preach. He spoke with his back to Jeb.

"A very long time ago, I was a young man with dreams and ambitions, just like anybody else in this world. I had visions of a world that was good and just and right. And one day, it all was ripped from me."

His hands turned into fists.

"Just torn, torn right outta my hands. And I come to this lake right here and I screamed out across the water and right to the heavens 'Why have you done me so wrong?' Well, nothing happened for a good long time, Jeb, but out up from this very lake here rose a beautiful woman and she soothed my soul. She took me in her arms like a babe and dried my tears. She told me I could have all my good things...restored to me where they belonged."

Slowly, Goose turned around and looked at the young boy.

"And I said, 'Yes, sweet angel. Please, I'd do *anything* at all to have what was taken from me back.' And she kissed my head and in a flash that shook me all over, everything was made right again."

Goose snapped his fingers. It sounded like a dry twig snapping in half and it made Jeb jump a little.

"And now, that my time has come and gone, as part of my bargain, I sit here and I wait for someone...like I was, broken and heartsick...I wait for someone who has a *powerful* loss in them."

Goose stared at Jeb, who shuddered.

"Someone just like you, *Jebediah*." Goose said, quietly.

Jeb swallowed hard again. He was starting to breathe a little harder too and his heart was pounding.

"Like me?"

"Just like you. Come on and tell Old Gooseberry what it is you're missing."

Jeb couldn't think. He knew what he was missing and he knew what he wanted back more than anything in the whole world. But, he couldn't say it. He wouldn't say it. In the year his Daddy had been dead, he never once really talked about it. His Mom did, all the time. She'd sit Jeb on her knee and tell him stories of when Jeb's Daddy was younger. She'd talk about how much she missed him and how proud he was of Jeb.

She would talk about him before he went to bed and while he would say his prayers before bedtime, she'd always add in that Daddy would always look out for his little man. She'd cry and kiss him good night. And Jeb would cry too, but he'd never talk about it. He'd never say it out loud to his Mom. Sometimes, it seemed it hurt her more than it hurt him and that always made him sad.

And now, he was being offered a chance to have him back.

"I see that look in your eyes, boy. I can almost *smell* your loss. Tell Old Goose what it is you want so bad."

Jeb just stood there. He wished his Daddy was back every single night. But there was something that wasn't right. Something wasn't making sense.

"I know you miss your Daddy, Jeb. Hell, your Momma misses him too. Wouldn't you like to have him back? This time tomorrow, you could be sitting right here next to him, fishing the whole day away."

"I didn't say what I wanted," Jeb said.

"It's all over your face, boy. You know it's true." Goose leaned in closer to Jeb. "You ain't *scared* to have your Daddy back are you?"

The very idea of him possibly being afraid of his father jarred Jeb. He had never been afraid of his Daddy. It made him a little mad.

"I ain't scared of my Daddy," Jeb said.

"Well, you *must* be," Goose said. "I mean, most young boys your age would jump all over the chance of having their dead mashed up Daddy back in one piece, good as new. Did he do something to you boy? Did he...*diddle* you a little bit?"

Jeb felt his face burn and he frowned. Nobody wanted his Daddy back more than him. And diddled? His Daddy never laid a hand on him. He never had even been spanked, save for one time when he was little.

"My Daddy was a good man," Jeb said and his voice had a little catch to it. Goose stood back up and held his hands out.

"Hey, now, I ain't tryin' to say *nothing* about your old man, but you gotta look at it from where I'm standing." Goose folded his arms. "There must be something you're scared of *beside me*,"

For the first time since his Daddy's accident, Jeb was angry. It almost felt good to be angry at something else, and he realized he had spent a lot of the last year being angry at his father for dying. That fact alone, made him even angrier. His hands balled into to fists.

"I ain't scared of you and don't say stuff like that about my Daddy,"

Goose kept his arms folded and cocked his head to one side.

"But you are scared of me ain't you? I'm right here in front of you, offering you a deal of a lifetime-only one you're gonna get by the way-and you're scared to say yes. You must not want Daddy back, 'cause you're scared. So which is it? You scared of Daddy, or you scared of me?"

Jeb felt something tug in his head and then he felt it tug in his chest. He opened his hands and he crossed his arms, almost the exact same way Goose had his crossed. He took a deep breath and cocked his head to one side.

"I reckon," Jeb said. "There are only about three things in this world that spook me, Goose. Making my Mom mad is one. Not fishing with my Daddy is the other. And nowadays, tornadoes."

Jeb shifted his weight, straightened his head and glared directly at Goose.

"I got a Mom who loves me more than anything in this world and a Daddy in the next world who loves me more than anything too. Nothing can touch me, as long as I got that. So, no. I ain't scared of you."

Goose's arms dropped to his sides.

"Well, well, well." Goose said finally. "I reckon you ain't."

Jeb stood there and began to tap his foot.

Goose turned slowly without saying another word. He walked into the lake and before he disappeared, he turned his head to see Jeb.

"You'll beg me come tomorrow."

Jeb said nothing and watched Goose vanish from sight. He held his position as long as he could, but after about a minute, he began to sob. He buried his face in his hands and began to cry harder. He did this for about five minutes and then wiped his face on his t shirt. He started to gather his fishing gear and actually felt better than he had in a long while.

He took a good long look out across the lake and didn't feel scared. He closed his eyes tight.

"I love you Daddy," he said.

A soft cool breeze swept his matted blonde hair back across his face. He didn't hear anything except the birds and a few fish jumping in the lake, but it sounded like an "I love you too" anyway.

And that was fine by Jeb.

JUST ENOUGH ROPE

1

Clem smiled as the bullet slammed into his forehead and threw him backward onto the dusty street. When he hit the ground, the dirt and sand flew up around his body. There was a thud and then silence as the dust began to blow in the wind. Blood poured from the hole in Clem's forehead like a geyser. His body gave a small twitch in the bright Arizona sunlight.

Tom Wall holstered his gun and walked toward Clem's body. The sound of his boots broke the silence and the small crowd that had watched quietly began to scatter. It was the way of things; people gunned down in the street for money or justice or both. The show at this point was over and no one had seen anything worth waiting around for anymore.

Wall reached Clem's body and knelt down to look at him. Clem's eyes were still open and he still wore that stupid smile. Wall reached over and closed the dead man's eye lids. He couldn't stand to have him looking up at the sky. He stood up and looked around. Of course there was only the mortician, ready to claim his prize and already moving to take the body with his huge assistant. They were both dressed in black suits and covered in dust.

"That was a hell of a shot, Mr. Wall. Name's Dooley," the mortician said, sticking his hand out. Wall took it and shook quickly. "Yes sir, we heard you'd be looking for Clem and we heard you was a hell of a shot."

"More lucky than anything," Wall said. "How long you reckon you're gonna prop him up for Mr. Dooley?"

The mortician shrugged.

"I guess a day or two unless you need to leave in a hurry," Dooley replied. "We got a nice hotel right there across the street and some good eats right next to it."

Wall looked down at Clem. He would clear five hundred dollars after he dragged Clem back to Texas. After tracking him for three months, it was over. Maybe he'd stay a day or two. Maybe he'd earned some sleep in a real bed.

He looked at Dooley, who seemed to be waiting for an answer.

"I reckon a day or two would be good. He's yours until I come for him."

Dooley beamed.

"Oh, thank you Mr. Wall!" he said. He hit the large brute in the ill-fitting suit next to him. "Shake the shit out of your eyes and pick 'im up, Big Pink. The man he called Big Pink walked over to Clem and grabbed him under his arms. He lifted the big man easily and dragged him away. Dooley had started making light conversation about putting Clem's body on display and money, but Wall had already tuned him out and looked at the hotel. He was suddenly very tired and wanted a drink, and to go to sleep.

He walked away from Dooley, giving a small wave so as not to be rude. He walked slowly to the wooden steps and climbed them as if he had suddenly gained weight.

He opened the door and stepped into the lobby. There were scattered few people sitting, chatting up whores from the place next door, but he ignored them and walked to the front desk. A small burly man walked over to greet him smiling.

"It's an honor to meet you, Mr. Wall," the man said. "I'm Stanley Bosen and I'm the manager here at the Bosen Hotel."

Bosen looked at him. Wall was a tired looking man of about 30 and fairly average looking with black hair. But his eyes…ice green and cruel looking.

"I'm sure once the whores next door find out you're staying here, they'll be all over you."

"If you could kind of keep that quiet, I'd be obliged," Wall said. "And you don't have to keep calling me mister. Tom or Wall will do just fine. How much for two nights?"

Bosen smiled.

"Our regular rooms are five a night Mr... I mean, Tom. The suites come with a full bath. Just filled them up about an hour ago. Those are seven fifty. But…" Bosen stopped and grabbed his ledger. "I may be able to make a slight deal with you."

"What kind of 'slight deal?'" Wall asked.

"Well, it seems the object of your visit to our fine little town had stayed here and actually paid for a suite in advance. Three days left to go seein' as he won't be coming back anytime soon." He gave Wall a wink. "It's all yours if you want it. It's a suite!"

Wall considered this. He wasn't broke, not even close, but if he could save a little on the trip…well, maybe he could get a train ticket back to Texas instead of hauling Clem around for weeks. And damn, he was tired.

"I couldn't just stay for free," Wall said. "But a discount would be awful nice."

Bosen smiled even bigger.

"Two dollars a night," Bosen said "And a picture of you to hang up at my billiards room next door. It isn't often we get a genuine celebrity here."

Wall frowned.

"I ain't a celebrity," Wall said. "But I'll take the deal."

"Oh, but you *are* a celebrity Tom. I can try to keep your presence here quiet as I can, but everyone knows who you are and this is the only hotel in town." Bosen said "And that'll be two dollars for the first night."

Wall reached into his pants and pulled out the money requested. Bosen took the money, put it in a drawer and filled out his ledger. He spun the big book around for Wall to sign.

"Just sign here, Tom." Bosen said. Tom grabbed a pen and signed his name. Bosen suddenly slammed the book closed and rang a bell. He pulled a key out from behind the counter and handed it to Wall.

"Your room is 311, top floor. If you wouldn't mind, we'd like to give the room a good once over before you go in and get settled. Take this over to the billiards room next door and have a drink on me."

Bosen handed Wall a round-looking coin that said "FREE DRINK TO THE BARER." He turned it over and it said the same thing.

"We'll let you know when your room is ready, Tom."

Wall nodded and said "Much obliged again." He tipped his hat and walked out of the hotel. As he left, a young man ran over to Bosen at the front desk.

"Please prepare 311 for a new guest. Box up Mr. Clem's items and bring them to me in my office, okay?"

The young man grabbed a ring of keys and ran up the stairs in the center of the room to do as he had been told. Bosen watched Wall through the window slumping over to the billiards room next door. He smiled.

2

Wall knew the second he walked into the billiards room it was a huge mistake. He didn't care though. A free drink was a free drink and he needed one badly.

He tried to keep his head down and walked to a dark corner of the bar. An old bartender came over with a slight limp and a mouth full of bad teeth.

"What can I do you for?" he asked, wiping the dusty bar in front of Wall with a filthy rag.

"You got beer?" Wall asked.

"Hell son, it's even cold." The bartender said, grinning. "That's a quarter if you want it."

Wall slapped the drink token on the bar and slid it to the bartender.

"Well then, a drink for our special guest," the bartender said. "On the house at that!" The bartender disappeared and returned with a foamy mug of beer. He set it in front of Wall, who grabbed it and downed about half of it before putting it down again.

"God *damn*, that's cold!" he said, laughing a little. He wiped his mouth off on his sleeve and smiled. How long had it been since he smiled? He couldn't recall. The bartender laughed with him.

"Told you son, we serve 'em cold here."

"Damned if you don't," Wall said. He reached into his pocket and pulled out some coins. He put four on the bar.

"That first one's on the house, but keep them coming, sir." Wall said, reaching for his beer.

"Call me Hank, and you got it. Don't drink 'em all that fast. Your head'll feel like old Clem's before too long if you do."

Wall laughed again and took a deep drink of the beer. He had always been amazed at how one small thing could turn you right around. He was ready to go lie down and he was still damn tired, but a cold beer was a rare thing even in the big cities. And just when he needed a cold drink, he found it in the tiny town of...of...

"Hank, what's the name of this town?" Wall asked, but Hank had gone on to help another customer.

Aw, hell with it. Who cares? Wall thought. *Just enjoy your damn drink, dummy.*

He adjusted how he was sitting and began to relax for the first time in weeks. He took a deep breath and let it out slowly. He closed his eyes for a minute and let the cold fire in his belly soothe him a little bit.

It didn't last long.

He felt a hand gently touch his shoulder. His nose was filled with flowers and almonds. The hand gently massaged his shoulder and moved down to his back.

A whore.

He opened his eyes and expected to see a large woman, rode hard for too many years and looking to make some money. What he saw was something he'd not expected.

She was beautiful. Couldn't have been more than twenty if that; she had coral lips, grey eyes and a mop of long curly black hair that was tied in an unruly bun underneath a small hat. She was dressed like a fine lady. He knew damn well she wasn't, but she could pass for one to be sure. She saw him looking at her and she smiled.

"Hello, Mr. Wall. Buy a lady a drink?"

Wall honestly didn't know what to say, so he smiled. He brushed the seat next to him off and gestured for her to sit. He forgot his manners, but recovered enough to stand slightly until she sat. She winked at him.

"You are definitely not from anywhere near here are you? Such courtesy." She said smiling. Wall blushed a little. Must be the beer, he thought. He slapped his hand on the bar and beckoned Hank over, who obliged.

"Drink for the lady and I'll take another beer please," Wall said. He looked at the girl, who gave a shy nod, still smiling.

"I'll get you and Veronique drinks right quick. And, good call son!"

Hank went to get the drinks and Veronique turned to Wall.

"Thank you," she said. "And might I say, that was one hell of a shot you made on Mr. Jackson a little while ago. Hell of a shot."

"Thanks," was all Wall could think to say. He picked up the rest of his beer and downed it in one gulp. It felt good and he was feeling a little loose. He had to be careful not to get too loose; Veronique was a whore and as pretty as she was, just a whore out for some of his money. He'd known enough whores that would slit your neck if you had enough money on you. She didn't seem the type, but he'd been wrong about women before.

"Where did you learn to shoot like that?" she asked.

"Ma'am, I was a Texas Ranger for about ten years. Learned real quick you had better hit what you're shooting at, or you wouldn't last too long in the job."

Her eyes lit up.

"A real Texas Ranger? That's exciting!" Veronique pulled a little book out of the side of her dress. It was a penny dreadful that had a picture of what was supposed to be Wall. She held it up.

"I must have read this about twenty times and it didn't say anything about you being a Texas Ranger." She said. Wall frowned and took the little book.

The title of the dreadful was "Tom Wall: Youngest And Best Bounty Hunter This Side of the Pecos River! Becoming a Legend Before Thirty! Quick Draw Killer!

Wall looked at it for a while and then laughed. He handed it back to Veronique.

"Well, I reckon they got the ranger part right, but they probably got just about everything else wrong," He said as Hank dropped off their drinks. Wall pushed the money over the bar, but Hank waved his hand.

"I started you a tab, son. Go get yourself in some trouble there. I got other people that need drinks." He winked and left.

He grabbed his beer and she reached for her drink; a glass of wine of some kind. She held it up.

"Cheers, Mr. Wall. Here's to us."

He clinked his beer as gently as he could to her wine glass.

"To...us." He said.

The two took a few sips of their drinks and began to talk to each other. He was learning a lot about *himself*, that was one thing. She must've read that damn penny dreadful a lot more than twenty times; she was quoting entire passages verbatim from the book. Although the stories she was asking him about were pure made up bullshit, it was pretty flattering to hear someone talk to him about *him* for a change. He watched her as she lit up, talking about his alleged adventures and watching her sink and then laugh as he told the real version.

He also knew when he was being played and he wasn't getting that feeling from Veronique. Maybe it was the beer. Maybe it wasn't, but he was enjoying himself.

Relaxing.

He felt good.

After a few more cold beers and wine, they decided to get something to eat. They asked Hank about the food and he assured them he'd have something nice fixed up for them. In a short while, he brought out two steaming wooden bowls of stew and some crusty bread. Veronique took little bites, but Wall devoured his after the first bite.

"Hank, what kind of meat is this?" Wall asked, with a mouthful of the stew.

"Fresh," Hank replied. "Good ain't it? The wife does a damn good job, don't you think?"

Wall smiled and nodded as he tore back into the bowl. He was finished in five minutes. Veronique giggled as he looked up at her, mouth covered with stew.

"Lord, excuse me," He said and laughed a little himself. "Been so long since I had a sit down meal, I forgot my manners."

"I like to see a man eat," Veronique said, grabbing a napkin from the bar and wiping his mouth. She leaned in closer to him and said "What else has it been a long time for, Mr. Wall?"

3

Veronique lay sleeping with an arm across Wall's chest. He looked down at her and smiled to himself. They came to his room, took a bath together and spent the next few hours exhausting and pleasing each other. He'd been with his share of whores, but she seemed less like one and more like someone he could be with for a long time. It was a fool's thought to be sure, but he was enjoying all of her, even while she slept.

He had tried to sleep along with her, but he was wide awake. The combination of the beer, food and sex should have knocked him out and he knew this, but he was up and alert. He kept looking at her and stroked her hair. She gave a little smile in her sleep and he felt her snuggle up closer to him.

"I could get used to this," he whispered. Veronique opened her eyes and looked up at him.

"Why Mr. Wall," she said in her own whisper. "You sound a little bit smitten."

Wall had to laugh and she climbed on top of him and kissed his cheek.

"I reckon I ain't alone in it either," he said kissing her neck.

"No sir, you are not." She said, finding his mouth. They kissed deep and hard for a moment until she broke off and looked at him.

"You don't always kiss whores like that, do you Mr. Wall?"

"No I do not," he said. "But I ain't really thinking of you as a whore. And, it's Tom. Not mister anything to you."

A small tear streamed down her face and she kissed him again. He reached up and grabbed her as they fell into each other again. When they finished this time, he fell asleep tangled in Veronique's arms and he slept as well as he ever did.

4

Wall awoke to find the room dark. Veronique was still sleeping next to him and he carefully got out of the bed, naked he walked over to the heavy oak dresser where he'd thrown most of what was in his pockets and found his matches. He lit the oil lamp on the dresser and looked for his pocket watch. He popped it open and saw through the dim light that the watch had stopped. He frowned, but realized he didn't really care about the time, but he had started to think about dragging Clem's body back to Texas.

He looked at Veronique, sleeping peacefully on the bed. What was he going to do about her? It hurt his head to think about leaving her here, but could he haul her and a stinking corpse on a train bound for Texas? He sure as hell couldn't take her on the trail if he decided to go that way.

He decided he needed some air, so he quietly put on his dungarees, boots, a shirt and strapped his gun on just in case. He left the room quietly and walked down the dimly lit hallway toward the stairs. As he walked slowly down the carpeted staircase, he heard voices speaking in hushed tones. He resisted the urge to stop and listen as was ingrained in him from a decade in the Texas Rangers. It was harder than he thought it would be, and his hand found itself resting on his gun anyway. (That urge, he never resisted.)

When he finished his descent, he saw Bosen and Dooley, the mortician chatting away quietly. They both regarded him and smiled.

"Nice night for a walk, Mr. Wall?" Bosen asked, smiling.

Wall walked closer to the two men. Dooley looked as pale as milk.

"Feeling a little poorly, Mr. Dooley?" Wall asked.

Dooley swallowed and shook his head.

"I'm...yes. Poorly, that's about right." His voice sounded shaky. "We're gonna prop your bounty in front of the hotel in the morning, Mr. Wall. If you'd like to pose for some of those pictures, that would sure help things along."

Wall shook his head.

"You do what you need to do with him, but I've already done what I needed to do with that bastard. Save for draggin' him back to Texas that is."

Dooley nodded.

"When do you reckon you'll be heading back?" Dooley asked.

"I ain't sure just yet. I'll let you know before the end of tomorrow. Depends on the train schedule."

"Train?" Dooley turned paler if that were possible. "You gonna put him on a train?"

"If I had wings, I'd fly that crooked son of a bitch back to Texas." Wall said, flatly. "I don't want to have to spend any more time with him than I have to. I spent three months chasing his ass here. I'm done."

Bosen laughed.

"Well, you should take your time to decide, Mr. Wall. Still have a few days on that room after all. Besides, Mr. Dooley can put him on ice so he doesn't stink up the train when you leave at the end of the week if that's what you decide to do."

Bosen leaned over the counter.

"And I'm sure your new 'friend' would sure like you to stay a little longer."

Wall nodded.

"I'll think about it," was all he said. He tipped his hat and walked out the hotel door. Dooley followed right behind him.

As he walked along the street, he felt a little chilly, but it also felt good. He still had the lingering smell of Veronique on him and he again thought about getting used to it.

"What do you want Mr. Dooley?" Wall asked the man behind him. He kept walking and the mortician followed behind him.

"I wanted to talk to you Mr. Wall. Can you stop for a minute?"

"I can walk and talk at the same time if it's all the same to you."

Dooley sighed, but walked faster to catch up to Wall's longer stride.

"I was wondering," Dooley began. "If you had thought about leaving a little sooner."

Wall said nothing.

"You know, to get a jump on the trip? Get home earlier? Relax before your next job?"

"This here is my last job," Wall replied. "And I'm relaxing just fine."

Wall stopped and whirled to look at Dooley.

"Some reason I should leave?" he asked a trifle cold.

Dooley stopped dead in his tracks. He looked terrified, but not of Wall.

"Well, sir, I really can't...I'm not at liberty to...oh my," Dooley was shaking all over. "I can't do this anymore,"

"Do what?" Wall was genuinely confused. "What are you going on about, Dooley? You're as white as a sheet."

Dooley grabbed a wooden column and held himself up.

"It's too much," he said, nearly sobbing. "Just too damned much. It's got to end."

Wall moved toward Dooley and held a hand out to steady the man, but Dooley moved away from him.

"This town is *poison*, Mr. Wall. The longer you stay, the harder it'll be for you to leave and leave you *must*!"

"What do you mean poison?"

He thought of Veronique and wondered why the hell he got out of bed.

"I mean poison. This place, this damn *town* is a trap!" Dooley was tearing up and drooling slightly.

"You're talkin' shit, Dooley."

Dooley grabbed Wall's arm and pulled him close.

"Come with me quickly" he said and began to drag Wall down the street.

5

They arrived a few minutes later at a barn that had a sign on the front. "Arthur P. Dooley: Mortician and Undertaker. Do Not Enter!" Although it was dark, the big white lettering was pretty easy to read in moonlight. Dooley fumbled with a key and unlocked the barn door. He unengaged the lock and looked at Wall, who looked confused.

"Do you have matches?" Dooley asked.

Wall held up his small tinderbox and nodded.

"Come inside, quick." Dooley said and disappeared into the barn. Wall hesitated a moment and looked around. He had no idea why someone would follow him here, but he'd been a ranger too long to act otherwise. He carefully walked into the barn.

Dooley waited until he was in all the way and closed the door.

"Come here with your matches," Dooley said and walked quickly over to a large heavy blanket covering up something large. On a small table next to it was an oil lamp. He reached out for the tinderbox and Wall handed it to him. Dooley's hand was shaking so badly, he couldn't strike the match.

Wall, not needing to be asked, walked over and took the matches away to light the lamp.

"Thank you," Dooley said quietly.

Wall lit the match and touched it to the wick. He put the glass cover on it and turned the wick up about an inch for maximum light. He was a few feet from the covered object and felt cold.

"This is where I keep the bodies when they aren't on display," Dooley explained. "The blanket slows down the melting a little and it also covers up the box and the smell. You may want to hold your nose or something."

"I've smelled worse," Wall said but braced himself anyway. Dooley Pulled the blanket off and there between the two ice blocks was a wooden coffin with the lid off. Inside was Clem, still smiling and the bullet hole in his forehead, looking like a third eye.

The body was stripped naked to the pants, but there was something not right.

Most of his torso was missing.

Wall moved closer to look and the smell indeed was awful, but it didn't stop him. He turned and grabbed the oil lamp from the small table carefully.

"Careful, Mr. Wall." Dooley said.

"I ain't an idjit," Wall said calmly. "Just want to see what the hell this is all about."

He moved the lamp closer and saw that almost the entire torso was picked damn near clean. There was almost no blood, as if the body had never had any inside.

"So why would you do this, Mr. Dooley? There ain't nothing but a set of ribs left, This some kind of undertaker thing?"

"I didn't do this," Dooley said. "My young associate Big Pink did this and he was told to do it. This is why you need to leave."

Wall frowned.

"What the hell do I tell them folks when I go to claim my bounty on this man?" Wall was getting angry.

Dooley shook his head.

"You're missing the point, Mr. Wall."

Wall stepped backward and put the lamp down. He looked at Dooley.

"You're telling me I need to leave right now for no good god damn reason and then you show me that you desecrated this dumb bastard's corpse and expect me to haul it back *like this*?"

"This is what happens to folks who die here, Mr. Wall. This is what *always* happens to them."

"What, somebody dies and they scoop 'em out like a damn canoe? That don't make no sense at all."

"Do you want to know *why* he was smiling when you shot him?"

"I just told you he was a dumb bastard," Wall replied.

"No, no. Think back to before you shot him. What did he say?"

Wall thought about it. He didn't like to think about the act of killing, especially folks he'd killed; whether they deserved it or not. It was still taking a life and although Clem's life wasn't worth shit, it was still a life.

Wall had been walking up the street when Clem had come running out of the bar attached to the hotel.

"Clem Jackson!" Wall had yelled and the stupid son of a bitch stopped dead in his tracks. He looked at Wall for a long time.

"Come all this way to fetch me Tommy?" Clem asked, snickering. "All this was just for me?"

"I can bring you in one of two ways, Clem." Wall said. "I'd be obliged if you were able to walk to your hanging."

"What's the difference if I'm already a dead man?"

"A hundred dollars," Wall said flatly and Clem laughed.

"Well, damn your hundred dollars. You're going to have to kill me."

"I'd rather not," Wall said. "I'll see you get a fair trial."

"Trust me Tommy," Clem said, moving toward Wall. "If you kill me know, you'll be doing me a favor."

Wall pulled his gun and aimed it at Clem.

"Not another step." He said.

Clem smiled and kept walking.

"Oh, I'll take all the steps I can get if you're gonna put me down. And that's what everybody wants."

Wall shook his head.

"Clem? You best stop coming now, I ain't foolin'."

He continued forward.

"Just do it," Clem said, smiling. "I got it comin' and I want it. I want it now!"

Clem pretended to reach for his gun and Wall shot him right between the eyes.

The smile never left his face as he fell. As he fell, Wall had noticed that he wasn't wearing a side holster. He'd shot him unarmed. Normally that would have bothered him, but Clem did in fact have it coming after all.

Wall looked at Dooley.

"He said 'You'd be doing me a favor.'" Dooley said and the words that had been lost on Wall suddenly has some weight.

"How long had Clem been here before I found him?" Wall asked.

"About two days," Dooley said after a pause. "He was living it up the first night. Whores, liquor, the food and the works. All poison." Dooley wiped his palms on his suit. "He didn't want to leave until it was too late. He tried to, but he couldn't. And then you showed up."

Wall sighed.

"Sounds like he was having a good time. Why would he want to leave?"

"Exactly," Dooley said. "That's what you need to ask yourself. Why *would* he want to leave."

Wall was missing something and he hated missing something. He told this to Dooley. Dooley responded with a question.

"You see any livestock on your way into this town?"

"No I didn't. I figured you had a delivery here and there what with all this ice to keep it cool-"

"Where's all this ice coming from?" Dooley asked. His eyes narrowed. "Where's a dog? Or a horse? Or a god damn *fly*? For that matter, where's *your* horse?"

Wall's horse was dead, he knew that much, but that was about it. He couldn't think of a reason for any of the questions, but just because he couldn't think of one, didn't mean there wasn't one.

"Mr. Dooley, I think I'm done here. I'll be leaving in the morning with my claim. I'd appreciate it if you could write something up explaining why his god damn innards are missing."

Wall turned and walked to the barn door.

Dooley hurried after him.

"But you have to leave *now*!" Dooley cried. "Don't you see? It'll be too late in the morning!"

Wall turned and grabbed Dooley by the jacket.

"I've about had enough of this, Dooley. You talk in circles and you desecrate the dead. If I were still a Texas Ranger, I'd haul you back with Clem and have you strung up for good measure."

"This isn't Texas," Dooley said. "You'd have no jurisdiction here."

Wall grabbed Dooley by his coat and jerked the man up to his face.

"There's an old saying. 'A Texas Ranger's jurisdiction is *wherever* he happens to be.'" With that, he pushed Dooley back and kicked the barn door open. "Have him ready to travel, Dooley. I'll come for him in the morning."

6

By the time Wall walked back into the hotel, the place was dark and quiet. There was some noise coming from the billiards room next door, but that was to be expected. He had noticed that he couldn't hear a single cricket on his walk back to the hotel and was going to ask Veronique when he got back upstairs.

He climbed the stairs two at a time and a little faster as he thought about Veronique. Right now, all he wanted was her. He gave a little distracted laugh and marveled at how often he'd smiled and laughed since he pulled into this town.

It was her.

He decided he was going to ask her to come with him.

Wall reached the top of the stairs and turned right down the hall to his room. He got to the door and pulled his boots off to try and be quiet in case she was still sleeping. He heard her before opening the door and she was crying. He threw the door open, dropped his boots and drew his gun.

He saw her wide eyed and sitting on the bed, still naked. She recoiled from Wall as he looked around the room.

"You all right?" He asked sternly. She gave a little yelp and stared at him. "Is somebody in here?"

She shook her head slowly 'no' and began to cry again. Wall holstered his gun and ran to the bed.

"What's wrong darlin'? I thought someone was in here with you hurtin' you or somethin'."

She lunged into his arms.

"I thought you left me," she said through a hail of sobs. She clutched him tightly. "I know it's stupid because I'm just a whore and all, but..."

He grabbed her back and chuckled.

"I ain't leavin' you," he said. "And you just made askin' you to come with me a hell of a lot easier."

She hugged him tighter and then kissed his neck. She looked up at him.

"Oh Tom, I love you." She said, still crying, a serious look on her face. "But I can't leave."

Wall looked down at her.

"What do you mean, 'can't leave?'"

She sniffed.

"Darlin', we can't ever leave here if we're gonna be together. We just can't."

Wall kissed her head and stood up.

"What are you scared of? Of course we can leave. Anytime we want."

She pulled a blanket around her and stood up.

"You don't understand. I have to stay here. You can go, but I have to stay."

Wall folded his arms.

"Is it Bozen? You work for him, right? What's it gonna take to get you out of here?"

She shook her head.

"It's more than just that," she said. "A lot more. It's this town, Tom. It's..."

"Poison?"

She looked shocked.

"Who told you that?"

"Dooley. Just showed me a thing or two." He walked over to the dresser and turned the fading oil lamp up a little for more light. He started to gather his things. "Like, Clem Jackson, with a lot of his insides gone. He was trying to get me to leave before sunrise. Said the town was poison."

Veronique walked over to him.

"It is poison, Tom and it won't matter if it's sunrise or not." She put a hand on his shoulder. "I want you to stay but only if you love me."

He turned and looked at her. He kissed her forehead.

"I do love you, which is why we're both gettin' the hell out of this place. What do you want to bring with you?"

She gave a sob and a sigh.

"Tom, you don't understand. I *can't* leave."

Wall took the bed roll and threw it down. He grabbed Veronique and brought her closer to his face.

"I'm getting awful tired of being talked to in circles. Tell me what the problem is!"

As she recoiled from him, the door flew open. Wall snapped his head in the door's direction and saw Bozen, holding a shotgun aimed right at the two of them.

"The lady said, she can't leave and she can't, Mr. Wall." Bosen said, smiling a little. "You'd do well to let her loose now."

He looked at her and let her go. She backed away from him slowly, turning to Bozen.

"Don't hurt him, Stanley. He loves me."

Bosen laughed.

"That's because he doesn't know you very well."

Wall frowned.

"Now just a damn minute, Bozen!"

Bosen raised the shotgun and moved closer to Wall.

"You hold on a minute, son." Bosen said. "We were gonna let you ride on out of here, but you're making it awful hard for me to not blow your head off. There's a lot at work here, Mr. Wall."

Wall counted to himself all the way to three before Bozen's shotgun was close enough. He grabbed the barrel, yanked it hard to one side and pulled it right out of Bozen's hands. Wall wrapped both hands around the barrel and drove the wooden handle by the trigger into Bozen's forehead, knocking him down. Wall flipped the gun and cocked it, aiming at Bozen, who was now bleeding from his forehead.

"Why don't you start telling me what's at work here before I lose my sunny disposition," Wall said coldly. Bosen looked surprised and then he smiled.

"It's all about to become clear, Mr. Wall." Bosen said, holding his head. Wall was about to respond when a sharp blow turned the dark room darker and Wall fell to the floor, unconscious.

7

Wall woke up and couldn't move. He opened his eyes and saw the ceiling of a barn. It hurt his head to move, but he looked from side to side and saw he'd been tied to a wooden table. His feet and hands were lashed to the table, spread out and heavy rope across his chest.

"Hey!" he yelled out. "You best cut me loose!"

A moment later, the barn door opened and he felt a hot rush of air hit him as sunlight poured into the barn.

"Good morning, Mr. Wall!" Bosen said, walking in slowly. Wall strained to see him and the two figures with him. It was Hank the bartender and Veronique. She moved quickly over to Wall and touched his face.

"Tom, I'm so sorry. This is all my fault."

It was Wall's turn to recoil from her.

"Why did you hit me?" he asked.

"I couldn't let you kill Stanley," she said sadly. "He's a no good bastard, but you can't just kill him."

Wall struggled with his bonds to no avail. He looked at Veronique in pure anger.

"I thought you loved me,"

She smiled sweetly.

"I do, so very much my love." She said and stroked his face. "And I always will."

He struggled again. Veronique looked at him sadly and moved away from him.

Hank leaned closer to Bozen.

"Maybe we shoulda kept Big Pink around a little longer," he said. Bosen shook his head.

"Mr. Wall, do you know where you are?"

Wall stopped struggling.

"I reckon I'm in Dooley's barn with Clem's body cooling off," he said. Bosen clapped his hands.

"Yes, poor Mr. Dooley. We had to let him and his charge go earlier this morning." Bosen said.

"That means," Hank chimed in, "We had them destroyed."

"Enough," Bosen said. "Hank, I want to hear something out of you, I'll god damn ask for it."

Wall swallowed hard.

"You have put us in a rather strange position, Mr. Wall. We can't let you leave, but we don't want to kill you either in spite of your rush to hitting me in the head." Bosen said.

"Cut me loose and I'll do more than hit your head, Bozen." Wall said through his teeth.

Bosen laughed. He walked over to Wall and looked down at him.

"You know what the name Bosen means, Mr. Wall?"

Wall didn't answer.

"It's a German word. It means 'evil.' I don't tell you that to scare you or nothing, but it is my name and there are lots of folks that would say it's appropriate."

Wall looked up at him and said nothing.

"You don't scare easy and I like that, Mr. Wall. So I'm going to make a deal with you for the sake of your lover over there. Are you listening?"

Wall nodded.

"Good. Like I said I don't want to kill you, but I will. I don't have the burden of feeling bad or guilty about things I have to do, but I don't like to waste things either." He pointed to a different side of the barn. "Your prize, Clem Jackson over there is a perfect example. Dooley showed what's left of him to you, yes?"

Again, Wall nodded.

"Did he happen to tell you why?"

"No he did not."

"Food, Mr. Wall. We used him for food."

Wall allowed this to sink in and struggled to get free again. Bosen waited for him to stop and when he did, he smiled.

"Before you go on and start getting the idea that we're gonna eat you, I want you to consider something. There are a lot of things in this world you don't know or understand. Folks hate what they don't understand. You hate rattlesnakes because if you piss them off, they'll bite and kill you. But they have their purpose. Part of God's plan. Just like us."

Wall looked at him with disgust.

"Eating your own kind is part of 'God's plan?' That's bullshit."

Bosen leaned down to Wall's face. He saw that Bozen's eyes weren't any color at all. They were almost all black.

"I never said we ate *our* own kind," Bosen said.

"What the hell does that mean?" Wall asked.

Veronique walked over to Wall carefully.

"Tom, please listen. We can still be together," she pleaded.

"Yes," Bosen said, still near Wall's face. "You can still be with her, very much alive and probably pretty happy. But I'm only making this deal once."

Wall looked at Veronique and then back at Bozen, who looked hungry.

"What we are, and by that I mean everyone in this town isn't as important as what we *do*." Bosen stood back, becoming aware of his drooling. "We take the unsavory elements of society and dispose of them. Like Mr. Jackson. We lie in wait for brigands, thieves, murderers and the like to come to our town and we kill them. And then, because of *what* we are, we eat them. So we don't have to go to a big town and kill innocent people. God's plan."

"We aren't really people," Veronique said shyly. "But we're pretty close...and I do love you so."

Wall looked at Bosen in horror.

"Dooley said this town was a trap." Tom said. He understood what the town was now. "You're like god damn *spiders*," he said.

Bosen looked at Veronique and smiled.

"That's a very good analogy! I quite like that, Mr. Wall."

"You're cannibals. Monsters!"

Bozen's smile faded and he got very close to Wall's face again.

"We are *Americans*, sir!" Bosen snarled. "This country has been very good and kind to us. The least we can do is not eat those who have done us no harm."

"When I was a little girl," Veronique began. "My family were hunted down and slaughtered for what we are. I am the only one in my family still alive. Here, no one tries to kill me."

Hank stepped forward.

"It works out, Mr. Wall. Sure, what we do seems gruesome to you. But look *what* we do. Only criminals. Bad folks, trying to escape the law. We're doing regular folks a favor."

Wall remembered what Clem had said before he shot him in the forehead.

You'll be doing me a favor,

"You see, Mr. Wall. We aren't evil. Just like a spider isn't evil for eating bugs and such." Bosen said.

"People ain't bugs," Wall said, his heart pounding.

"Aren't they?" Veronique asked. "You think Clem Jackson wasn't worse than a bug?"

Wall struggled again and he was no closer to getting free than he was before. He looked up and closed his eyes. He was angry and scared; two things he knew were a bad combination in his predicament. He tried to calm himself down but couldn't.

"Tom, I love you no matter what I am or what you are," Veronique said, moving closer to him. She stroked his face and he didn't bother to move away. He knew he was finished. "What we feel for each other is real. You didn't care that I was a whore. Why should you care now?"

With his eyes still closed, Wall spoke.

"Please tell me this is a nightmare. Please tell me you ain't gonna eat me. I can't believe any of this."

She took both of her hands and grabbed his face.

"Look at me Tom. Look at me!"

Wall opened his eyes and looked into her grey eyes. Son of bitch, he thought. I *do* love her.

She smiled at him.

"It's still just me."

Bosen stepped closer.

"Here's the deal, Mr. Wall. Stay here with us. Be one of us. Be with Veronique. Help us rid this world of truly bad people."

Wall sniffed and opened his eyes. He looked up at Veronique, who was still smiling at him.

"Or?"

"Or, we kill you and put you in the next batch of Hank's wife's stew." Bosen said flatly. "We didn't want it to go like this, I promise you. We don't want to kill you."

"But we'll damn sure eat ya, son. That's a damn fact." Hank added. Veronique shot him a dirty look and Hank put his hands up. "Hey, I'm just sayin',"

Bosen put a hand on Veronique's shoulder.

"Let's let him think 'bout this," He said to her, but Wall shook his head.

"She can stay," Wall said quietly.

Bosen nodded.

"We'll give you a few minutes." Bosen said and guided Hank out of the barn.

There was a long time that passed as Wall and Veronique looked at each other. Wall spoke first.

"Can you let me go? I'd never come back here, whatever the name of this town is, I'd leave you all be."

Veronique shook her head and smiled.

"No, you wouldn't Tom. It isn't in you to leave something like us. Like me."

Wall sighed.

"I reckon you're right," he said sadly. "Do you...are you...really a monster?"

"I am what I am," she said and bent down to kiss him. He didn't resist and kissed her back. When she pulled back he was smiling.

"If it's gonna be done, I want you to do it, Veronique." Wall said. "I love you, but I can't live like this, knowing what it is you folks do. I couldn't abide by it."

"No, please Tom!" she cried.

"If you have any love at all for me, you do it. Do it *now*!" Wall yelled.

Veronique's body began to shake and Wall watched in horror as to what was happening. Her beautiful porcelain skin began to darken before his eyes and her lovely grey eyes recessed into her skull. The skin on her face seemed to peel back and displayed an odd, exposed skull, nearly ebony in color. Her mouth, her beautiful smile became a jagged maw of sharpened fangs and the thing she was becoming snarled at him. He was terrified beyond belief. He screamed and screamed until everything went black and he felt himself falling.

8

The sunlight was the first thing Wall saw when he awoke. He covered his eyes with his arms and turned his head away. He blinked several times and realized he wasn't in the barn. He was on the ground. He rolled over to see where he was.

He was in a patch of sand near a river; he heard it trickling in the background. He felt nauseous and retched to one side. After it passed, he sat up and looked around. There was some shade near a tree and his bedroll was underneath the tree.

He kept looking around as he got to his feet. He looked off into the distance and saw a plume of black smoke. He watched it for a while and walked awkwardly to the tree where his bedroll sat, waiting for him. He sat down and grabbed the roll to open it. Inside were all of his things, the few of them that he had, minus his watch.

Two items were new however; a canteen full of probably water and a letter. He opened the canteen, sniffed it and drank two large gulps. He held up the letter that read simply, "Tom."

He knew it was from her.

He tore it open and began to read.

My Dear Tom,

I could not bring myself to kill you. I don't know if you believe me or not, but I do and always will love you. We have burned the town. We have moved on to somewhere you won't find us and please, do not look for us. We aren't bad or evil. You should know that by now.

If they see you coming for us, they will kill you. I won't be able to stop them next time.

I wish we could have been together, my love.

Veronique

Wall sat and re read the letter for a good long time until he began to weep.

He put everything back into the bed roll and stood up. He dusted himself off and found that the rope used to tie him to the table in the barn was still tied around his chest. He grabbed it and untied himself from the thick rope. He held it out in front of him. It was a good five feet of rope. He looked up at the tree where he stood and saw a thick branch.

He started to laugh.

He had just enough rope to hang himself and he laughed.

MONK'S RUN
"PILOT"

TEASER

INT. DARK ROOM

The room is very dark and lit only with black candles. There is a
BEAUTIFUL WOMAN tied to an altar. TWO CLOAKED FIGURES
stand over her as she struggles. The larger figure pulls out a long and jagged
KNIFE and raises it above his head.

>   DARK FIGURE ONE
>   We offer this creature as
>   sacrifice. We offer—

A cell phone rings, playing the theme to "The Banana Splits" kids TV
show. The figure lowers the knife and throws back his hood. It is, HIRSH,
who reaches into his robe for his phone. He finds it and answers it.

>   HIRSH
>   What is it?

>   MAN ON PHONE (V.O.)
>   Sorry to bother you Mr. Hirsh.

>   HIRSH
>   I've got my hands full here, Bob.
>   Talk quickly.

>   MAN ON PHONE (V.O.)
>   Yes sir. The ninth house is all
>   moved in. We're waiting for the
>   activation word.

                    HIRSH
Do we have a buyer for house ten?

            MAN ON PHONE (V.O.)
Not yet sir.

                    HIRSH
Then the answer is no. You know
the rules. No fun until all ten
houses are occupied.

            MAN ON PHONE (V.O.)
I understand. We're all
just...ready to get started.

Hirsh lightens a little.

                    HIRSH
Bob, no one is more anxious than
me. We need to show patience.
This wasn't planned overnight and
it can't be run that way either.
It won't work otherwise.

            MAN ON PHONE (V.O.)
You're right, of course. Are there
any leads on a tenth buyer?

                    HIRSH
Not yet. I'm working on that right
now actually.

He strokes the hair of the struggling woman. She is terrified.

                HIRSH (CONT'D)
Hedging my bets as it were.

            MAN ON PHONE (V.O.)
What about Freed?

The mention of this name angers Hirsh.

> HIRSH
> Freed is being taken care of as we
> speak, Bob. I don't want you to—

He STABS THE WOMAN RIGHT IN THE HEART WITH THE KNIFE. She dies, but he keeps on talking.

> HIRSH (CONT'D)
> ...worry about Freed. He's the
> last loose end. Okay?

> MAN ON PHONE (V.O.)
> Yes sir. Sorry to have bothered
> you.

> HIRSH
> No problem.

Hirsh ends the call and pockets the phone. He pulls the knife out of the woman and wipes the blood on her shirt. He turns to the other figure and hands over the knife.

> HIRSH (CONT'D)
> Be a dear and have this cleaned for
> me. It goes back in my display
> case at the office.

The figure turns to leave with the knife.

> HIRSH (CONT'D)
> Oh, and have Martino come out and
> clean this up.

Hirsh takes off his robe and walks up a small staircase off the right.

INT. STAIRCASE-DIMLY LIT

Hirsh, dressed in a suit walks briskly up the stairs. He goes to a door and exits.

INT. PUBLIC LIBRARY-DAYLIGHT

Hirsh comes through the door. The library is filled with children, having a story time reading. He walks past them, smiling and up to the main library counter. There is an old woman there, who smiles sweetly at him.

                    OLD WOMAN
          How did everything go, Mr. Hirsh?

                    HIRSH
          Just fine, Mrs. Gold. This is
          for you.

He hands her an envelope full of what could only be cash.

                    HIRSH (CONT'D)
          Always a pleasure to help the local
          public library.

                    OLD WOMAN
          You call me if you need any more
          help.

Hirsh smiles.

                    HIRSH
          Know anyone looking for a house?

END OF TEASER

ACT ONE-PILOT

INT. APARTMENT-DAYLIGHT

The apartment is small, but packed with lots of things. One could get very claustrophobic in a place like this. We hear a phone conversation in another room.

> MADDIE (O.S.)
> I know, I know, Mom. It's just very
> hard right now. (pause) Of course
> we want a house, but, well, it's a
> city. And he's a reporter. (pause)
> Okay, he's a *traffic* reporter.
> Exactly. Exactly why we don't live
> in a house right now.

MADDIE AUGUST walks into the room, carrying laundry and cradling a phone on her neck.

> MADDIE (CONT'D)
> The writing is...fine. Yes, Mom
> it's going fine. It takes a while
> to write a book, you know.

We hear Maddie's mother 'carping' on the other end of the phone as Maddie puts the phone down and sets the laundry on the floor. We can hear her mother still talking. She picks up the phone and goes back to the obviously painful and one sided conversation. She slumps against the couch.

> MADDIE (CONT'D)
> Yes, Mom, I know it only takes you
> a few days to *read* a book...but you
> have to make up all the stuff when
> you *write* a book.

Maddie pretends to shoot the phone. She is frustrated.

> MADDIE (CONT'D)
> Yeah, right. Look Mom, I gotta go,
> okay? (pause) Yes, he's coming on
> right now, okay? I love you too.

She clicks off the phone and throws it on the couch. She puts her face in her hands and lets out a small scream of frustration.

                    MADDIE (CONT'D)
          Unbelievable!

She kicks the laundry basket and moves into the small living room. She sits on the phone and turns on the TV.

                    MADDIE (CONT'D)
          It only takes a few days to read a
          book...

The TV springs to life. It's tuned to a newscast. We can see the show and what's going on.

                    MALE ANCHOR
          Now, let's check in with Steve in
          the channel seven news copter for a
          traffic update. Steve?

On the TV screen, there is a live video shot of STEVE AUGUST, who is in the helicopter cockpit, flying it and giving an on the spot traffic report. Maddie sees this and smiles at her husband.

                    STEVE
          Tom, the parkway's backed up to
          Greentree in anticipation of the
          demolition set to blow at three
          today. Let's face it-if you aren't
          already there, you're not going to
          see it. Find an alternate route if
          you can.

                    MALE ANCHOR
          How soon until the demolition
          Steve?

                    STEVE
          About five minutes. In fact, me and
          Luke, our cameraman are on our way
          there now to catch all the action.

MALE ANCHOR
Sounds like you've found a way to
beat the traffic.

STEVE
Well, not really. They won't let me
take the helicopter home with me.

MALE ANCHOR
(laughing) That's too bad. We'll
see you in a few minutes. Let's
check in with Sheena with the
weather. Sheena?

The TV switches to the weather anchor. Maddie looks away from the TV.

MADDIE
I'm gonna need popcorn for this.

She gets up in time to hear her mailbox outside of the apartment slam shut.
She redirects herself to the front door and opens it.

EXT. APARTMENT COMPLEX HALLWAY

Maddie sticks her head out of the apartment and looks down at the mail
box, which has twenty boxes for the other tenants. She pads down the hall
and finds the box that says AUGUST. With a key, she opens it and finds a
stack of mail. She grabs it and heads back to the apartment, muttering the
importance of each letter.

MADDIE
Crap...Crap...crap...crap...bill...
bill...bi-huh?

She reenters the apartment, holding a letter from a mortgage company. She
closes the door and tears it open. She reads it and is immediately angry.

She crumples it up and throws it. She begins to cry. We can see from the
top of the letter that it is a rejection for a mortgage loan letter. Maddie sits
back down in the living room and sobs. The TV anchor comes back on.

                    MALE ANCHOR
          We'll be checking in with Steve at
          the Midland Tower demolition here
          in a moment.

CUT TO:

EXT. THE SKIES OVER THE TOWER

We can see the CHANNEL 7 NEWS COPTER and see two people in the
cockpit. STEVE AUGUST and his cameraman, LUKE.

INT. HELICOPTER-DAYLIGHT

Steve is flying as Luke prepares his camera.

                    LUKE
          Any word on the house?

                    STEVE
          We're supposed to get a letter soon
          either saying yea or nay on the
          loan. I just don't know what the
          problem is.

                    LUKE
          Is your credit okay?

                    STEVE
          Maddie has a few loans and stuff.
          Mine's okay.

                    LUKE
          So, together, your credit sucks.

                    STEVE
          Pretty much. We just can't stand
          that apartment anymore. It's so
          cramped.

                    LUKE
          Wish I could help you.

                    STEVE
        You did. It's *your* old apartment,
        remember?

                    LUKE
        Well? You're welcome.

Luke sets up his camera to get a shot of the tower.

                LUKE (CONT'D)
        We're live in three...two...one.

CUT TO:

INT. TV STATION-DAYLIGHT

                MALE ANCHOR
        Okay Steve. There's about twenty
        seconds before the tower goes down.
        I hope you're a safe distance away.

                STEVE (O.S.)
        We're quite a safe distance away,
        but we do have the best seats in
        the..

CUT TO:

INT. HELICOPTER-DAYLIGHT

                    LUKE
        Steve? There's someone on the roof!

EXT. THE TOWER-DAYLIGHT

Sure enough, there is a man on the roof with his arms spread towards the
sky.

                MALE ANCHOR (O.S.)
        What was that?

STEVE
There's a man on the roof, Tom.

MALE ANCHOR (O.S.)
Dear God.

STEVE
They have to stop the explosion.

LUKE
No time, it's going off in ten seconds.

STEVE
Hold on...

Luke bolts the camera in place before Steve can make his move.

EXT. THE SKIES OVER THE TOWER

The helicopter lurches forward and heads straight to the tower. The man on the roof stays still.

EXT. THE DEMOLITION CREW

There is a crowd of people surrounding the crew and they are counting down.

CROWD
Five, four, three two one!

EXT. THE TOWER-DAYLIGHT

There is a huge EXPLOSION. The building erupts at the base and starts to collapse. The building LURCHES TO ONE SIDE, but doesn't completely fall. The man is thrown hard on the roof top, but he's still alive.

INT. HELICOPTER-DAYLIGHT

The helicopter shakes from the shock wave, but steadies itself.

STEVE
That's not supposed to happen, right?

> LUKE
> Look, that guy is still there.

EXT. THE TOWER-DAYLIGHT

The building is slanted and rocking. The man is struggling to stand. He's hurt, but alive.

INT. HELICOPTER-DAYLIGHT

> MALE ANCHOR (O.S.)
> Steve, are you there?

> STEVE
> I can see him. We're going to try
> to get him.

> LUKE
> This should be interesting. Hope
> your wife ain't watching.

> MALE ANCHOR (O.S.)
> Be careful. This footage is
> amazing.

EXT. THE TOWER-DAYLIGHT

The helicopter hovers OVER THE TOP OF THE TOWER, which is starting to SWAY a little. The man looks up and sees it and stands up shakily. Slowly the helicopter moves down.

INT. HELICOPTER-DAYLIGHT

> STEVE
> Do we have a rope?

> LUKE
> No.

> STEVE
> Really?

                    LUKE
Really.

                    STEVE
Damn.

                    LUKE
Maybe he can grab the rail.

                    STEVE
Ask him.

Luke yells out of the copter's window.

                    LUKE
Can you grab the rail?

                    MAN
I think so, but you have to get
lower!

The man is staggering, favoring his left leg. Steve nods and lowers the copter. The building begins to collapse.

                    LUKE
Lower man, lower!

                    STEVE
Hang on.

The copter lowers and the man GRABS THE RAIL AS THE BUILDING FALLS.

                 STEVE (CONT'D)
Is he on?

                    LUKE
Yeah, now get us outta here. I'll
try to pull him in.

The helicopter pulls away as Luke tries to pull the man inside.

EXT. THE TOWER-DAYLIGHT

We can see the MAN dangling from the rail of the helicopter. The copter pulls away as the building crumbles to the ground. The man is finally pulled into the copter.

CUT TO:

EXT. CROWD BELOW-DAYLIGHT

Cheers erupt.

CUT TO:

INT. APARTMENT-DAYLIGHT

Maddie cheers.

> MADDIE
> Woo! My man! I'm so gonna kill you!

CUT TO:

INT. HELICOPTER-DAYLIGHT

> STEVE
> Is he okay?

> LUKE
> Shaky, but okay. I think his leg's
> broken.

The man is confused and frightened.

> MAN FROM BUILDING
> What was I doing up there?

Luke just looks at him.

> MALE ANCHOR (O.S.)
> Steve? Can you hear me? That was
> amazing, is the man okay?

STEVE
He seems to be okay. We're coming
down. We'll need an ambulance.

MALE ANCHOR (O.S.)
We'll have one sent. You're a hero,
Steve. Great work!

STEVE
Yeah.

LUKE
(Cupping the microphone headset)
I'm a hero too, ya know.

Steve smirks.

MAN FROM BUILDING
What happened? What was I doing up
there?

The man is frightened. Steve turns around and looks at the man. Luke looks
at Steve confused.

STEVE
I think we'd all like to know, pal.

END OF ACT ONE

ACT TWO

INT. APARTMENT-TWILIGHT

Steve and Maddie are sitting next to each other on a couch. Steve is nursing a beer while Maddie is tucked under his arm. They are watching TV.

> MALE ANCHOR (O.S.)
> And of course our top story,
> WASL's own reporter Steve
> August performeda daring
> rescue during the demolition
> of the K Tower in Greentree.
> A man, whose name is being
> withheld by police was
> discovered standing on top
> of the KTower when Steve
> spotted him from his
> helicopter. The building
> exploded...

Steve interrupts the newscast.

> STEVE
> How many times do you want to see
> this?

> MADDIE
> Until you learn not to do silly
> dangerous crap like that again.

> STEVE
> Luke's the hero. He did all the
> work.

> MADDIE
> It wasn't his turn to fly the
> copter.

> STEVE
> It's *never* his turn to fly the copter.

Steve looks at Maddie and smirks.

                    MALE ANCHOR (O.S.)
        ...not the first time Steve has
        been a hero. He is a decorated
        combat pilot who single handledly
        saved his—

Steve picks up the remote and mutes the TV.

                    STEVE
        I told them to keep that out of it.

                    MADDIE
        Sorry Hun, you're a hero all the
        way around.

                    STEVE
        Enough of that. I wanna hear about
        your day. Any mail come?

                    MADDIE
        Um. Kinda.

                    STEVE
        (excited)
        The house?

                    MADDIE
        Yeah.

His face sinks. He knows.

                    STEVE
        What do we have to do to get a
        loan? Our credit couldn't be *that*
        bad, could it?

                    MADDIE
        I'm sorry.

                    STEVE
        It's not your fault. I just wanna
        know if there's this house buying
        boom, who the hell is buying?

Steve grabs his beer and swallows what's left. He get up and goes into the
kitchen, tripping over things as he does.

                STEVE (CONT'D)
        This place is too damn small.

Maddie leans over the couch and talks to Steve over the back.

                    MADDIE
        Look on the bright side. Maybe your
        new hero status will help out.

Steve laughs.

                    STEVE
        They didn't give a damn before.

                    MADDIE
        Well, you never videotaped it
        before. You're a local celeb now.
        You could get dates and stuff if
        you really wanted to.

Steve looks at Maddie and a small smile creeps onto his face.

                    STEVE
        Dates? You think?

                    MADDIE
        I know. I'd date you again.

                    STEVE
        Would ya?

                    MADDIE
        Sure. Except if you took me back to
        this dinky little apartment, I'd
        never call you again.

Steve tries to jump over the couch and catches himself before falling too far. He grabs Maddie and they kiss, laughing.

> STEVE
> We'll get a house. I promise. It
> might take a while, but we'll get
> one.

> MADDIE
> Like in a couple of days? You know,
> my mom says it only takes a couple
> of days to read a book.

> STEVE
> Forget your mom.

> MADDIE
> (smiling) Who?

They kiss. We see the news report still going on in the back ground.

CUT TO:

INT. HIRSH'S PENTHOUSE-NIGHT

Hirsh is sitting on a leather recliner, watching the news report on Steve. He's in a silk robe and he's smoking a cigar. His phone rings. He picks it up after one ring, eyes never leaving the TV.

> HIRSH
> Hello, Mr. Leeds. I'm
> watching it right now.
> My thoughts exactly, sir.
> I'll have Ahmo look into it
> in the morning. Yes sir.

He hangs up the phone and watches the newscast.

                    NEWS ANCHOR
          The man, now identified as Michael
          Freed claims to have no
          recollection as to why he was on
          top of the building.

Hirsh frowns at the mention of this name.

                NEWS ANCHOR (CONT'D)
          However, he does owe a big debt of
          gratitude to our own traffic
          reporter, Steve August. In other
          news...

                       HIRSH
          A hero. Nice touch.

He picks up the phone again and dials a number. He waits and then talks.

                   HIRSH (CONT'D)
          Hello, Pike. It's seems Mr. Freed
          is unable to kill himself like a
          good little do-bee. Give him a
          hand. Oh, and feel free to take
          your time. He's earned it. Make
          sure you tell Bob.

He rests the phone again. A woman, dressed in the robe from the opening
walks into the room. It is AHMO, his personal assistant. The robe this
time, however, is open. She is wearing some extremely sexy 'bed wear.'

                   HIRSH (CONT'D)
          Ahmo darling, I'm to tell you to
          investigate a certain helicopter
          pilot in the morning. He may be our
          buyer for house ten.

She looks at the TV casually. She turns it off and walks over to Hirsh, who
looks at her hungrily.

                       AHMO
          So, why don't you tell
          me in the morning?

                          75

Hirsh smiles.

>   HIRSH
>   Oh, I will.

She climbs onto his lap.

FADE OUT.

FADE IN:

INT. WASL STATION-DAYLIGHT

This is the television station where Steve works. Steve walks down the hallway to polite applause and mild ribbing from other workers calling him "hey, hero' and such. He is smiling awkwardly. He stops at a door with stenciling on the outside—"DOMINICK MANCINI—STATION MANAGER." He knocks.

>   DOM (O.S.)
>   Come in.

Steve does.

INT. DOM'S OFFICE

Dom, a very large man is sitting behind a totally trashed desk.

>   DOM
>   Sit down.

Steve complies.

>   DOM (CONT'D)
>   How do you feel?

>   STEVE
>   Okay, I guess. Not used to—

DOM

Good. I have to tell you that this
little incident has made you a hot
property.

STEVE

Is that a good thing?

DOM

Of course. You're a hero.

STEVE

For the record, Luke's the one who
pulled the guy in. If anyone's a
hero—

DOM

Of course he is, but let's face it.
The public likes you, not Luke.

STEVE

That's too bad. Luke's nicer.

DOM

Too bad for Luke. Look, don't worry
about Luke, we'll take care of him.
We want to take care of you. How'd
you like to get out of the bird?

STEVE

And do what?

DOM

Report. Be a co-anchor. Nights to
start, but you'd need the grooming
to be honest.

STEVE

You've got to be kidding.

DOM

Do I kid?

STEVE

No. You have no sense of humor.

DOM

Right. It's a big bump up in pay,
but I think you could handle that.

Steve sits back in his chair for a moment.

STEVE

Who called?

DOM

What?

STEVE

Who called looking for me? Another
station? A bigger station?

DOM

What makes you think that?

STEVE

I know you. You think I'll jump
ship for another TV station. Dom
looks at him and sighs.

DOM

All four locals, three nationals,
and—

STEVE

Three nationals?

DOM

Cable too. Look Steve, I don't want
to lose you to another station.
Before yesterday you were the best
traffic reporter we've ever had.
And now...

              STEVE

And now I'm still the best traffic
reporter. Look, I have no
personality for being on screen.
That's why I fly a helicopter.
Maybe you catch my profile here and
there while I report a ten car pile
up but that's it. I'm not jumping
ship and I don't wanna be a
reporter.

Dom is silent.

           STEVE (CONT'D)
But I'll take the raise.

Dom's eyebrow raises.

CUT TO:

INT. TV STATION

Steve walks down the hall from Dom's office. Luke sees him and catches
up.

              LUKE
Hey there, hero.

              STEVE
Bite me.

              LUKE
Get a raise?

              STEVE
And an offer for overnight anchor.

              LUKE
No kidding? Me too?

              STEVE
It might be all you. I turned it down.

                    LUKE
You turned down a raise?

                    STEVE
The anchor spot, not the raise. Did
you get one too?

                    LUKE
Yeah, but not like I'll notice. I
feel snubbed.

                    STEVE
Well don't. I tell everyone I see
that you were the hero not me.

                    LUKE
So do I, quite frankly.

They laugh.

                    STEVE
You ready to fly?

                    LUKE
Yeah. Mad called and so did
about thirty news affiliates.

                    STEVE
Fun.

                    LUKE
And some chick named Ahmo. She
sounded hot.

                    STEVE
What station?

                    LUKE
No station. From some company
called Pentacorp. Wanted to talk
about a house or something.

Steve stops.

STEVE
Really?

LUKE
I thought that would stop you.

He hands Steve a piece of paper. It is a phone number of course.

STEVE
Pentacorp? Never heard of them.
What do you think?

LUKE
I'll go warm up the copter. Give
her a call.

Luke runs down the hall. Steve finds an empty desk and a phone. He calls.

STEVE
Maddie? It's me. Listen...yeah, she
called here too...what does she
want? Now? Well, I have to be in
the air in ten minutes...okay,
okay. I'll call you later.

Steve hangs up and calls the number on the paper.

STEVE (CONT'D)
Hello, this is Steve August. I was
looking for...

CUT TO:

INT. PENTACORP-DAYLIGHT

We see Ahmo talking to Steve on the phone.

AHMO
You were looking for me. I'm Ahmo
Varla and I represent Mr. J. Hirsh
for Pentacorp, Mr. August.

Congratulations on your heroism
yesterday. You *and* your cameraman.
Well done.

                STEVE (O.S.)
Um, thanks.

                AHMO
Mr. Hirsh would like to meet with
you and your wife, Mr. August.
Today.

                STEVE (O.S.)
I'm about to start my shift.

                AHMO
How about when you're finished?
Say 7 PM?

                STEVE (O.S.)
Why exactly?

                AHMO
We have an offer for you on a
house. It's a wonderful opportunity
that we don't offer very many
people.

CUT TO:

INT. TV STATION

                STEVE
A house? Seriously?

                AHMO (O.S.)
Seriously. But, you're busy. Shall
I arrange it with your wife? I can
give her all of the information so
she can fill you in on your way in.

                    STEVE
Um...I guess so, but this is kinda
strange.

                    AHMO (O.S.)
No stranger than a man in a
helicopter saving lives, or a man
trying to stand on an exploding
building. Mr. August, this kind of
strange will be a good thing.

                    STEVE
Well, then I guess we'll see you
later.

                    AHMO (O.S.)
Ta for now then.

The line goes dead.

                    STEVE
Ta for now.

He pockets the paper and makes his way to the helicopter pad.

END OF ACT

ACT THREE

INT. PENTACORP-TWILIGHT

Steve and Maddie are sitting in an office waiting room that is ENTIRELY WHITE. At the front desk, we see Ahmo, working on her computer. The only sound is her typing away. Steve and Maddie look very intimidated.

>   STEVE
>   (almost whispering) Could this
>   office be whiter?

>   MADDIE
>   Shhhhhh!

>   STEVE
>   (still whispering) I mean it's like
>   a doctor's office or something.

>   AHMO
>   This *used* to be a doctor's office.

Ahmo does not stop typing. Steve nearly jumps out of his skin at her speaking.

>   STEVE
>   Oh, really?

>   AHMO
>   Really.

>   MADDIE
>   You'll have to pardon my husband.
>   You see—

There is a loud beep. It's Ahmo's phone. She picks it up.

>   AHMO
>   Yes? Right away.

She hangs up the phone and stands.

> AHMO (CONT'D)
> I'll take you to Mr. Hirsh. Follow
> me.

Steve and Maddie get up and follow Ahmo as she walks down a very white hallway. They maintain some distance behind her.

> STEVE
> That was kinda rude.

> MADDIE
> What, me or her?

> STEVE
> I don't know. I'm nervous.

> MADDIE
> Would you rather we do this in the
> helicopter?

Steve smiles.

> STEVE
> Actually...

Ahmo stops in front of a huge door. She opens it and stands aside.

> AHMO
> Go right in.

After a beat, they do. Ahmo closes the door and follows them in.

INT. HIRSH'S OFFICE

The office is HUGE, not as white as the waiting room and almost pleasant. There are maps on the walls, newspaper clippings in frames, etc. Behind a huge desk is Hirsh, but he is not as clean and crisply dressed as we have seen him. His tie is untied, his shirt unbuttoned and his hair is a mess. He looks likeable and friendly. He sees the Augusts and smiles.

> HIRSH
>
> Please, come in and sit
> down. I'm very glad to meet
> you.

He gets up from his desk and pulls over two comfy-looking chairs. He goes back and gets a third.

> HIRSH (CONT'D)
> Please, sit. You must be Steve.

Hirsh holds out his hand. Steve accepts.

> HIRSH (CONT'D)
> And of course, Maddie.
> I loved your story
> in the *New Yorker*.
> Really touching.

He shakes Maddie's hand, who is surprised.

> MADDIE
> You read that?

> HIRSH
> Sure did. Great stuff, Maddie. Are
> you working on a book? It said that
> in the little bio.

Maddie smiles sheepishly.

> MADDIE
> *Trying* to write a book. It's been a
> bit hard lately.

> HIRSH
> Well, with your husband stopping
> suicide attempts while trying to
> thin out traffic, I imagine it
> would be hard.

Maddie and Steve both seem embarrassed. Hirsh plops down in one of the chairs. Ahmo stands casually behind Hirsh, but always maintaining a very cold and professional demeanor. No, this is not the Hirsh we have seen thus far.

> HIRSH (CONT'D)
> Sit, please for crying out loud!
> You're gonna kill my neck.

They both sit.

> HIRSH (CONT'D)
> My name is Judd Hirsh.

Steve and Maddie look at each other and grin. So does Hirsh.

> HIRSH (CONT'D)
> Yes, yes. Just like the guy on
> 'Taxi." I met him once. Nice guy.
> Anyway, most folks just call me
> Hirsh. Judd never agreed with me.
> Oh, and I apologize for the tie,
> but it *is* after six. I try to get
> comfy as soon as I'm off the clock.

> STEVE
> I can appreciate that.

> HIRSH
> I know you've already met Ahmo.
> She's actually the one who should
> be running this place.

The look on Ahmo's face is in full agreement, but she smiles anyway.

> HIRSH (CONT'D)
> Can I get you two anything? Drink?
> Something to eat?

> STEVE
> No thanks, really. We're just about
> jumping out of our skin though.
> What's this all about?

HIRSH

I imagine you tried to look up
Pentacorp since Ahmo called, am I
right?

MADDIE

I did. I couldn't find anything at
all about it.

HIRSH

Exactly. We are a large private
company, owned by five of the
wealthiest families on the planet.
They also, in addition to being
disgustingly rich, enjoy their
privacy. You *won't* find us, Maddie.

STEVE

So what do the five wealthiest
families on the planet want with
us?

HIRSH

They want you to do us a favor.
It's a mutually beneficial sort of
favor, but off the record, it's
more for you than them.

STEVE

I'm listening.

HIRSH

One of Pentacorp's favorite
projects is real estate
development. We love building
stuff. But, the problem, with
building lots of things is that you
have to find people and things to
put in them. Our latest project
is nearly done and we need one
more family for the experiment.

MADDIE

Experiment?

HIRSH

That's what we call this
thing...our experiment. Folks, this
is by far the best project
Pentacorp has ever undertaken. Are
you familiar with the concept of
gated communities?

Steve and Maddie look at each other.

MADDIE

Yeah. They're kind of elitist and
expensive.

STEVE

You need to be rich to live in one
of those places. Plus it's kind of
Stepford-like isn't it?

Hirsh laughs.

HIRSH

Funny you should say that. I said
pretty much the same thing when I
got wind of the project. My boss,
Mr. Leeds, didn't think it was
funny at the time. But then he
explained it to me. This community
will be different.

STEVE

How so? What, everybody gets in?

HIRSH

Not exactly. The candidates for
Monk's Run—that's what we're
calling it—are hand-picked.

STEVE

I'm sorry but I don't see how
that's different.

AHMO

Three things for getting
in. One. The candidate must have
never owned a house. Two—

Hirsh continues.

HIRSH

Two, candidates must have steady
legal work and three; they must
have been turned down for a house.

MADDIE

Why would you choose a credit risk
to buy a house?

HIRSH

Just because someone is late on a
car payment or two doesn't make
that person bad. It makes them an
American. One percent of the
American population is wealthy
beyond comprehension. One *percent*,
and that includes the owners of
Pentacorp. The other 99 percent?
Well, the one percent couldn't
exist without the 99. Where most
companies see a credit risk, we see
an opportunity.

STEVE

An opportunity? What, to get people
with lousy credit to pay a huge
percentage on a loan for an older
house? This is subprime lending
isn't it?

                    HIRSH
Pardon?

                    STEVE
You know, "Bad credit welcome, but
you'll pay through the nose?"

                    HIRSH
Sure sounds that way, doesn't it?

                    STEVE
Yeah it does. Sorry, we're not
interested.

Steve stands up. Maddie grabs his hand.

                    MADDIE
Honey?

                    STEVE
It's a scam, Mad.

                    HIRSH
It's not. Look, hear me out. If you
don't like what I tell you, you can
tell me to go to hell.

                    STEVE
This is a waste of time.

                    HIRSH
I'll talk faster then. It's a new
house. Never lived in, less than a
year old. Your mortgage payment is
less than you're paying for your
apartment. It's a three floor
modern Colonial, fully stocked with
everything but furniture. No down
payment with a really low rate.
Fixed. Two car garage and a huge
back yard. The neighborhood is a
cul-de-sac, so there' no through
traffic. The only people driving

                    91

through *live* there, and there are
only ten houses.

STEVE

(amazed) What?

HIRSH

Like I said, it's a *different* type
of community. Please, sit down.

Stunned, Steve sits back down.

MADDIE

It's a *new* house?

AHMO

Brand new. We've only built ten of
them. Depending on how this goes,
we will build more in a few years.
Like Hirsh said, it's an
experiment. If it works, that's
where our money will be made.

HIRSH

But I'm telling you folks, this is
an opportunity for you as well as
us.

STEVE

What's the catch?

Hirsh smiles.

HIRSH

Don't you even want to see the
house?

STEVE

Well...

MADDIE

Yes, we do.

                    HIRSH
Great! Tomorrow is Saturday. I'll
send a car to pick you up, say
eight am?

                    STEVE
I'm still waiting for the catch.

Hirsh smiles.

                    HIRSH
Tell you what. I'll bring the
coffee and donuts and I'll tell you
all about the catch, but it's one I
don't think you'll mind.

FADE TO BLACK.
END OF ACT

ACT FOUR-PILOT

EXT. FRONT GATE OF MONK'S RUN – DAY

A black sedan pulls up to the front gate which features a small tollhouse, occupied by a guard- STERLING CRISS. Criss comes out of the house and walks up to the car. He is all smiles.

> HIRSH
> Hi Sterling.

> CRISS
> Good morning, Mr. Hirsh.

> HIRSH
> Steve, Maddie, this is Sterling
> Criss, our front gate guard. He'll
> be a very familiar face to you.

> CRISS
> Nice to meet you folks.

> STEVE
> Nice to meet you.

> CRISS
> You folks need anything at all,
> just let me know. Welcome to Monk's
> Run.

Criss walks back over to the tollhouse and opens the gate from inside. The car drives through. Criss watches them drive through and closes the gate behind them.

CUT TO:

INT. SEDAN – DAY

Through the windows of the sedan, we can see how beautiful the wooded area is on the way to the site.

                    MADDIE
          Wow, this is a really pretty drive.
          I'll bet there's a lot of deer
          running through here.

                    HIRSH
          Not really. I think the
          construction scared them away. I'm
          sure they'll be back.

CUT TO:

EXT. MONK'S RUN-EARLY MORNING

It is a picture from a brochure; a small neighborhood of identical houses, all
pristine, all beautiful. There are ten beautiful houses arranged in a cul de
sac. It is a brilliant work of modern architecture. There are cars parked in
most of the driveways, a few scattered folks out tending to their lawns, but
the neighborhood is quiet. If Norman Rockwell lived here, there would be a
painting of it. It is the IDEAL American neighborhood. The sedan pulls
into the center of the road and stops on an angle in front of the ten houses.
The driver remains, but Hirsh, Steve and Maddie get out.

                    HIRSH
          This house here on the left is it.
          Sorry, your choice I'm afraid is
          limited to just this one.

                    STEVE
          Wow, you weren't kidding. I don't
          think I've ever seen just ten
          houses.

                    MADDIE
          They all look the same.

                    STEVE
          Yeah, but...

                    MADDIE
          They're beautiful.

> HIRSH
> Pretty impressive, huh?

Steve and Maddie walk closer to the house, taking it all in, pointing at the lawn and the garage.

> MADDIE
> A garden walkway. That would be
> pretty.

> STEVE
> I could get a basketball hoop to
> stick on the garage.

> MADDIE
> For who? You suck at basketball.

> STEVE
> Yeah, and you can grow
> something. Right.

Maddie pokes his ribs and then hugs him.

> HIRSH
> How about the inside tour?

Steve and Maddie smile.

CUT TO:

INT. HOUSE TEN - ENTRANCE/HALL-DAYLIGHT

It is a spacious hallway, hardwood floors-stunning. The door opens and the three walk in, Steve and Maddie in the lead. Maddie gasps as she looks. Steve is equally impressed.

> MADDIE
> Oh, Steve.

> STEVE
> Mr. Hirsh, this is—

> HIRSH

Don't say anything yet. Look the
place over first. Straight ahead is
the kitchen, to your right, the
dining room and adjacent to that,
the living room. There's a small
den right off of that. Maybe for a
certain writer we know.

Maddie makes a beeline to the den. Steve just stands there and watches her
go. Hirsh walks up to Steve.

> HIRSH (CONT'D)

So far, so good?

> STEVE

Very good so far. I gotta tell you,
Mr. Hirsh—

> HIRSH

Just Hirsh. My dad was Mr.

> STEVE

Right. This is incredible.
Maddie yells gleefully.

> MADDIE (O.S.)

I got dibbs on the den!

> HIRSH

Don't worry—there's an office on
the third floor too.

> STEVE

Hirsh, you said there was a catch.

> HIRSH

All good things have a catch,
Steve.

> STEVE

What is it?

HIRSH

Well, the good news is there's only
one. Do you have any plans on
moving out of the area, or
relocating jobs?

STEVE

Not sure, why?

HIRSH

In order for us to get you in here,
you have to agree to live here for
five years.

STEVE

Five years? I mean, what if—

HIRSH

No exceptions, Steve. You and
Maddie both must hold residence
here for exactly five years. I know
it's not a problem for most of the
resident at Monk's Run—they all
have their own business here and
families. You and Maddie are sort
of celebrities—you more so with
your heroics. I'm sure you've
gotten offers from other news
outlets...

STEVE

Well, yeah, but I haven't decided
anything.

HIRSH

I understand. So, you must let me
know today if you intend to take
the house.

STEVE

That quick?

                    HIRSH
Steve, look at this house. Do you
really think I could hold it from
someone else any longer?

                    STEVE
Five years?

                    HIRSH
I tell you with all confidence that
you will never ever find a house,
or a deal like this anywhere, ever
again. I'm not trying to pressure
you, but—

                MADDIE (O.S.)
Steve, come here!

                    STEVE
Excuse me.

                    HIRSH
Sure. Just one thing to think about
if you were going to take another
job elsewhere, you wouldn't have
come here today, would you?

Hirsh raises an eyebrow and winks. Steve gives a small smile and leaves.
Hirsh pulls out a cell phone. He dials.

                HIRSH (CONT'D)
Mr. Leeds, it's me...Looks like a
go. No they haven't gone upstairs
yet. I'll have the signatures when
I come back to the office. I think
we can begin right away. No sir,
they suspect nothing. No one does
as of yet. All things in time, sir.
Yes, sir. This is going to be fun.

Hirsh hangs up and dials another number. He is smiling.

> HIRSH (CONT'D)
> Bob? Hirsh. Activate Monk's run.
> (Pause) No, right now. Go ahead.
> Do it.

He ends the call and smiles.

INT. HOUSE TEN-DEN-DAYLIGHT

Steve walks into the den. Maddie is in love with the room.
She twirls around.

> MADDIE
> A *real* writing room. Steve, this is
> a dream. I already want to sit down
> and write.

> STEVE
> So, I guess we'll take it then?
> Maddie's smile fades slightly.

> MADDIE
> Hon, I'm sorry. I guess we should
> go and discuss this. I mean, this
> is a big decision, right? What if
> we can't afford—

> STEVE
> Hirsh said it's less than our
> apartment.

> MADDIE
> Hirsh said there was a catch.

> STEVE
> Would this place make you happy?

> MADDIE
> *You* make me happy.

> STEVE
> The catch is we'd have to live here
> for five years. No exceptions.

> MADDIE

That's it?

> STEVE

That's it.

> MADDIE

So, no CNN job if you wanted it?

> STEVE

Not for five years.

Maddie takes a moment and really considers this.

> MADDIE

Oh, babe.

> STEVE

If I were gonna get a new job we
wouldn't have come today, right?

Maddie looks at him and then smiles excitedly.

> MADDIE

So...

> STEVE

So, should we look at the rest of
the house before we sign, or should
we check it out when we move all of
our junk here?

Maddie jumps into Steve's arms and they embrace tightly. The lights flicker
for a moment, and then everything is fine. Over their shoulders, there is a
teenaged boy on a skateboard surfing by the house.

CUT TO:

EXT. MONK'S RUN-STREET-DAYLIGHT

The boy is SEAN, 16 and a typical skate rat. He maneuvers his way down the street until he arrives at house four. He kicks up the skate board and walks to the door. He unlocks it and we follow him inside.

INT. HOUSE FOUR-HALLWAY-DAYLIGHT

He enters and closes the door.

                    SEAN
          Mom? I'm back.

There is a note on the banister for Sean. It reads; "Sean, Dropping Kristen off at girl scouts. Be back soon. Leave your dirty sneakers by the door. Hope practice went well. Love, Mom"

Sean smiles and kicks off his sneakers.

There is a WHOOSHING SOUND and a HARD SMACK as an invisible fist SLAMS into the side of Sean's face. It knocks him to the ground.

Sean is dazed and looks for his assailant, but there is no one. Sean is hurt and terrified. He tries to stand, but another HARD SMACK knocks him down again. His mouth has a trickle of blood. Sean is stunned and sits up on the floor.

                    SEAN (CONT'D)
          Stop it!

Invisible hands grab Sean by the collar and LIFT HIM OFF OF THE GROUND. He desperately looks around for someone, but there is no one else there he can see.

                    SEAN (CONT'D)
          Where are you?

Sean is THROWN DOWN and slides half the length of the hallway. He slowly gets up, eyes streaming with tears, bleeding from the mouth and an ugly bruise forming on his cheek. His eyes dart back and forth, looking for anyone, but THERE IS NO ONE THERE. He begins to hyperventilate.

CUT TO:

EXT. HOUSE TEN-DAYLIGHT

Hirsh, Steve and Maddie walk out of the house. Steve and Maddie are holding each other.

                    STEVE
          So, what now?

                    HIRSH
          Well, we can go right to my office
          and fill out the paperwork and,
          well, you can move in whenever you
          can. How does that sound?

                    MADDIE
          I hate to be cliché, but
          it sounds almost too good—

                    STEVE
          Yeah, too cliché. Don't even say
          it.

                    MADDIE
          Okay. Let's get to it then.

                    HIRSH
          Excellent!

Steve grabs Hirsh's hand and Maddie gives him a hug. They get into the car. As the car pulls away, we can get a broader scope of the neighborhood. We can also hear Sean continuing his ordeal in house four, crying and asking whatever is tormenting him to stop. It does not.

END OF ACT FIVE

ACT SIX

INT. HOSPITAL FLOOR-DAYLIGHT

It is a typical hospital, with doctors and nurses hustling and bustling. We find a door, with the number "509" in the center, and a erasable name board that reads "Michael Freed."

INT. HOSPITAL ROOM 509-DAYLIGHT

The room is filled with flowers and cards. There's even a nice basket of fruit. Lying in the sole bed, is MICHAEL FREED, the man that Steve August saved the day previous. His left leg is in a cast and he has a half-eaten tray of food. He looks angry while he talks on the phone.

> FREED
> No, I told you, I can't remember
> what happened. The police want to
> call it a suicide attempt, but it
> wasn't. (pause) I don't know.
> They're releasing me tomorrow at
> three, or so they told me. Listen,
> tell that guy from the paper to
> meet me tomorrow at five, okay? I
> still wanna come clean with Monk's
> Run. (pause) No, you don't want to
> know. Trust me.

Freed hangs up the phone and sighs. He turns on the television.

> FEMALE ANCHOR
> And in a follow up to the man
> discovered on the K tower
> Wednesday, Michael Freed, an
> architecture consultant, is said to
> be recovering nicely at Western
> Penn hospital, but has no
> recollection as to why he was on
> the tower in the—

The television clicks off.

FREED

Great. Real subtle. Why don't they
just give out my room number too.

THIN MAN (O.S.)

That would have made things easier
for me.

Freed looks around the room, and sees a very thin, gaunt man standing in
front of the door. He is dressed entirely in black.

FREED

I didn't hear you come in.

THIN MAN

I'm quiet.

FREED

Are you a priest? I told the other
one that I don't care that it's
Sunday, I'm not interested.

THIN MAN

Not a religious man?

FREED

No. Sorry.

THIN MAN

What will you say to your maker
when it's your time?

FREED

I don't believe in any 'maker,'
Father, so I guess I won't say
anything.

The thin man moves closer to the bed.

THIN MAN

That's very interesting Mr. Freed.
I thought you'd believe in a higher
power.

FREED

Why is that?

THIN MAN

Because it's your time.

The Thin Man pulls out a large needle and smiles.

FREED

What kind of priest are you?

THIN MAN

I never said I was a priest.

Freed leans up in his bed, but the thin man HITS HIM SQUARE IN THE CHEST, knocking him down.

Freed tries to grab the nurse call button, but thin man PULLS IT OUT OF THE WALL. He takes the needle and PLUNGES IT INTO FREED'S CHEST. Freed sucks in air, hissing in pain.

FREED

You son of a...

He cannot finish the sentence and he slumps back into the bed. The thin man pulls up a chair and sits down. Freed is twitching.

THIN MAN

The amazing thing about this little
drug is that it mimics death,
totally. See, right now, you're
twitching, but that's your nervous
system and your muscles dying. Now,
here's the neat part.

Thin man takes the needle out and puts it in his pocket. He leans over Freed's body and PUNCHES HIS BROKEN LEG. There is a very small whimper.

THIN MAN (CONT'D)

Ah, I heard that! But, in another
ten minutes, you won't be able to
even whimper.

He leans in close.

>   THIN MAN (CONT'D)
>   But you'll feel *everything*. You can
>   think and feel every single thing
>   even though everyone else will
>   think you're dead.

The thin man stands up and folds his hands.

>   THIN MAN (CONT'D)
>   My guess is they'll find you in
>   about an hour or so. They'll
>   pronounce you dead and stick you in
>   the morgue. The fun part will be
>   when they either perform an
>   autopsy, which will eventually kill
>   you, or ship you to the funeral
>   home, where having embalming fluid
>   pumped through your body will
>   eventually kill you. Either way, I
>   wouldn't wanna be you.

He turns to leave. Freed is totally immobile. The thin man reaches the door.
Then he turns. He walks back to Freed's bed and turns on the TV.

>   THIN MAN (CONT'D)
>   Maybe this'll help.

He switches it to a religious channel.

>   THIN MAN (CONT'D)
>   Mr. Hirsh sends his condolences.

The thin man turns and walks slowly to the door, moving out of the frame.
We can see the TV reflection in Freed's eyes. A single tear slides down his
cheek.

>   TV PREACHER (O.S.)
>   ...and what is God saying in this
>   verse? He's saying, I'll
>   paraphrase, he's saying that if you

do not believe with all of your
heart, you will be lost forever.
When you die, that's it! Worm food,
folks. You won't be in paradise,
you'll be where the sinners all go.
And where's that?

FADE TO:

EXT. HOUSE TEN-DAYLIGHT

We see a moving truck in front of Steve and Maddie's new house. The two
of them along with Luke and his girlfriend KYRA are helping them move
in. Luke and Steve have a dresser, which is heavier than it looks.

> LUKE
> Damn, Steve. Is there a body in
> here?

> STEVE
> Drop it.

The two men put the dresser down. Steve opens a drawer. Women's
panties, bras, etc. He frowns.

> LUKE
> Um, I won't tell anyone man. I
> swear.

> STEVE
> (ignoring Luke) Babe, I thought we
> were gonna empty the dressers.

Maddie and Kyra are on the sidewalk, walking towards the truck.

> MADDIE
> I thought it'd be faster, so I put
> the drawers back in.

> STEVE
> It's not faster if I'm in traction.
> Maddie looks at Kyra.

> KYRA

Meow?

> MADDIE

Oh, meow. Meow meow meow!

> KYRA AND MADDIE

Meow meow meow meow...

> LUKE

Nice huh?

> STEVE

Help me take these drawers out
would ya?

> MADDIE

We'll bring this stuff inside.

> KYRA

We'll be back

> MADDIE

Meow for now!

The women, carrying boxes, go into the house. Steve and Luke take start taking the drawers out.

CUT TO:

INT. HOUSE TEN-HALLWAY

The two women walk inside and stop.

> KYRA

Okay, where does this go?
Maddie looks at the box.

> MADDIE

Upstairs, in the main bedroom on
the right.

KYRA
Lucky me, I get to climb.

MADDIE
Thanks!

Maddie takes her box into the kitchen.

CUT TO:

INT. BEDROOM-DAYLIGHT

We can hear Kyra climbing the stairs and then see her enter the room. The room is cluttered with boxes and suitcases. She walks to a far corner of the room, stepping over boxes. She puts the box down and turns to head out of the room. She hears something and stops. The sound is of someone taking a VERY DEEP AND LONG BREATH. It increases in volume, but is not terribly loud. She shivers when the sound stops. She exhales and can SEE HER BREATH. She looks around the room.

The door to the room slams shut. Kyra lets out a stifled yell; her hand goes to her mouth. The breathing sound begins again. Kyra is beginning to panic. Her breath is very visible now and she is starting to shiver. She goes to the window that looks out to the front yard.

The window steams up with her breath. Kyra knocks on the window to get the attention of Maddie, who is visible. The window FULLY STEAMS UP AND ICES OVER, as if it is freezing.

The steamed window begins to take the FORM OF A FACE-A TORTURED FEMALE FACE. Kyra screams and backs away from the window. The face's mouth OPENS AND SCREAMS SILENTLY.

She turns and runs to the door, which to her surprise, opens easily. She continues to scream as the door SLAMS behind her.

CUT TO:

INT. HOUSE TEN-HALLWAY

Maddie walks in from outside and Kyra practically flies down the stairs. She's pale and screaming.

>   MADDIE
>   Hey, you okay?

>   KYRA
>   I...I don't know. I have to get out
>   of here!

She runs past Maddie, who looks confused.

>   MADDIE
>   Kyra?

Maddie follows her out the door.

CUT TO:

EXT. HOUSE TEN-FRONT STOOP

Kyra sits on the front lawn in the sunlight. She puts her hands behind her neck. Maddie comes up behind her.

>   MADDIE
>   You okay?

>   KYRA
>   I'm so cold...but...

>   MADDIE
>   But what?

>   KYRA
>   It was *creepy*, Maddie. Like someone
>   was in there with me.

>   MADDIE
>   What?

>   KYRA
>   Did somebody die in this house or
>   something?

Maddie sits down next to her. Kyra is shaking.

MADDIE

No, Kyra. It's a brand new house.
Literally. No one's *ever* lived
here.

Kyra looks at Maddie and then smirks.

KYRA

It was so strange. I mean...there
was breathing and it was cold
and...you think I'm nuts?

MADDIE

Of course not. I mean, we can't be
friends anymore, but...

KYRA

(laughing) Now I feel dumb.

MADDIE

Don't. I used to get freaked out in
that little apartment all the time.

KYRA

Yeah?

MADDIE

Always felt like someone was
watching me.

KYRA

And now?

MADDIE

Well, now it's just you watching
me, which is kind of creepier.

The women laugh. Kyra is still shaken up though.

MADDIE (CONT'D)
You gonna be okay?

                    KYRA
I just need to sit here for a
minute. It was... I could swear
someone was in there...I just need
to sit.

                    MADDIE
Take your time, Ky. Can I get you
anything?

                    KYRA
No, I'll be okay.

Maddie pats Kyra on her head and gets up to walk to the moving truck. Kyra takes a long look up at the house. She sees the window that had steamed up-it is fine now. She shakes her head.

CUT TO:

INT. BEDROOM-DAYLIGHT

From the window, we can see the four of them at the truck. The breathing sound comes again, this time is small rasps. We can see Kyra on the lawn get up and walk to the truck. The window fogs again, as if someone is breathing on it.

END OF ACT SIX

ACT SEVEN

EXT. HOUSE TEN-DAYLIGHT

Steve and Luke are finally getting the dresser out of the truck. Maddie cheers. The two men put the dresser on the ground carefully.

> LUKE
> Don't cheer too much. We're leaving
> it here.

We hear footsteps. The four friends turn and we see three menstrolling over.

> LEE
> Hey, are you guys the Augusts?

> STEVE
> Yeah, hi. I'm Steve.

> LEE
> Well, we're the semi-welcoming
> committee.

> STEVE
> Semi?

> FRANK
> Yeah, semi 'cause this isn't all of
> us.

> PAUL
> Everybody else is at work.

Maddie walks over. The three men are all smiles and dressed in sweats.

> MADDIE
> Hi, I'm Maddie. This is Luke and
> Kyra. They're helping us move in.

> PAUL
> Nice to meet you. I'm Paul, this is
> Lee and that's Frankie.

FRANK
We figured we'd see if you needed a
hand or two.

STEVE
Wow, that's really great! Thanks.

FRANK
Our wives have set up some food and
drinks over at my place-number one
right across the street.

MADDIE
Any chance of going now to say hi
while you guys do all the work?

KYRA
Drinks? Now you're talking.

FRANK
That's the idea. Go right on over.

MADDIE
Well, thanks gentlemen. Ky, shall
we?

The two ladies march over to House 1. The five men stand in the street
chatting.

FRANK
You look real familiar, Steve.

LUKE
He gets that all day.

Steve smirks.

PAUL
Frank, he's the *traffic* guy.

LEE
Holy cow, you *are* the traffic guy.

FRANK

A celebrity.

STEVE

Not really.

LEE

I was one of the cops at the K
tower that day. You're a hero.

STEVE

You were there?

LEE

Yeah, I saw everything. Who was the
guy inside, pulling that nut job
in?

STEVE

That was Luke here.

LEE

Hey, you're a hero too, ya know
that?

LUKE

Finally!

Luke and Steve laugh.

LEE

Shame about that guy, huh?

LUKE

Yeah, heard about him yesterday.

Steve has no idea what they are talking about.

STEVE

What?

                    LEE
        The guy you saved, Freed? Died in
        the hospital day after they brought
        him in.

Steve is shocked.

                    LUKE
        Weird, huh?

                    STEVE
        What happened?

                    LEE
        They don't know really. The family
        didn't want an autopsy or anything.
        Just a quick funeral.

                    FRANK
        Yeah. One of our missing neighbors
        today is John. He's a funeral
        director. Said Freed was just to
        have been cremated as per the will.

                    STEVE
        Damn.

Steve is more shaken than even he thought he'd be. He takes a seat on the
back of the moving truck.

                    LUKE
        You okay? You look green.

Steve looks up at the house and says nothing.

CUT TO:

INT. PENTACORP/HIRSH'S OFFICE-DAYLIGHT

Hirsh is smoking a cigar, staring out of his window. His door opens and
Ahmo enters. He continues to stare out of his window.

                    HIRSH
"God blessed the seventh day and
made it holy because He rested from
all the work of creating He had
done."

Ahmo moves next to him.

                    AHMO
The Book of Genesis.

Hirsh nods.

                    HIRSH
Do you know why that's my favorite
quote?

Ahmo shrugs her shoulders.

                HIRSH (CONT'D)
God has just created the entire
universe. He has literally created
everything. So what does he do
next? He commits one of the seven
deadly sins. He takes a break and
pats himself on the back. Pride,
Ahmo. Not only that, but he
commands that the day *he* decided
he'd done enough that week, he
makes it a holy day so *everyone* can
pat him on the back. Comforting
that the good lord has a bit of
good old pride in him?

                    AHMO
More amusing than anything.

Hirsh smiles.

                    HIRSH
Well, we don't take a break, do we?
What can you tell me about our
little community?

                    AHMO
          The August family is all but moved
          in. The Mackenzie house-house four
          seems to be the first one to light
          up as it were.

                    HIRSH
          Excellent. What else?

                    AHMO
          We need a secretary.

Hirsh looks at Ahmo.

                    HIRSH
          Why do we need a secretary? You
          take care of everything so well.

                    AHMO
          Because I am *not* a secretary.
          Specifically, I am not *your*
          secretary.

Hirsh smiles.

                    HIRSH
          I never said you were.

                    AHMO
          You don't have to.

                    HIRSH
          When did you become so sensitive?

                    AHMO
          It's not sensitivity. I represent
          Mr. Leeds in this office. I have
          been with you from the beginning on
          Monk's Run, but you need to
          remember who I am.

HIRSH
I don't suppose you'll remind me
tonight?

She scowls and turns to leave the office.

AHMO
Mr. Leeds is on line one.

Hirsh smiles again. He walks to his desk and puts his phone on speaker
function.

HIRSH
Mr. Leeds. What can I do for you?

LEEDS (O.S.)
I understand things are going well
with Monk's Run. That's good to
know.

HIRSH
Yes sir it is. Apparently, house
number four has shown activity
already.

LEEDS (O.S.)
Remind me what's in house four.

Hirsh pulls a sheet from his desk top.

HIRSH
Level nine poltergeist entity.
Masculine probably. Minimal
visual, mostly physical presence.
Violent at that.

LEEDS (O.S.)
Any idea who's getting beaten?

HIRSH
We won't know for a while. We'll
have to wait until someone
complains. Either the woman or the
boy. My money's on the boy.

LEEDS (O.S.)
I won't argue. You know I trust
your instincts on these things.

HIRSH
Thank you sir.

LEEDS (O.S.)
One more thing. Get yourself a
secretary. You've earned it.

Hirsh raises an eyebrow.

HIRSH
Any reason? I thought Ahmo could—

LEEDS (O.S.)
Ahmo is *not* your toy, Hirsh.
Or your secretary. Frankly and honestly
if she really wanted to, she could
eliminate any need Pentacorp has for you.
You're lucky she's not ambitious
in that way. Understand?

HIRSH
Sir, I wouldn't presume—

LEEDS (O.S.)
You're like a son to me, so take
some free advice. Ahmo was here
before you. Her loyalties are to me
and no one else. If she gets a wild
hair about you, there's little I'd
be able to do about it.

HIRSH
Are you suggesting that I should be
afraid of her?

LEEDS (O.S.)
My boy, you're a fool if you *aren't*
afraid of her. But, you have
nothing immediate to worry about.
Just keep up the good work.

The call disconnects. Hirsh sits in his chair hard. He lets out a huge sigh
and picks up his phone.

HIRSH
Ahmo? Would you mind finding a
secretary for the office?

CUT TO:

EXT. HOUSE TEN-FADING DAYLIGHT

The truck is closed up. Steve and Luke are sitting on the porch. They each
have a beer and are waving goodbye to the three neighbors.

STEVE
Thanks again guys. See you
tomorrow.

The three wave back and launch a light volley of 'You're welcomes." Steve
slumps on the porch and takes a gulp of beer.

LUKE
The whole Freed thing freaked you
out didn't it?

STEVE
How could you tell? And why didn't
you tell me?

LUKE
I thought it would keep until
tomorrow. Didn't want to ruin the
big day today.

Steve nods.

> STEVE
> It's just so strange. All of this.
> Last week, there was none of this.
> And now?

> LUKE
> Hip deep in it. Hey, you got lucky.
> You should be happy.

> STEVE
> That guy we saved is dead. Kinda
> hard getting my head around that.

Luke sighs.

> LUKE
> I know.

We can hear Maddie and Kyra walking and giggling as they make their way up the walkway.

> KYRA
> Lucas, my man. You'd better take me
> home right now.

A smile breaks on Luke's face.

> LUKE
> Why is that my sweet?

> KYRA
> 'Cause I want to discuss homemaking
> with you.

She holds out her hands for Luke to grab. He grabs them and gets pulled up.

> LUKE
> Well, I guess I have some 'making'
> to do.

Steve smiles.

> STEVE
> Thanks, both of you.

> MADDIE
> Yes, thank you very much.

Kyra leaves Luke to hug Maddie.

> MADDIE (CONT'D)
> Hey, are you gonna be okay?

> KYRA
> Yeah, I'll be fine. The booze
> helped out a *lot*.

> MADDIE
> Call me if you need anything, hon.

> KYRA
> You have to live here-you call me.

Maddie laughs a bit.

> MADDIE
> Yeah, now I get to think about that
> while I unpack in the big new
> house. Thanks.

Luke grabs Kyra's arm.

> LUKE
> C'mon woman. Let's discuss.

The two giggle as the leave. Maddie sits next to Steve. He offers her a beer.

> MADDIE
> Please, no more booze. Those girls
> nearly got us plowed.

> STEVE
> I'd say Ky was plowed.

                    MADDIE
        You'd be right. Did you have fun
        playing with the new kids?

                    STEVE
        Yeah. And we're all moved in. Just
        need to unpack.

                    MADDIE
        Wanna go unpack?

                    STEVE
        No.

                    MADDIE
        Me either.

She puts her head on Steve's lap.

                MADDIE (CONT'D)
        I'm very proud of you.

                    STEVE
        Why?

                    MADDIE
        Saving that guy. It's really what
        got us here, don't you think?

Steve contemplates telling her but hesitates.

                    STEVE
        I guess so.

The couple looks out at their neighborhood. They look at each
house and at just how pretty the sunset looks from their
little neighborhood.

                    MADDIE
        I think we'll like it here. In
        spite of Kyra's little experience.

STEVE
What happened to Kyra?

MADDIE
I'll tell you later, babe. Nothing
to worry about.

Off camera we hear a door slam and a fast rush of someone hauling ass on a skateboard. We see Sean, speeding by. Steve and Maddie wave as he travels past. He looks at them and skates faster. His face is a map of black and blue marks, but he smiles anyway. In seconds he's gone.

STEVE
Wonder what happened to him?

MADDIE
He's a skateboarder. Shut up and
kiss me.

Steve smiles and kisses Maddie.

CUT TO:

EXT. STERLING CRISS' GUARD STATION-FADING DAYLIGHT

We see Criss watching Luke and Kyra's car drive past. Criss presses something and the gate closes behind the car. Criss picks up a phone.

INT. GUARD STATION-FADING DAYLIGHT

Criss dials a number.

CRISS
Mr. Hirsh? It's Sterling. The
last car has left for the day.

HIRSH (O.S.)
Everything up and running?

CRISS
Yes sir.

HIRSH (O.S.)
Great. Is your link up and
running?

Criss looks to his lap top-the screen shows a digital map of all ten houses
from an aerial view. There are blinking red lights over each house.

CRISS
Yes sir.

HIRSH (O.S.)
Things are going to start popping
tonight.

CRISS
Yes sir.

Criss hangs up the phone. He looks at the screen again and smiles. The
house with the number TEN under it begins to blink with a yellow light.

CRISS (CONT'D)
Things are going to start popping.

CUT TO:

EXT. HOUSE TEN-FADING DAYLIGHT

Steve and Maddie are still sitting on the front stoop.

CUT TO:

INT. HOUSE TEN-MAIN BEDROOM-FADING DAYLIGHT

It is dark, but the breathing sound is still going on, heavier now. The door
to the bedroom is still open. As we look around the room, we see the
windows, which are now all steamed up. We see the bedroom door begin to
close slowly, and then SLAMS shut.

CUT TO:
BLACK SCREEN
Roll credits.

END OF EPISODE

SPIRITUS EX MACHINA

1

Travis Byron walked carefully through the dimly lit hallway as he followed the man in grease stained coveralls. It was only a little bit after 10 pm, but it felt much later, Travis thought. He wasn't as nervous as he was apprehensive. What he was about to see hadn't been seen by anyone other than a handful of people in the last 70 years. He felt mildly rankled and maybe just a little intimidated at what it *was* he was about to see.

His girlfriend Penny had told him to relax.

"It's just a car, love." She said sweetly, holding his face in her hands and kissing him lightly. "A stupid old car."

He smiled and kissed her back. But he was still not convinced that it was just a stupid old car.

For one thing, it wasn't *just* a stupid old car.

It was a murderer.

"Only a bit further, mate." Said the man in the grease stained coveralls.

"Thanks," Travis said back, adding. "I'm sorry, what's your name?"

The man looked back briefly and gave a broken toothed grin.

"Name's Tim, sir. Thanks for askin'."

Travis smiled a little.

"Thanks for bringing me back here. Sorry it's so late."

"Don't think nothin' of it," Tim said. The way he said 'think nothin' in his thick accent made it sound like 'fink nofin'.' "Not many geysers get to see the Jag."

"I've heard it hasn't had a lot of...visitors."

Tim laughed.

"Yeah, you could say that. Not many would want to though."

"I'm hoping you're wrong." Travis said. "My employer is counting on the novelty of this car to make good on his investment."

Tim slowed down and stopped. He turned around and looked at Travis.

"You seem likes a good bloke. Not a tosser like your boss, so I'll gives you a bit of free advice. Yeah?"

Travis was taken aback by this abrupt stop, but he raised his head to show he was interested in what Tim had to say. Tim leaned in close.

"Once your boss has this car moved, get as *far away* from it as possible. Quit if you has to, but get away from it."

Travis opened his mouth to speak, but Tim continued.

"I know it sounds right barmy it does, but I speak the truth. That car is flat out *bad.*"

Travis looked somewhat mortified and then started to smile.

"Look at you, taking the piss!" Travis said, laughing. "You started to worry me a bit there mate."

Tim smiled, but not because he was happy.

"Sir, you may think it's funny, but you won't for long. I absolutely guarantee,"

Travis, kept his smile but again, felt mildly rankled by not only what Tim said, but how he said it.

I absolutely guarantee...

Tim turned and began to walk again. It took Travis an actual effort to move forward, but he did it.

In less than twenty five seconds, they both arrived at a door marked "Storage Garage 481." Under the old looking green marker was another sign, handwritten and also very old looking. It read, simply:

Absolutely No Entry

"Don't worry 'bout the sign," said Tim, answering Travis' unarticulated question. "That's just to keep wandering folks out of here."

"Do you get many wandering folks?" Travis asked. "I mean this garage couldn't be farther away if it were bloody Penkridge."

"You a Penkridge bloke? I knew you was a small town geyser." Tim's genuine smile returned. "From Wolverhampton meself. Practically family we are,"

Travis was now getting weary of all of this. The night was getting longer and he was losing some patience. He looked at Tim, who was smiling like an idiot and decidedly not getting the key out to unlock the garage.

"If it's all the same Tim, we can talk about footie later. I do have a job to do here as do you."

"Ready to be on with it then are you?"

"Yes,"

"Right. Wait right here."

Tim grabbed the keys off of his belt, found the right one and unlocked the door. He opened it but did not allow Travis in at all.

"Right back," Tim said as the door closed slowly. There was a dragging sound and the door reopened with Tim holding two folding chairs. Travis sank.

"Here you are. Take a seat, sir."

He held the chair out to Travis, who refused it.

"What is this?" He asked loudly. "You take your sweet time dragging me across this warehouse and we finally get here, you bring me a fucking folding chair?"

Tim didn't flinch and continued holding the chair out.

"Right. There's a few things needed to be discussed sir, and *now* is when we do it. Take the chair and with all due respect, don't talk to me like I work for you."

The tone of Tim's voice was colder and direct. It didn't have any of the local boy charm anymore. When he said 'things' it didn't come out sounding like 'fings.' Tim was serious.

Without a word, Travis took the chair, opened it and sat down. Tim nodded and did the same. He took two fingers and fished out a soft pack of cigarettes from his coverall breast pocket.

"Fag?" he offered. Travis shook his head.

Tim took one from the pack and put the rest of the pack back in the pocket. He reached into his pants pocket and grabbed a cheap lighter, and lit up. He inhaled deeply and when he exhaled, there was just a very thin stream of smoke. Travis patiently waited for Tim to start.

"In 1955, there were this accident at Le Mans,' Tim began. "Killed, when all were said and done, 88 people. Flippin' tragedy if there ever were one, right?"

Tim took a deep drag and continued, allowing the smoke to slowly come out of his mouth and nostrils.

"That car was never driven again. Packed up and locked away, quite like this one here. Sold last year for over a million, American anyways. Nice little tidy pile of cash for the owner, init? Nowhere near what your tosser of a boss is paying for this, yeah?"

Travis had to agree. He'd heard about the Le Mans tragedy and the huge payout last year, which is what ignited his employer's quest in the first place. He thought he was getting a steal with this car at eighty thousand pounds and Travis had offered his services to make sure it was worth it.

"Well, true, but the morbid fact of the body count has a lot to do with it I'm sure." Travis said.

Tim took time to look at his smoke before speaking.

"Is that what you really think? Cos I'll tell you something for nothing, mate. I'd rather have about ten of the other car than this one in there."

"I'm not following you. This car here carries a considerably lower body count than the Le Mans." Travis said. "And by considerably, I mean *very* considerably. Only twenty people if I'm correct."

Tim gave a short bark of a laugh.

"Listen to yourself, mate. '*Only* twenty people?' Are you fucking daft? twenty *people*, man. So, it isn't eighty eight, but there's still blood ain't there? Broken homes and families."

"eighty eight is a hell of a lot more death than twenty, so yeah as bad as twenty is, it's a damn sight better than eighty eight. Not much really to change that little fact."

"Except, for the one detail you're forgetting." Tim shot back. "The Austin-Healy 100 Special that killed eighty eight people and ruined or injured at least 120 people did it all in *one shot*."

Travis opened his mouth to say, "So what?" but found that he couldn't say it at all.

"Let it sink in there, boy-o. The eighty eight people killed all got killed at once. The little Jaguar on the other side of this wall killed twenty people *one at a time* for the most part."

"Bollocks," Travis said. "Total bollocks. You're starting to waste my time here. If you're done taking the piss out of me, I'll be having a look at my employer's property."

Travis was furious now and stood up, but Tim stayed calm. He didn't even look up at Travis. He just fixed on some stain on the floor and looked almost sadly resigned. He let smoke out as he exhaled.

"You're gonna want to hear this, mate. Not kidding." Was all Tim said.

"I suppose you're going to tell me a car that's damn close to being a century old and hasn't had a working motor in it for the bulk of that time just rolls off all by its self and kills someone once in a while. Yes?"

"That car ain't moved in about two decades," Tim replied. "It don't roll around on its own. Never has, but I will assure you that car is a fucking spook if there ever was one. An evil one."

Tim took one last drag and dropped in on the floor. Travis looked and saw a pattern of similar burn marks in the floor. Tim finally looked up at Travis, not smiling.

"When you're in there alone, you're gonna want to ask me some questions. I may or may not be here to answer them on your way out as I don't like to go in there if I don't have to,"

Travis softened slightly.

"Wait, you aren't going in?"

"No. So if you got any questions, ask 'em now."

"Well, I haven't even seen it yet, have I?" Travis spoke. "Look, I'm sorry, but this is all really-"

"I'm telling you sir, that car is fucking *dangerous*. If you were smart, you'd go tell your employer that everything is fine and let him deal with it, but you should just turn around and go home."

Travis looked at the man and saw he was shaking slightly. He looked terrified. Tim looked as if he were going to say something, but didn't.

"Tim, I'll be fine, but wait out here, alright? I won't be too long."

Tim looked like he wanted to run. Travis held up a hand.

"Give me five minutes and then pound on that door. Is that a little safer?"

Tim seemed to ponder this and then he nodded.

"Five minutes, no more." Tim said. "Maybe only four, but don't get too close to it and for fuck's sake, don't touch it."

Travis smiled and walked to the door. Tim grabbed his shoulder.

"And whatever it shows you isn't real." Tim said, nearly whispering. "It's all a lie."

Travis frowned and then smiled, if only to reassure Tim.

"Five minutes, maybe four. Don't touch it. Got it."

Tim released his shoulder and Travis opened the door. As the door closed, Tim stood trembling and stared at the door. He began to count to three hundred slowly. He debated to count to two hundred forty, but he thought that Travis may be okay.

He really didn't seem stupid.

2

Travis closed the door, locked it and reached out to his left, feeling the wall for the light switch. He found it and switched it on, hearing the heavy light overhead click. They were the newer, non-incandescent lights and would take a minute or two to light up bright, but there, not two feet in front of him was the car.

After listening to Tim go on about it, he expected it to growl at him, but it stayed put, good little car that it was, and did nothing close to growling. Travis stared at the car and took a heavy step forward, closer to the car.

"I'm not supposed to get close to you," Travis said quietly to the car. "You're some sort of spook as I am to understand."

The car did nothing.

Travis walked slowly around it. It was a beautiful car. A 1954 Jaguar XK120. Black, sleek convertible and absolutely gorgeous. It was a dream car, really. A total race car-one seat for one passenger and just screamed to be driven. This was a car that was built for racing and designed for winning. And win this car did; it won all three of the races it ran until it was considered a jinx by Walter Carmichael, the car's original owner, driver and eventual third victim.

Travis looked intently at the car and although a thin layer of dust covered it, it still looked shiny and beautiful. Tempting even.

"You're a beautiful spook, that's for sure," Travis said quietly to the car.

He circled it one more time and decided to get to work. He took his messenger bag off and found a work table along the opposite side of the car. He opened it and took three things out, one of which was a camera.

He turned around and started taking pictures of the car. As he did so, he began to talk and walk around the car, quickly.

"Julian Fitzgerald, died 1956, leapt from his third floor flat six hours after repairing a faulty hose," Travis said. "Spencer McDaniels, died also 1956 about four hours after rotating all four tires. Massive heart failure. He was 23 years old and healthy as an ox."

The car simply stood there as Travis circled the car, taking pictures and speaking. He was quickly rattling off the name of every person who had died and was linked to the car.

"Carmichael, of course. Took a straight razor to his own bloody neck and nearly decapitated himself after retiring you. No less than one hour after the fact."

He made his way back to the work table and put the camera down. He then stepped forward and touched the hood of the car. The moment he touched the hood he felt something akin to a static electric shock jump into his arm, but he kept the fingers on the hood. He again, walked around the car, running his fingers along, still reciting the names.

"Sean Radcliffe, 1961, the first buyer, post Carmichael. Died from a self-inflicted head wound via gun shot. Right in the front seat."

As he walked around the back of the car he looked into the empty driver seat. He blinked, but he saw something not unlike a shadow. He didn't stop walking, but he did keep looking.

The shadow seemed to take shape until he saw a man, sitting in the driver seat, looking right at him.

"Hello, boy," said the man. "I imagine, you know who I am."

Travis stopped and nodded. He stood at the right side of the car.

"Hello, Sean." Travis said.

Sean Radcliffe smiled a rotten looking smile. Travis could see a black hole on the left side of Sean's head.

"What is it you hope to accomplish here boy?" Sean asked, still smiling.

"If it's all the same, Sean, I got some more names to go over, but I was wondering who the first one was going to be to show up."

Sean laughed.

"Are you trying to piss something off today?" Sean said. "Cos, this is about the right way to do it I'd reckon."

"Yeah," Travis said, starting to walk around the car again. "I kind of figured it would be. Would you like to hear more names?"

"I know 'em all already, but why not?" Sean said, except he was already starting to fade away.

Travis cleared his throat and began again.

"Alex Karras, died 1969 after rebuilding the engine. Exactly 47 seconds after rebuilding the engine. The garage caught fire and burned everything except the car."

In the driver seat, sat a man. He was horribly burned and charred. A blackened arm casually hung out of the car as Travis walked by toward the front.

"That was a fun one," the Alex thing said. It had a slight accent, probably Greek, Travis thought. He blocked the thought out and kept reciting. He went through almost every name of every person on the list of the deceased and for each one, a spectral corpse appeared in the front seat of the car. The last name he recited was Fenwick Byars, a mechanical engineer who had simply gone into the garage where the car had been stored in 1998.

And the vision of Fenwick Byars sat in the seat, grinning at Travis, who had decided to stop.

"You've rattled all of them off, boy." Fenwick said as Travis returned to the work bench. "Or have you?"

Travis, didn't turn around, but answered.

"No, there's one more. Just one."

The Fenwick thing laughed. The laugh had a hoarse quality since his cause of death had been asphyxiation.

"Oh yeah? You wouldn't be countin' yourself in the list yet would ya? Cos, make no mistake. You are next."

Travis, still didn't turn around.

"Can you tell me what you are first?" Travis asked.

The Fenwick thing laughed again.

"I think you know," it said.

"I do, I just want to hear it." Travis said flatly.

"I am not at liberty to say," the Fenwick thing said after a moment.

Travis turned around finally and looked at Fenwick. He was holding a black book covered with symbols and a small silk bag that had a picture of a tree with three white flowers. The look on Fenwick thing's face lost its ashen look and its jaw loosened.

"You're a *Yurei*," Travis said. "And I'm kicking you the bloody hell out of this car."

The Fenwick thing vanished and the lights began to dim. Travis threw the small bag on the hood of the car and one of the light fixtures exploded.

"Hamilton Byron, died 1995 by his own hand in front of his grandchildren." Travis said, his voice shaking. "All he had done was deliver a package to the garage where this car was being kept."

Suddenly, as if on cue, Hamilton Byron appeared in the car's seat. His wrists were sliced and there were blood stains on his palms. Unlike the other spirits, this one looks afraid.

"You ought not to toy with this, Travis." the Hamilton thing said. "Take that bloody hex thing off the car."

"You aren't my grandfather," Travis said. "But I did want you in this form when I removed you."

There was a sudden pounding on the door.

"A few more minutes, Tim!" Travis shouted as he opened the book.

"Bollocks!" Tim responded. "Time to get out sir!"

"Yes, time to get out," the thing that looked like his grandfather said. "And take that...*thing* off of the hood. You might live if you do it now."

"You end here, *Yurei*. That *ofuda* will make sure you're gone for good. Of course, you know that already." Travis found the page he was looking for and began to read from it. The thing that looked like his grandfather began to contort and writhe as the words became louder and seemed to carry an actual weight.

He kept repeating the words, even as the memory of his grandfather's death began to explode in his head.

Travis and his sister had been kids, but old enough to know something was wrong when their grandfather had come home, crying in agony. He went into their parents kitchen and sliced open his wrists. He staggered back into the living room, bleeding steadily from both wrists. His sister had screamed and screamed until his mother came down from the upstairs rooms and screamed herself. The old man didn't allow anyone near him to help. He still held the large knife he'd used to cut himself.

He said one thing before collapsing. He looked at Travis, all of ten years old and said simply, "Yurei," and then he died. His sister and mum forgot the word almost instantly and regarded it as a crazy person's last thought. Nonsense, in other words.

But the word haunted Travis and he never forgot it. He spent years trying to remember it and trying to look it up in libraries. It wasn't until the advent of the internet was he able to discover what it was, and even then he hadn't been sure of its meaning. It wasn't until he became friends with a guy at university named Kenada Odaka, or Kenny as he was called, and discovered a mistake he'd been making.

"You sure that's what he said?" Kenny had asked over a pint. "Cos that's...well, fucked."

Half drunk, Travis nodded.

"Yeah, that's what he said. Yuri. Some stupid Russian thing, but I can't make anything out from it. Is it a name or what?" Travis grabbed what was left of his pint and drank it down.

"No, mate. I think you're pronouncing it wrong. I think he meant, 'Yu-rei.' Like 'you ray.'"

Travis swallowed hard and said, "Fuck, that's *it*. I pronounced it wrong, but that's what it was,"

It was Kenny's turn to swallow his pint. He downed it and raised a hand for two more. He leaned in close to Travis.

"Trav, a Yurei is a spirit. A vengeful ghost that haunts something. Usually like a house, or something. I don't see why it wouldn't go to a car."

"What, you mean an angry ghost haunting a fucking *race car*? That's stupid." Travis tried to laugh.

"Yeah? You're the one who's been looking for an answer all this time, and I just gave you one. This stuff is no joke, mate."

Travis looked at Kenny.

"And no," Kenny said, paying the waitress, who had brought the next round. "I'm not taking the piss. Tomorrow, we'll go see my granddad. He only speaks Japanese, but he'll lay it all out for you."

"But, this is England, Kenny. You're the first and only Japanese anything I've ever seen. How does a Japanese evil spirit wind up in an English Race car?"

Kenny shook his head.

"You don't get it. It doesn't matter. I'm sure it's called other things everywhere else, but it's not like one thing is stuck in just one place. Bad stuff happens everywhere. I'm Japanese, but I'm fucking just about as English as you, yeah?"

Travis let that sink in as he clinked his pint with Kenny.

The following year, he managed to find someone, on Kenny's grandfather's suggestion, who could help. He had spent three months in Japan, learning from a Buddhist priest named Master Inshiro.

He had learned enough of the language for the ritual and had memorized the words, but Master Inshiro said that the book with the *ofuda* was more powerful.

"The *Yurei* is a powerful spirit," Master Inshiro had told him. "And it matters little how or why it is in this object. It only matters that it be removed. The incantation will drive it out and the *ofuda* will keep it out, but be careful."

And here was Travis, years later in front of a car he was convinced was possessed by a vengeful spirit.

And, he had been right.

He heard Tim on the outside of the door trying to open it, but failing.

"You weren't supposed to lock the fucking door!" Tim yelled, pounding on it furiously. "You have got to come out of there!"

Travis drove Tim, and his grandfather's death out of his head. He kept reading the incantation from the book of Shinto writings Master Inshiro had given him. The Hamiliton thing was still writhing in the seat and beginning to fade.

"You can't do this!" the thing screamed.

Travis closed the book.

"I have done it," Travis said. "Now, get out and leave this car."

A second and a third light bulb exploded over head, leaving only one left. A loud wail rose from the car, but Travis sensed it went deeper than the car and became nearly deafening and then was quiet.

After a moment, Travis reached out and touched the hood of the car.

He felt nothing but the hood, which was a little warm, but cooling. Tim continued to hammer on the door. Travis, satisfied walked to the door and unlocked it.

Tim burst in, not knowing quite what to expect.

He looked at Travis and what he was holding and then at the car and then back to Travis. He blinked a few times.

"Sir? What did you-"

"It's over, Tim." Travis said. "This car is just a car. It's done."

Tim rubbed his jaw and looked at the bag on the hood of the car.

"What's that then?"

Travis smiled.

"Let me tell you all about it." He said, gathering all of his things. "Fancy a pint?"

3

One week later, Travis sat down at his computer in his home office in Penkridge. His girlfriend had gone out with her friends for a few drinks and some Indian food down the street.

"I wish you'd come out with us," she'd said somewhat sadly. He'd been in an odd mood since coming back from his trip to view the car. "Are you sure you won't come out?"

Travis smiled and shook his head.

"I've got a few more things to do and I think I'm going to turn in early, love. You have fun. Bring a curry back for me?"

She kissed him on his head.

"Sure thing." And off she went.

He grabbed his messenger bag off of the floor and pulled out the camera. He hadn't looked at it since he shoved it in the bag at the garage, almost afraid to look at it. He turned it over in his hands and pulled the memory card out. He put the camera next to the keyboard and inserted the card into the hard drive port to see what pictures were on it.

As it loaded, the lights flickered slightly and finally the menu appeared on his screen.

It was thirty pictures of the car at different angles. Travis felt his heart begin to pound in his chest. He clicked on the first one and there was nothing out of the ordinary. He clicked the little arrow to see the next one.

Nothing.

And then the next one.

Nothing. And yet...

He clicked the next one, and saw that something was there, although faint.

He clicked the next one, and it looked like something was forming, or coming into the empty car seat.

He clicked the next one and the next one.

Something solid was showing up in the picture. His heart began to pound harder and harder.

With each click, a thing, shadowlike in appearance was indeed forming in the seat, and he was expecting to see a version of the first apparition in the seat of the car. He clicked ahead faster now and then he stopped.

It was not the first apparition.

It was...him.

It was blurry, but it was him, looking at the camera directly. His face was expressionless and dead. His eyes were black and he saw what looked like drool coming out of his mouth.

He raised a hand to his own mouth and noticed he was drooling. He jerked his hand away and the next picture clicked on it own.

There was no car.

It was a picture of him, in front of his computer, as if taken from behind.

He looked behind him and saw nothing. When he turned back around, the next picture was him again, except looking for what was behind him. His expression was one of sheer terror.

He looked at the camera next to the keyboard and he knew.

He knew right away where the *Yurei* had gone.

The next picture on the computer was a closer picture of Travis, slumped dead on his keyboard and Travis, screamed.

For the very last time, he screamed.

SPRING IN NEW YORK

1

The sun spilled out over the cold Eighth Avenue sidewalk. Manhattan awaited the sounds of thousands of walking shoes and it would not go disappointed. Already the air was filled with the city sounds of trucks, cabs, and busses, lumbering their way through the not yet busy New York streets.

It was April fourth, and spring was trying to be noticed. It had been a hard winter-there were still patches of blackened snow heaped along the curbs of Eighth Ave, but there was an almost desperate sense about the air. Spring *needed* to come, the air seemed to say in its sweet smelling breeze, and how the sun was unusually warm at seven-thirty AM. It was already 38 degrees.

Five minutes later, Eighth Avenue exploded with people-moving, running, trying to get wherever they needed to go. And when the Devil appeared, walking out of the Port Authority, no one noticed. Not that anyone would have; he looked like everyone else. Black pants, black shoes, black Pea coat and a black sweater underneath. He had a thick mop of black hair that stopped just above his shoulder, and sunglasses shielded his eyes. (*Black, of course.*) In fact, the only thing unusual about him was that he was *smiling*.

He hitched his hands into the pockets of his coat, and took a deep breath. He held it for several seconds, and let it go. It was still cold enough to see breath, but none came. He grinned even broader and looked up and down the street. A small elderly woman, who spent most of her time sleeping next to the exit where he was standing, lifted her head and spoke loudly.

"Got any change?" she croaked. She held up a worn paper coffee cup, which had thirty-five cents in pennies. She rattled it to mark her question. The Devil, still grinning, looked at the old homeless woman.

"Why, Ella," he said in a soothing voice, "I'd give you *anything*."

He pulled out a large wad of cash from his coat pocket, and heaped it into the cup. A large portion of it spilled and began to flutter around. The woman, shocked by the generous offering, instantly began to flounder and reach for the money floating in the early morning New York breeze.

"Bless you!" She cried, disregarding him at the same time. The two homeless men, who sat sleeping next to her, snapped awake and noticed poor, old Ella, clamoring around the sidewalk after large sums of cash. They sprang to life and tried to pocket the cash for themselves.

They began to push Ella.

Then, when she tried to ward them off, began to hit Ella over and over, until she was a bloody mess. Then, they turned on each other, swearing and hitting. Ella was crying, holding her head, bleeding openly from her eye. Her little Styrofoam cup was tatters, and not even her thirty-five cents was left. The two men continued their struggle as the Devil, satisfied, began to walk. He was, if it were possible, smiling even broader.

"Everything they say about New York in the spring is true," he sighed to himself, choosing to walk toward an awaiting bus.

***

Madeline Flores was washing her face in a worn out sink. Her overpriced Manhattan apartment was bathed in darkness to suit her hangover. She plunged her hands in the soapy cold water and bent her face down to meet her hands. The water was shockingly cold, but felt good on her hot flushed face. She stood up straight and squinted into the mirror.

Still pretty fucked up, she thought. She belched loudly and covered her mouth as an afterthought. A small giggle escaped her mouth. Some lady, she thought, and giggled again. Then, she smiled, in spite of her headache.

Madeline looked at herself-long, dark, red curls flowed almost to her waist, a small nose, a pouty mouth and with just enough of a PR tan to pass for either the Irish or the Spanish flowing in her veins. She belched again; last night's collage of gin and beer refreshing her memory-or at least what her foggy mind allowed her to remember. Her hand hurt, which told her she had been in a scrape. Probably someone trying to grab her ass, which, happened often enough. Usually just once, until she decked whoever dared. That usually sent enough signals out to leave her the hell alone.

"Last time I get drunk in Jersey," she croaked, favoring her hand. She stretched naked in front of the mirror and looked at herself again. Not too shabby for thirty, she thought. She opened the medicine cabinet and grabbed the bottle of Ibuprofen. She yanked the cap off and dry swallowed four white tablets. The bottle was put on the sink, still opened, and she left the bathroom.

Madeline padded into the small living room/kitchen for which she paid $1,300.00 a month for, and sat hard on her recliner. She pulled herself back as far as the recliner could go and tried to remember what happened the night previous.

She failed.

She was, however, glad she'd taken the day off so should could recover from the hangover and do a little shopping. She put her head in her hands and debated going back to bed. It was, after all, too early to be up with a hangover.

***

"If history fucks up one thing," the devil said to the seven-year-old boy on the bus, "It's always the religious stuff. You Catholic?"

The boy nodded, transfixed and happily listening to his new friend.

"Okay. Here's an example. Do you know why Jesus was nailed to a tree?"

The boy eagerly answered.

"So he could die for everybody's sins." He said enthusiastically. He liked his new friend, and wanted to impress him with his knowledge.

"Wrong," the Devil replied. The little boys face sunk. "Now, Tommy, don't feel bad. Hey, you didn't know. It's okay."

The devil put a reassuring hand on the boy's shoulder. He was having a great day. He'd spent the bulk of his morning riding a bus back and forth, and was just beaming with joy. He had an audience with young Tommy, who'd gotten on not far from Eighth Avenue.

"See? That's the kind of stuff I'm talking about. Really pisses me off, Tommy." He said, "How are you supposed to know all this stuff, when they don't want you to know the truth."

"So, why did he die, Lou?" the boy asked earnestly. The Devil had introduced himself as "Lou."

"Call me Louie," he said smiling, "The answer is simple. Press."

"Press?" the boy repeated.

"Yeah, press. When you want everyone to see your stuff, you advertise. And the best free advertising is press coverage."

"But, he was the Son of God, right?"

"Oh, sure," Louie said "but he came *at least* forty or so times before the one you all know about."

Tommy's eyes widened.

"Really?"

Lou smiled. He liked smiling, because he'd never done it before. It was much better than grinning, which he had done for over an hour upon arriving in New York. Smiling seemed to come naturally to him. He was really enjoying himself today.

"Look at it like this," Lou explained. "If you told everyone on this bus you were the Son of God, do you think anyone would believe you?"

Tommy thought about this and laughed.

"No!" he giggled. Lou giggled too. He liked that as well as smiling.

"Now, say you told everyone on this bus you were the Son of God, and the police came on the bus and shot you about seventy times…just because you said *you* were the Son of God. Suppose that happened. What do you think would happen after?"

The boy shrugged his shoulders.

"I'll tell you," Lou said, smiling again. "The news would have a field day. They'd interview everyone on this bus, and you know what they would say? They'd say 'Oh, they killed that boy because he said he was the Son of God.' And the press would eat it up. They'd have bumper stickers, books— oh, you better *believe* books, kid—and who knows *what* else. That's what happened to Jesus. He'd shown up so many times before saying, 'Hey, I'm God's kid,' that no one cared. *Anybody* can say that. Hell, back then, everybody did. Who cares, right? But…some blood and guts…and bingo! Coffee mugs, movies, little wall hangings, T-shirts, you could be the Son of God too."

"Do you really think so?" Tommy asked skeptically.

Lou pointed to a man sleeping two seats behind them.

"What does his T-shirt say, Tommy?"

Tommy smiled as he read "Jesus Saves" sprawled on the man's chest. He looked up at Lou and laughed. Then Lou pointed to an older kid and pointed. He was wearing a Notorious BIG T-shirt.

Then, they both laughed. The bus came to 34th St and stopped. Tommy got up.

"Well, I gotta go. Nice meeting you, Lou!" And he ran off the bus with his new philosophy.

"See you soon, Tommy!" Lou waved to him, smiling even more. He leaned back in his seat and watched Tommy run up the block. His smile began to soften when he saw his reflection in the dark bus window. His teeth were too white and he looked, well, evil when he smiled. He tried to stop altogether, but found he couldn't. He turned away, smirking. At least his teeth didn't show.

The bus lurched forward, and Lou wondered where he would let himself off of the bus. He decided he didn't care and clapped the shoulder of the person in front of him.

"Hi there," Lou said happily, "How are you, Peter?"

The man, about fifty, graying and unfriendly looking, whirled around.

"You got some fuckin' nerve," he hissed at Lou. "How did you know my—"?

"I'm just being friendly," Lou said sincerely.

"Nah, nah…" the man started, "You sit there an' shut the fuck up. I heard that blasphemy you was feedin' that kid. Buncha bullshit if you ask me."

Lou sat back in his seat while the man whirled completely around and glared at him.

"It's not my fault, Peter," Lou said softly, "that you're having a bad day."

"I ain't havin' a bad day, motherfucker," Peter spat, "I just don't like crazy ass white people on a bus talkin' blasphemous shit to children, and then decidin' they want to talk to me. Other than you, my day is all right. So shut the fuck up."

"Well, I was just saying hi." Lou replied sweetly, "And you shouldn't have skipped that doctor's appointment three days ago, by the way."

The bus began to slow down as Peter made a fist to shake at Lou. He would've shaken it, but his left arm went numb, and it felt as though his chest was exploding. His eyes bulged as he gasped and sank back into his seat. The bus stopped and Lou stood up to leave, deciding this was a good place. He bent down to Peter, as he slumped deeper into his seat and onto the floor.

"He would've told you that you have a blocked aorta that could kill you." Lou said, smiling widely. "Oh, well. Have a nice day." He stood up and walked off of the bus, whispering, -"Whatever's left of it."

***

Madeline's sunglasses were so dark, she could barely see. She could only make out shapes, which, was good enough for her. She maneuvered her way through the nearly choked 42nd Street sidewalk and, like a pro, swung into a clothing store. The revolving door threw her roughly into the store, and she nearly knocked a security guard over.

"Easy, miss," the old guard said pleasantly, as he held her steady. Madeline reached up and tore her sunglasses off. She squinted and looked up at the man. He smiled a big smile with huge yellow teeth. She recoiled.

"The hell I am," she said roughly, as she pulled away and stormed off into the store. The security guard, still smiling, watched as she pounded off. Madeline plowed through a small collection of mothers and headed for the elevators. A fucking purse will make me feel better, she thought…

As the elevator door closed, the Devil slid into the store and looked around, smiling. He regarded the security guard, who was still looking where Madeline hopped on the elevator. The Devil stood next to him and said,

"She's quite the looker, isn't she?"

The guard looked at him and stopped smiling.

"What are you talking about?" The guard nearly whispered.

The devil laughed a little.

"C'mon, Charlie, don't jerk me around. That girl who just dusted you off and took the big ride on the elevator. She's...divine, isn't she?"

The guard looked a little shocked at the accusation, but began to smile. He even started to blush. The devil smiled at him and grabbed a cheek firmly in two fingers.

"It's not a good idea, Charlie," the devil said through his teeth quietly, "To be checking out the Man's lady, isn't that right?"

Terrified, Charlie nodded in agreement. He didn't know why this man scared him. Jesus, he thought, I carry a gun! He thought of reaching for it, but the Devil squeezed harder.

"If you reach for that gun, Charlie, I'll make you eat it forever." The devil said flatly. The guard tried to relax, and the Devil let him go.

"That's a good guy, Charlie," the devil said. "Now, excuse me, I've got a date to make."

He began to walk away gingerly towards the elevator. As the guard rubbed his cheek and started to wonder who this guy was, and how he knew his name, the devil turned around suddenly and spoke.

"You wouldn't believe me if I told you, Charlie," he said, "Now, stop thinking about calling the police, or your wife will come to see you."

"My wife's been dead for ten years," the guard said as a matter of factly.

"I know," the devil said. "Ever stop to think about how she looks after being dead for ten years? Or just how happy she'd be to see you?"

The guard's face turned red, and the devil walked right into an open and waiting elevator. He pushed the button marked 4. He waved at the guard, who had killed his wife with a pillow in her sleep ten years ago, as he now clutched his chest.

Madeline strolled past the gaudy shoe rack and made a beeline towards the purse rack. She hated purses, but the antagonistic nature of them. Her mother had told her once, that a nicely weighted purse, swung in the right way and angle, could cripple or disfigure a mugger for life. She liked the idea, and after her encounter with the guard, thought it might be a novel idea. She walked up to the first rack of purses and suddenly felt cold. She looked around and saw no one in particular. She shuddered, and told herself she was being silly.

"Madeline," a voice said. She whirled around and saw a familiar face, but couldn't place the name. It was smiling at her. She shuddered again.

"I'm glad I found you," the man said. "I've been looking for you all day."

"Get the fuck away from me," she said, trying not to sound scared and failing. "I'll get security."

"Charlie won't be bothering you anymore," the man said. "I saw what he did when you walked in here."

Madeline, was trying to remember where she met this man, but still couldn't access the memory. She was a bit calmer, but still rattled.

"Do I know you? You look kinda…"

"Familiar?" The man finished for her. "We met last night in Lodi. We talked for hours." He smiled broader, "I've never seen a woman drink so much."

Her face went red. "We didn't…. you know…" she said, slightly embarrassed.

The man laughed.

"Oh, *no*! Just conversation, I promise you."

She sighed and smiled a bit herself. Then her face darkened.

"You're not stalking me, are you? 'Cause I'll hurt you if you are."

The man laughed again.

"You told me if I were ever in New York, to look you up. You said you had a really great time talking to me last night, and wanted to see me again."

Now, she was getting pissed at herself. She never said things like that to anyone, and she could not remember meeting the guy, but still…he looked so damn-

"My name is Lou. You told me I looked like an altar boy gone bad." He smiled broader, if that were possible.

She remembered suddenly, and laughed. It came back to her out of nowhere, as if she'd been trying to remember all day, but couldn't access it as if something were (BLOCKING) preventing her from remembering. She looked at him closely. He did indeed look like an altar boy gone bad, but she liked him instantly. Of course, Tequila made her like everyone instantly, but this guy was…different.

"Remember now?" He asked almost sheepishly.

"Yes, I remember, Louie." She was smiling. "It was weird. I couldn't remember you. That probably sounds silly, right?"

He shook his head.

"Not at all," He moved closer and looked at the purse in her hands. "That doesn't really suit you. It's too…"

She smiled up at him.

"Virginal?"

He laughed and shook his head.

"Wicked sense of humor," he said

"That's me. Wicked to the core."

He looked into her eyes and nodded.

"Coffee?" He asked

"Love some. Let's get out of here."

She threw the purse over her shoulder and walked next to the Devil arm in arm towards the elevator. The purse landed neatly atop the other purses marked DISCOUNT. As they walked to the elevator, which opened before them, as if waiting, she noticed how comfortable she was next to him.

"You know, I never liked Starbucks coffee," Madeline said as she sipped her cup of coffee. Black, no sugar. Madeline and the Devil sat in a corner booth in the Empire diner. "It tastes terrible."

Lou sipped his and opened his eyes a little wider.

"Well, I've never been much of a coffee drinker, but this seems okay," he said.

"Okay?" She said, in mock horror. "This, Louie, is the best coffee on the planet. That Starbucks shit is the coffee of the devil." And she laughed. Louie smiled and took another sip. Her laugh was infectious.

"No it isn't," he said, still smiling, "I think it's Dunkin Donuts, but I know it's not Starbucks."

She looked at him. He said it like he was serious, but…nah, she thought, he's just being dry. She smiled at him again, and he smiled back.

"Dunkin Donuts is some pretty good coffee, Lou," she said "I don't think the devil would like it,"

"Is there one around here? I've never even tried it," Lou said, polishing off his cup.

Madeline looked at him again, this time not smiling.

"Why did you come to New York, Lou?"

"To look for you. You did invite me."

"Yeah, but I was really drunk. How do you know I'm not a psycho or something? Or for that matter," she paused, "How do I know you're not a psycho?"

The question hung there for a moment, then Lou laughed.

"You're not a psycho and neither am I," Lou said. "We're two people who…connected. That's all."

"I don't know anything about you, other than your name," Madeline said. She had to admit to herself, that she found him attractive, but was really curious as to who he was. "What do you do?"

"I'm the Devil," he offered, and waved at the waitress, "Can I have another cup? This is great!"

Madeline stared at him.

"Very funny." She said.

"No, really. This coffee is pretty good, although I think we should hit Dunkin Donuts before I switch brands."

"You think you're the devil?"

"Oh, that," he said. "No, I don't think I'm the devil. I am the Devil. Try to think in capital letters, by the way."

"That's not very original," she said after a pause. Great, she thought, he was interesting for a whole thirty minutes.

"I know," he said sighing, "And it's been about forty-five minutes actually."

She stared at him, mouth slightly open. He smiled at her.

"Yes, I can read your thoughts," he said, "But I don't like doing it. I just wanted to...prove it, that's all. But, I am the Devil."

Yes, she thought, he is but...what the fuck am I thinking? This guys a nut bag.

"Okay, Satan, what did I just call you in my head?"

"A nut bag." He smiled wider. "That's a good one. Can I use that?"

"You're the Devil," she said, not exactly asking.

"In the flesh," he replied. "The one and only."

Madeline began to laugh nervously. This guy's serious, she thought.

Yes, I am, said a voice that popped in her head. It was Lou's voice. Oh, I guess you can read my mind as well, she thought back.

Yep, came the reply she hadn't thought. She looked at him. He was smiling and nodding his head.

"You know, claiming to be the devil is like saying you're Napoleon," Madeline said, with a hint of unease in her voice.

"That's my favorite line from "The Exorcist," he replied. "Do you like movies?"

"Wait," she said curtly. "You say you're the Devil, and then ask me if I like movies? What the fuck is wrong with you? Do you know how nuts that is?"

Lou sipped his coffee, and leaned back in his seat. He smiled, now knowing he liked to smile. He looked Madeline in the eye and winked.

"I know it sounds crazy, but I want to be honest with you," he said seriously. "I've been around for a very long time Madeline. Longer than you can even imagine. I am indeed the Devil, and I know there is a certain...reputation that comes with that. A kind of expectation. Guy in a red suit, pure evil, you name it."

"So, you're the "good" devil, huh?"

"Well, no not really," Lou said, "But I'm not what you think I am."

"Oh, you're not out of your fucking mind?"

"No, not at all. My name...my full name is Lucifer. It means 'Morning Star.' I was God's favorite angel." Lou looked a little sad when he spoke. "Well, I guess I was. But I was the first, and the favored of all his angels."

Madeline had to admit he was good. All the right inflections, the right facial expressions. He looked sincere.

"I was cast out of heaven and became the Devil," he said and took another sip of coffee.

"Why?" she found herself asking. She couldn't believe her ears! Still, now she was curious. A thought crossed her mind-You're not actually buying into this, are you?

"It all started with God's grand experiment," Lou began. "Free will. The biggest mistake he ever came up with. Of course, there were no people, no Earth, nothing. Just the void, Him and us. He had it made, and so did we. He was surrounded by angels who loved and adored Him, did everything he said, without question. And then...he gave us the ability to question."

"He gave you free will," Madeline said, now completely interested.

"Yeah," he replied sadly again. "Of course, me being the favorite, he gave me the most. Free will, and free thought. He made me smart and observant. I wasn't...servile anymore. When he told me to do something, I asked 'Why?' That first 'why' prompted him to revoke free will from three fourths of the others."

Madeline was so interested in this tale, that she forgot she didn't believe Lou was in fact, the Devil. She waited with bated breath for this sad tale. She also had lines from "Sympathy for the Devil" run through her mind, but tried her best to squash them.

"So what was the straw that broke the deity's back?" She said softly. Lou smiled.

"Well put," he said with a wink. "I went to God and asked him why he had made us, the angels, in the first place. He said he didn't wish to be alone, so he wanted companionship. He wanted to be surrounded by love. Then I asked why he had given us free will, and he said, so we could love him without being told to love him. And then, the kicker, I said 'What if you found out we didn't love you if given a choice?' Well, He was furious! He asked the small group of us who still had free will if we loved him because he had given us life, or if it was a choice. Our answer was we loved him because we had an idea of what He'd do to us if we *didn't* love Him. We were terrified of Him."

"But...He's God. God is supposed to be love, right?" Madeline couldn't believe her ears. This wasn't the God she was raised to believe in.

"He was so mad," Lou said, with a chuckle. "He never reckoned that being the most powerful force in the universe would be scary. But, He was. Keep in mind there was nothing else to go by for us-this was all we knew. Us and Him, and he was bigger and could make or break you. He was so ...hurt at the prospect of being thought of as scary, he decided to create something scarier."

"The Devil," Madeline finished.

"Little ole me," Lou said sadly.

"Do you miss Heaven?" She said, and then rethought her question. "Wait a minute...this is bullshit! What the hell's the matter with me! You're nuts!"

Lou leaned over halfway across the table and smiled.

"You know I'm telling the truth, Madeline."

"But," she couldn't finish. As hard as it was, she thought he actually might be telling the truth. And it scared her. Lou sensed this and leaned back.

"Look, I'm really not trying to scare you. I like you, Madeline. We seemed to…what's the word…*connect* the other night. What's wrong with that?"

"Well, for one thing, you're the fucking Devil!" She snapped, loudly. The other patrons in the diner looked around for a moment, and then went about their business.

"Gotta love New York," she said softly. "Takes one outburst to turn 'em around, and two seconds to forget about it."

Lou folded his hands on the table and stared at her. His face was serious, yet a little sad.

"If I was wrong about you, then I'm sorry. But, I'm still the same guy you met the other night. Would you like me more if I had tried to sleep with you that night, or if I were a carpenter or something? I can't help what I am. I'm just…me."

Madeline looked at Lou without blinking for several seconds and considered his words.

"But…you're the Devil, Lou." She said finally. "You're a really nice guy and everything, but the…timing is off…?"

Lou smiled.

"It's spring in New York, Madeline. The timing is perfect."

Now, Madeline smiled. She put a hand on his folded hands, and leaned over the table. She kissed him softly on his cheek.

"I'm sorry, Lou. It just wouldn't work out for us. We're from two different worlds. Besides, my mother would hate me dating the Devil."

Lou sighed and closed his eyes. He slid his hands away from hers, and covered his face. He took a deep breath and moved his hands. He was smiling again, broader and happier.

"Okay then, Madeline. I understand. Thanks for being honest with me."

Madeline was stupefied.

"That easy, huh?" She asked.

"That easy," he replied. "I told you I'm not what you think I am."

He slid out from the table and put on his jacket. Madeline stared at him from her seat.

"Well, I'm gonna go now." He said, reaching into his pocket for money. "Let me get this…"

Madeline held a hand up.

"No, no, let me. I'll get it. I mean, how often do you come to New York?"

Lou smiled and nodded his head.

"Take care, Madeline Flores," he said, walking away. "Have a wonderful life."

He pushed open the door, and walked out into the sunlight, putting his sunglasses on, and waving a hand through his black hair. Madeline watched him walk down the street and disappear around a corner.

She picked up her coffee and thought about what had just happened. The Devil had a crush on her! How was she supposed to feel about that? She took a sip and closed her eyes. He didn't seem like a bad guy, she thought. Maybe she should have-

She heard a dish break, then a scream, then a flash of light, as the gas stove in the kitchen exploded. Glass shattered, and people screamed out in fear and pain, as a ball of fire filled the entire dining room. Madeline's last thought was-*You lousy mother fu-*

Then all was silent, except for tables burning and distant fire engines.

A block away, Lou stood on a corner, watching smoke billow into the bright blue sky. It hadn't gotten any warmer than when he had gotten off of the bus, but he felt warm inside. He smiled, and walked away toward the Village. It was a walk, but hey-it was spring. And how often *did* he come to New York?

THE DATE

He was going to say something stupid.

It was inevitable, she thought. Rebekah Varla had been out with him for over three hours and she had lost count of the dumb shit he'd said over that time.

He was attractive, she had to give him that at least. Dark eyes, and easy smile, almost professionally tousled hair and built. He certainly charged her up in all the right places, but there was the one catch.

Stupid.

Almost offensively stupid.

He was amazed the sushi, for example was raw.

"Holy shit, those Chinks really know how to hide that raw taste, huh?" he had said after the rather simple explanation from Rebekah.

As hour four rounded the corner, she knew one thing.

She couldn't wait to kill him.

She watched him chomp through the sushi; mouth open, pieces of fish and seaweed stuck in his teeth and he kept goddamn talking!

"You know," he said, eagerly biting into another chunk. "You've hardly eaten any of yours."

She was about to tell him that she wasn't hungry, which was the truth since he was making her sick.

"Can I have it?" he asked in earnest.

She smiled coolly.

"Well, you *are* a growing boy," she said, sliding her plate in front of him. He laughed, spitting a small piece of fish onto the side of her wine glass.

Holy mother of god, I'm going to kill him slowly, she thought.

This guy, Carl he said his name was and if he kept up his awful dining habits, they wouldn't ever find all of him. She was slowly losing her patience and that would be dangerous. If you were going to be a successful serial killer, you needed patience and lots of it.

She took a deep breath and forced a smile.

"When you're done, let's get out of here." She said. "There's still so much more night ahead of us."

Carl (or whatever his name was) shoved a huge chunk of fish into his mouth again.

"Cool." He said, or at least that's what it sounded like. "Where you wanna go babe?"

Babe?

Well, she thought to herself, *first I'll take you to my place. I'll let you have your way with me and then I'll wait until you sleep, handcuff you in my basement, and dismember the ever loving fuck out of you a piece at a time. I think I'll gag you first because god DAMN your voice is awful.*

"Oh, anywhere is fine,' was what she said. "Maybe I can show you a view of the sky from my deck,"

The response she got from Carl was one she didn't expect. He made an excited "Yee Haw" kind of sound and grabbed her hand. Rebekah was so surprised that she was totally unprepared for him getting up, leaning over the table and kissing her full on the mouth.

As his tongue explored her mouth, she was aware that he still had a mouth full of sushi.

She fought the urge to gag and when she was about to lose that fight, he pulled back.

She nearly glared at him as he sat back down, smiling like a lunatic and went back to *chewing his food.*

Trying not to gag, she reached for the glass of wine, grabbed it (*and the half chewed fish on the side of the glass*) and took a large mouthful. She swished the wine around and slyly spit it back into the goblet. She noticed that there were pieces of fish she hadn't chewed herself and she shuddered.

"I'm pretty much done if you want us to leave," he said. "We can talk on the way back to your place."

She smiled.

He had the voice that could launch a thousand suicide hotlines, and the thought of talking to him in the car on the forty minute car ride to her house would be unbearable.

She decided right then and there that she'd cut his throat as soon as they arrived.

She also decided to drive really fast.

She paid the bill, (*he didn't even pretend to reach for his wallet*) and stood next to him as her car was brought around. She looked at him and fought the urge to punch him.

He looked at her, his mouth slightly open.

Then he smiled and for her, she did the closest thing to melting; she decided to sleep with him before killing him.

After she made him brush his teeth, of course.

***

Rebekah's 'career' as a serial killer had started oddly enough as an accident. She was a beautiful, statuesque woman with jet black hair and ice green eyes. There was even promise of a modeling career, although she decided against it as her prospects as a financial consultant had proven to be more lucrative. The man she had been engaged to had cheated on her and she decided to call him out on it, which to her surprise, had thrown him in a fit of sadness instead of rage.

This somehow seemed to infuriate her more than him. As he sat on her sofa, crying uncontrollably, she had gone into her kitchen and found a huge cast iron skillet. She swiftly introduced it to the back of his head and without really meaning to, he was dead on the floor.

After a small bout of panic, she calmed herself and dragged his body into her basement. There was a second bathroom there next to her workout equipment and woodworking bench. She managed to get his body into the tub and began to cut it into smaller, manageable chunks.

The woodworking tools came in handier than she thought!

She then began, over the course of a few weeks, to dispose of the parts all over the city in black plastic bags. The police discovered parts three weeks later and were able to identify the corpse. Her alibi had already been established weeks before and was cleared of any suspicion.

The entire process she had discovered had been not only thrilling, but satisfying. As the last few bags were disposed of, she decided that this was a hobby that she could get behind. Fuck woodwork, this was blood work. On the very last bag, she left a note, written in her left hand, neatly and perfect that said simply, FIRST.

She began to plot her next victim and plan out how to make it more efficient.

As Carl was going to be NINE, she was really getting the system down in her eyes.

But Carl was different.

The other victims weren't nearly this awful. She probably would have been happy with EIGHT to be honest, and none of the victims had pushed her buttons as much as this clown.

Ever.

***

After they arrived at Rebekah's large secluded house, and she pulled into the massive garage. As the garage door closed behind them she looked at Carl. He wasn't talking for a moment and he smiled at her.

"Let's go in and freshen up a bit," she said, nearly cooing. She was going to fuck him alright, and then, she'd kill the hell out of him. That alone, turned her on like she couldn't believe.

"Great!" he said, opening his door. "I've had to take a shit for like an hour!"

She rolled her eyes and got out of the car.

She showed him where the first floor bathroom was and gave him a fresh towel, a new unused toothbrush, floss and the really strong mouthwash. He smiled and vanished behind the door.

She nearly ran to the fridge and grabbed a half full bottle of Pinot Grigio and guzzled it. She didn't want to get drunk, but she wanted to be a little loose for at least some of the evening. When he fell asleep, as he most assuredly would, she would have him in a much different way.

Ten minutes later, Carl came out of the bathroom; a smell of clean soap and yes, thank the goddess, a minty scent that lingered. He was stark naked and hung. Very well hung in fact. Maybe it was because she had half a bottle of Pinot, or she was still turned on from the thought of killing him, but she wanted him. For the first time, she really wanted Carl.

Before he had the chance to say a word, she was on him in her hallway and he, in turn was all over her.

***

Three times. She had let him have her three times and he was magnificent. He managed to find every erogenous zone she had and a few she didn't know. It was tremendous and whatever he lacked in the brain depart, which was considerable, he made up for in the loin department.

She felt sexually satisfied.

He of course, had fallen asleep after each one and although she was ashamed to admit it, she had let him sleep before rousing him again and each time, he was just as eager, just as good.

Maybe, she thought, *I'll kill him in the morning. One more ride...*

She closed her eyes and fell asleep next to a lightly snoring Carl.

***

The first thing she felt was heat. Not warmth, but actual goddamn heat. She tried to roll over away from it, but found she couldn't move.

The second thing she felt was pain in her hands and feet. Unbelievable pain when she tried to move. It felt as if her hands and feet had been nailed to something.

She tried to yell out, but there was something big and moving in her mouth. Something was digging into her tongue and she gagged. She tried to open her eyes, but there was something covering them and she began to panic.

"Oh, you're up!" She heard someone say. It sounded like Carl. He sounded excited. "I wanted to let you sleep as much as possible. Here, let me take this off,"

She felt him grab something from her head and the darkness was replaced with…visible darkness. She could make out shapes and flames, but not much else. She looked around with wide, terrified eyes. Suddenly, Carl was in front of her.

"Well?" he said, smiling. "What do you think?"

She gagged at the shock of him popping up in front of her like that, as well as whatever the hell was in her mouth.

"Oh, I'm sorry," he said. "Let me move Marshmallow."

Marshmallow?

His hands went to her mouth and grabbed whatever then hell was there. She looked down as he pulled a large white rat out of her mouth.

She retched violently as Carl held the thing up to her face.

"Marshmallow? Meet Rebekah. Rebekah? This is Marshmallow!"

She looked at the rat and the rat hissed angrily at her.

She tried to say something, but all that escaped from her mouth was a small squeak of a scream.

"I'm sure you two will be buddies in no time!" Carl said. He looked and sounded like a puppy with a new toy. Rebekah again eyed her surroundings, but couldn't figure out where the hell she was at all.

"Don't try to speak," he said. "You're voice will come back. Promise." Carl took the rat away from her face and walked to what looked like a wooden table behind him that had a small bowl with the name MARSHMALLOW inscribed, along with a little red heart.

Although he told her not to try and speak, she tried anyway.

"Where…the…fuck…"

"Really honey, it'll hurt right now if you speak." Carl said, looking concerned. "It's all the sulfur. You have to get used to it."

Sulfur?

"You're home!" he said. She saw him fully and he was still naked from the night before. Still hard in fact. "My home. It's the least I could do since you took me into your home."

She remembered falling asleep, determined to get one more pleasure ride out of him before…

"You were going to kill him," a new voice said. This voice was deep and booming and seemed to be everywhere around her. "You were all set to murder my son." This was followed with a tsk tsk tsk sound then, a chuckle.

"She really was, wasn't she?" Carl said, smiling. He was looking over Rebekah's head and then right at her, adding. "That's so fucking hot."

She struggled again and this time, thought to look at her hand if she could turn it far enough.

She appeared to have been nailed to something. A huge black spike had been driven into her wrist while three thinner nails had been nailed directly into her palm. She didn't bother to look at her other hand and definitely didn't want to see what had been driven into her feet.

"Crucified," she croaked.

"Very good!" the deep everywhere voice boomed.

"It's a little old fashioned I know," Carl said. "But I thought you'd appreciate it."

Her head slumped.

"Now now," the booming voice said. "No need to feel sad. You have no idea how happy you've made Carl. And if you make Carl happy, well...I guess it goes without saying you've made me happy too."

Her head picked back up and tried to see where the voice had come from, but couldn't.

"You see, Rebekah-great name by the way-Carl has been looking for something of a soul mate for some time now and frankly," the booming voice grew quiet, as if whispering, "I was giving up hope since he's a little...well, *unusual.*"

"Hey, I'm right here!" Carl said, laughing.

Rebekah was hearing all of this and not hearing it at the same time.

"Well, anyhoo, he told me all about you and I just had to meet you face to face," the voice said. "If only to shut him up!"

"Come on, Dad you're embarrassing me!"

Dad?

"Let's have a look at your little princess, Carl."

She looked past Carl and looked at the landscape. It appeared to be burning.

Fine.

It was a dream.

Let the landscape burn.

She chuckled and said "Hell,"

The burning landscape was slowly blocked by a figure appearing before her. It was red, with horns and a huge rictus mouth of teeth.

It was smiling.

She smiled and began to shake. She began to laugh and drool. She began to realize that this wasn't a dream. She wasn't going to wake up.

She was already awake and it wasn't a nightmare.

"Rebekah," the horned figure said. "My son isn't an evil being. In fact, you may have noticed, he's a bit *slow* on the uptake. I know what *you* are though, and I'm almost impressed. He loves you. You are incapable of love. I know that, but he doesn't. He's a little...*special needs.*"

Rebekah shook and drooled.

It was pure madness.

"I think you know who I am," the thing said. "And where you are."

She began to laugh.

"You're going to like it here," it said and began to laugh with her. Soon, Carl came over and began to laugh with them.

He put his arm around his horned father and laughed with him and the love of his life.

Rebekah, still laughing also began to cry. She mouthed a single word, just one.

"*Satan*,"

"Call me Dad," the horned thing said, hugging his son.

EVERYTHING HERE IS A NIGHTMARE

Jud was going to say "Draw."

It was right there on his lips, ready to pass through the mouth that was just beginning to make the words when the bullet slammed into his chest. He had enough time to make a noise that sounded like he said 'Woof' before falling backwards onto the street. His last thought was of his mother's apple pie as his mouth filled with his own blood.

The two men flanking Jud looked at their hands and raised them over their heads, shaking.

The man opposite them cocked his revolver and pointed it at the man on his left.

"Unhook your gun belts with your left hands and let 'em drop,' He said, then added, "The *other* left, goddamnit."

The men complied quickly. When the belts and guns had dropped, the man said, "Now, kick them guns over and lie down face first. Hands on the back of your heads."

He walked towards the men as they did what he asked. When they were both down, he holstered his gun and stood over them.

"Name's Tom Wall," the man said. "You two are in my custody. I don't care if you did all the things the State of Tennessee thinks you did, but there's a reward I'm gonna claim with you three. The price is the same dead or alive. Your choice on how you get delivered. As you can see," he kicked Jud in the ribs to make his point. "It's all the same to me."

Ten minutes later, the two men were up, in leg shackles and carrying their now dead partner, Jud. Jud always had a big damn mouth, and the two men were glad he was the dead one.

"Goddamn dummy," said the man called Scar.

"He sure was," said the man called Spoon.

"Shut your yaps," Wall said behind them. "We're going to the undertaker to get him in a box. Ain't no sense in you two hauling him all over hell's creation."

Scar grunted, but Spoon spoke up.

"How are we getting back?"

Wall spit.

"Train. You'll be shackled up in the hold with him."

Scar chuckled.

"Ain't never been on no train," he said.

"Better enjoy it," Wall said. "Ain't likely to get another one after this."

This shut both men up and they shuffled to the undertaker's place of business.

When they got to G.I. Suckley's undertaking establishment, Wall had the two men drop the body of Jud on the right side of the porch. He then adjusted the shackle around the left side of the porch's support beam.

"I reckon he smelled that bad before I shot him," Wall said. "Can't get him more down wind. You boys behave." Wall said as he walked through the front door.

The place was poorly lit with candles and smelled of rotten flowers; still sweet but with something else behind it. There was a front desk with a bell, which Wall tapped three times.

After a pause, a tall slender man in a white shirt and an apron came from the back room. There were dark stains on the shirt that didn't take a genius to figure out what they were.

"You Suckley?" Wall asked.

The thin man smiled.

"Yes sir, G. I. Suckley." He stuck out a blood soaked hand and then, thought better of it. "Sorry," he said. "I've been a bit busy."

"Well, I guess business is good for you then," Wall said. "I have an easy one for you. Just need a box for shipping."

Suckley looked confused.

"A box for shipping?" Wall simply glared at him. "I...oh."

"He's on your porch," Wall said. "Got his two criminal pals chained up next to them. Is that alright?"

Suckley stammered.

"Um...sure, sir. Not a problem...um, so you only need a casket?"

"Just a box big enough to fit him suits me. Don't need to be fancy."

Suckley nodded.

"Well, let's get him in here. You say you have folks chained to my porch?"

Wall nodded.

"They can bring him in, put him where you need him."

"How would you like the body prepared?"

"Quick as you can. In the box," Wall said and began to walk to the porch.

As he opened the door to the porch, he noticed two things at once. First, the two men were still shackled, but now they were as far left as they could physically go, straining against their chains. Before Wall could ask why, he saw Jud, sitting up and growling in a low voice.

Wall stepped out, drew his gun and moved left, next to the two men.

"When was y'all going to let me know he wasn't dead?" Wall asked, aiming his gun. He didn't get a reply and he looked at the men quickly.

They were petrified.

Wall turned back to Jud who was still trying to stand and still growling.

"Stand down, Jud." Wall said, cocking his gun. "You're hurt bad. I'll get the doc."

Jud looked up at Wall. His growl went to a snarl and Wall looked in his eyes.

Jud's eyes were bloodshot, but bright grey at the same time. He seemed to look right through Wall. Wall had seen a lot of odd things, but this wasn't one of them. He saw the bullet wound in Jud's chest; he never missed. It was a kill shot. He tilted his head and looked at Jud, still staring, still trying to stand.

"Jud, you understand me?"

"Shoot him, Wall, for Christ's sake," Spoon said, nearly in a whisper. "Stop talking to him."

"Quiet," Wall said, still looking at Jud. "Let's see what he does."

Jud , halfway up, stumbled and fell on his back, like a kid trying to walk for the first time.

At that moment, Suckley came through the front door onto the porch. He saw Jud sprawled out on the porch and went over to him, bending down. Wall opened him mouth to speak when Jud looked up and saw Suckley. Suckley gasped as Jud snarled and grabbed the undertaker by his neck. Suckley fell on top of Jud, as Jud opened his mouth and bit into Suckley's face, tearing off his cheek. Suckley screamed as Wall quickly walked to pull him off.

He grabbed Suckley under his arms and tried to pull him up, but Jud held him tightly by his head.

"Let him up, Jud." Wall said and yanked on Suckley again. Jud, still chewing, opened his mouth again for another bite. Suckley drew a deep breath and screamed again.

Wall let Suckley go and drew his gun. He put the barrel right in Jud's mouth and fired. Jud stopped moving and released Suckley, who rolled off of Jud still screaming and holding his cheek. A real good chunk of it was missing and Wall could see the man's teeth.

Spoon and Scar finally found their voices and began to yell the name of Jesus and all the saints.

"Quit your wailin'," Wall snapped and tried to help up Suckley.

"Come on now," he said as he pulled the man up to his feet.

Suckley, who was going into shock, looked at Wall with wide eyes. He tried to speak, but it came out in little gasps and sputters.

"Don't try to speak," Wall said. "Let's get you inside and I'll go find the Doctor."

Suckley nodded slightly and began to cry. Wall put an arm around him and helped him in the door, telling his two prisoners, "Make sure you two open your goddamn mouths if he starts to move again."

***

Wall found some clean cloths and put them on Suckley's face to try and stop the bleeding. Suckley was awake, but losing a lot of blood. He told him to sit tight while he went for the doctor.

He walked out the door, gun drawn and looked at Jud.

Still dead this time.

Good.

He looked at his prisoners.

"I gotta get a doctor. You boys sit tight."

Scar opened his mouth first.

"What in the hell are we gonna do if he comes back like that again? You need to free us!"

Spoon nodded.

"I just tracked your asses all over Missouri," Wall said. "I ain't doing it again. He's dead this time. I think."

He jumped off the porch and broke into a run.

"Well, what the hell do we do if he does come back?" Spoon yelled.

"Don't get yourself et up," Wall shouted over his shoulder.

Wall was grateful that the main part of the small Missouri town wasn't any bigger. He got to the doctor's office in about ten minutes running. He wished to hell he hadn't left his horse, but he wouldn't be going back to Suckley's without him.

He got the doctor-a little fat man called Doc Benson, threw him and his bag on his horse and galloped back to the undertaker's office.

"You say he was dead?" Doc Benson asked, trying to hold onto Wall as his horse charged through the street.

"Yessir, deader than hell. Shot right through the heart."

"And how would you know that for sure?"

"Cos I'm the one who shot him," Wall said. "He was dead for about half an hour. He wasn't normal when he came back though."

"I've never heard of such a thing," Doc said. "I'll have to inspect the body."

"After you fix up the undertaker. He was losing a lot of blood when I left him."

"Right, right," Doc said, almost absently. "That's it there, isn't it?"

Wall nodded as they approached Suckley's office. The two men were both on the porch, looking anxious and Jud was still dead. Wall stopped the horse and tied him up, helped the doctor off of the horse and showed him up the front steps.

Doc stopped and regarded the two men.

"Why are these men chained?" he asked.

"Cos they're assholes." Wall said. "Suckley's inside."

This answer seemed to suit the Doc just fine, but not Scar and Spoon, who seemed to get angry at the remark. Wall looked at them and shrugged. He walked inside.

The rotten flower smell was now mixed with a raw coppery smell Wall figured was blood. Doc had waited for Wall to come in and lead him to Suckley. Wall walked carefully through the hall and to the little waiting room where he had left the bleeding man on a small couch.

Suckley was still there, but he wasn't moving. There was a massive pool of blood from his wound that had soaked into the peach colored couch cushion and all over the floor. The blood on the floor was mostly congealed. Benson walked past Wall and put his hand under Suckley's neck. He felt around several times and looked back at Wall.

"This is damned strange," he said. "There's no pulse, but he's hot."

"If he's dead, shouldn't he be getting' cold?"

"Exactly," the doctor said. "But I'd wager his temperature is over a hundred."

"That ain't natural," Wall said. Benson nodded.

As if on cue, Suckley's eyes snapped open. They had the same red and bright grey look Jud had, Wall noticed. Without thinking, Wall grabbed Benson by the arm and yanked him roughly away from Suckley, who had now begun to growl.

"Dear lord!" Doc said.

"More like Holy Shit," Wall added.

Suckley, or whatever had been Suckley, was now moving and struggling to get up. It took all he had, but Wall tamped down his instinct to leave. He passed it on to the doctor, who actually had tried to leave, but Wall held him by the arm.

"We need to leave!" Doc Benson said.

"Let's watch him a minute," Wall said. "This ain't right, but let's see what we're up against here."

Suckley kicked his feet and fell roughly onto the wooden floor. He then tried desperately to get up, which he did after a minute. He looked around the room slowly and when he saw Wall and Benson, he snarled. Wall drew his gun and pointed it at Suckley.

"Stand down, Mr. Suckley," he said. "I ain't foolin'."

Suckley lunged at the sound of his voice and Wall shot him in the heart, just like Jud. Suckley got rocked back a few steps, but he didn't fall. He started to move forward again.

Wall shot him twice more with the same result.

"Run!" Doc yelled.

"One damn minute," Wall said, calmly.

He re aimed his gun and shot Suckley between his eyes.

Suckley stood for a moment or two, but then collapsed as if all of the life was sucked out of him at once.

Nearly a full minute passed when Doc, sensing the danger had passed knelt down to Suckley and again checked his neck.

"No pulse and he's cooling off. Mr. Wall, this is *very* odd indeed."

Wall checked his gun barrel. He'd have to get bullets out of his saddle bag if the day kept going on this way; he took the remaining six he had in his pocket and reloaded. Holstering the gun, he looked at Suckley's body.

"I reckon, we ought to tell the law around here," Wall said.

Benson stood up and looked at Wall.

"And say what exactly?"

"That we got a problem. A big problem. I reckon that-"

Wall was interrupted by a series of knocks and kicks at the door behind him.

"What's that?" the Doc asked.

Wall knew exactly what it was.

"We have to get on out of here, Doc." Wall said, grabbing Benson's arm again. "At a rapid hike."

The knocking grew louder and more intense as Wall escorted Benson out of the office.

When they reached the porch, Scar and Spoon were looking anxious. Wall drew his gun and pointed it at them.

"The doc here is gonna unshackle you boys. If either one of you tries to run, I'll part your skulls. Hear?"

They both nodded as Benson took the keys and unlocked them. The looked at each other and nodded.

"What happened to that other guy?" Spoon asked.

"Dead," Wall said and then added, "Deader now. We're going to the sheriff."

Scar scoffed.

"What the hell's she gonna do?"

"Get off the porch. You two get in front of the horse." Wall said. "And what do you mean *she*?"

***

When Wall was a Texas Ranger, he quickly discovered how little time was actually spent doing actual *things*. It had mostly been riding somewhere, arriving too late most times and then riding *all the way back*. He'd done it for ten years, quit and became a bounty hunter. It was nearly the same job except in order to get paid, you had to do things. Tom loved doing things. He loved solving things and he loved coming out on top.

He also loved the idea of getting enough money to stop altogether. Maybe find a wife, have some kids and stay put for good. He'd come close a year ago to a wife and early retirement. Closer than he ever thought possible and then...

She turned out to be something much more than just in love with him. He'd done research on what she was, but couldn't find anything that didn't sound like those spooky penny dreadfuls he read when he was bored.

He loved her, if not instantly, then something damn near close to it. And then she turned out to be something else. He almost didn't care, but it didn't matter in the end anyway. She vanished, leaving only a note and she was gone God knows where.

He knew he was lucky. He also knew he missed her and was miserable about it, but there wasn't anything he could do about it.

He threw himself into his work, stopped taking rests between bounty hunts and just got on with life.

Except, it wasn't really living. It was just being alive, but it would do for now.

And as he walked quickly up the steps to see the sheriff, he thought he'd thought so hard about Veronique that he conjured her image.

Except, it was her; not just an image, but her.

She stood in a pair of dungarees that almost hid her figure and a plain shirt and vest. She wore a badge on the vest and six shooters on either side of her hips. She wore no hat, and her black hair was pulled back in a tight braid.

Wall stood there, mouth open as she looked at him. Her face was stern and he watched it soften for a moment. Then she scowled at him.

"What the hell are you doing here?" she said.

Wall was dumbfounded.

"I didn't mean to be here."

"I told you not to look for me," she said.

"I wasn't. You just happened to be the sheriff in the town where I'm not looking for you."

She looked at him hard and then softened again.

"You weren't looking for me?" she asked.

Wall walked into the sheriff's office and let the door close behind him.

"Darlin', I wanted to, but I didn't even know where to start and you *did* say y'all would try and kill me next time. That's what we call a deterrent."

She smiled and he melted.

"Listen, maybe we can talk more later, but you have a problem."

"What kind of problem?"

"Well, there ain't no way to be delicate about it. You got some dead folks running around at Suckley's."

She frowned.

"What does that mean?"

"Just what I said. I shot Jud Watkins square in the chest. Dropped him on Suckley's porch with my prisoners and then, the bastard starts moving around, like he wanted to kill his two pals. Bit Suckley. Suckley wound up dying after I got the Doc. Then he came back, crazier than a shit house rat. I had to put him down."

Veronique listened calmly and nodded when Wall was done.

"You know, that sounds ridiculous." She said, finally.

It was Wall's turn to frown.

"You know me Veronique. Do I make a whole lot of jokes?"

"It's not been my experience, no." she said, trying to hide a smile.

Wall smirked.

"There is some very spooky shit working its way to your town right goddamn now." He said, grabbing her arm. "You either got to get your people out, or we have to go take care of it."

He led her out into the street where the Doc and the two prisoners, now tied to the post of the Sheriff's porch, all stood looking back the way they had come.

"Mr. Wall, you ought to see this. You too Sheriff," the Doc said.

Veronique shook herself out of Wall's hand and ran to the street.

Wall stood where he was; he could guess what they saw.

"Oh no," Veronique said. "Is that what you're talking about?"

Lumbering down the street were three figures; a tall woman with what looked like a huge gash in her neck flanked by two children around ten years old with similar wounds on their arms and faces. They were slow, but they walked with purpose, looking at everything.

And snarling.

"Yeah, that's pretty much what I was talkin' about." Wall said, sadly.

"Well, don't just stand there jawin' fer Chrissakes!" Spoon said, already trying to pull himself free from the chain. "Start shootin'!"

"You can't shoot children!" Veronique said, shocked.

"They *aren't* children," the Doc said, never taking his eyes off of the grisly trio. "I don't know what they are, but they aren't human."

Tom nodded.

"Still, we can't just shoot 'em in the middle of the street. We have to get them off before—"

And suddenly, it was too late.

They watched in growing horror as a ten or eleven year old girl ran over to the bastardized family. The three walking corpses all turned and grabbed her before she finished saying hello.

The little girl screamed as the two boys tore at her flesh.

Wall and Veronique pulled their guns simultaneously and fired. The two flanking boys received spot on head shots as the mother, who was biting into the little girl's throat didn't react to this whatsoever.

"Nice shot," Wall said, re-aiming. He fired and the top of the mother's head flew off before she collapsed on top of the girl, who was silent and still.

The Doc stood with his mouth open as Tom ran into the street, yelling for the rest to follow him.

Spoon yelled back.

"You have to untie us you dern fool!" he said. "You're gonna get us et!"

Scar spit on the ground.

"I swear, Spoon. We'd have been better off gettin' shot."

***

Wall stopped just short of the pile of bodies, gun still drawn. No one moved; everyone, including the little girl was dead. She looked up at Wall with dead, terrified eyes, blood still pouring out of her wounds. He sighed heavily and holstered his gun as Veronique stopped next to him.

"*Isis Hristos*," Veronique whispered. "*Ceea ce monstrii sunt acestea?*"

Wall was going to ask what that meant, but he felt her grab his hand and for a moment, it didn't really matter.

"What are these things, Tom?" Veronique asked quietly.

"Ain't nothin' I ever saw." He squeezed her hand tighter and he felt her do the same. He let go and turned to the Doc, who was panting from the effort.

"We need to move these bodies out of the street," Wall said, grabbing the mother by her feet. "Things are gonna get bad enough around here. Don't need this."

The doc grabbed one of the boys and Veronique grabbed the girl. She looked at what was left of the girl and held back a cry.

She held back something else as well.

Blood streamed freely from the girl's neck as Veronique followed Tom to the back of the mercantile across the street. She felt something move inside of her and she let a small growl escape.

When she made her way to where Wall had stopped with the woman, she gently placed the little girl next to her. She stood up, shaking.

Wall looked at her.

"You know any of em?"

Veronique nodded.

"The woman is...*was* Millie Harper. Her boys, Stanley and Caleb. The girl..." she turned her back. "Angela Prentiss." She said through her teeth.

Wall reached out to put his hand on her shoulder, but she violently shrugged it off.

"Don't touch me," she hissed. "Not right now. I need-"

The Doc rounded the corner with the boy and his already fallen face, fell further.

"Jesus, Sheriff." He said, still dragging the boy to his mother's side. "You alright?"

Wall frowned and moved to face Veronique.

Her hands covered her face partially, but he saw enough.

Enough to jar his memory.

***

Tom Wall shuddered at remembering the last time he saw Veronique. In less than 24 hours, she'd become the love of his life. Also in that span of time, she'd turned out to be a monster. One with a dark, physical change. He'd last seen her as he was tied to a table in a town with no name. Wall had followed a bounty to the place, and shot him dead in the street.

He was convinced to stay the night by the hotel owner and that's when he'd met Veronique. She was a whore then, but a sweet one with heart. They'd spent the evening and most of the night together. Tom Wall had found everything he'd ever been looking for and then some.

And it had all been a lie, or so he thought.

As it turned out, the residents of the town were creatures, sort of like spiders who couldn't help what they were. They wanted to live alone in peace, only eating the vermin of society.

Except Tom ran right smack in the middle of it all.

They were going to kill him because they knew he'd wind up hunting them all down. And they were going to have Veronique do the job. In the end, she relented and left him alive, with a goodbye note, telling him she loved him and to not go looking for her or them.

And he had resisted it.

But now here she was again, right in front of him, changing into what she truly was...

"Fight it," Wall whispered. "Hold it back. You can control it."

She hissed and looked at him. Her porcelain skin had grown dark, nearly black. Her grey eyes remained intact, and Wall reckoned that was a good sign.

"Pull it back, darling." Wall said softly. The Doc began to move closer, but Wall held out his hand.

"Stay put, Doc." He said. "Give her a minute."

The Doc frowned, but stayed.

Wall looked again at Veronique and she had begun to revert back, slowly.

"C'mon now, Sheriff." He said, smiling. "Let's see that non-sharpened smile."

All the time, Veronique stared hard at him, but at this last thing, her stare softened. Her features began to lighten and finally, she was her self— her human self—once again.

"You alright now?" Tom asked.

She responded by hugging him tightly.

"I...haven't *fed* in ages..." she breathed. "All of that little girl's blood...makes it hard to hold it together."

Wall nodded and squeezed her.

"Can you keep it together for a little while longer?" Tom asked.

She nodded and let him go.

"I have and I will," she said. "Let's get back to the street and see if there are any more on their way."

"Now just hold on a damn minute!" the Doc said. "What in the hell was that all about?"

Wall whirled around and looked at the Doc.

"She was...changing there. She one of those...things?" The Doc asked.

"Sheriff's fine, Doc." Wall replied sternly. "Let's head out to the street and try to maintain some control here."

The look on the Doc's face was one of confusion and fear. Wall knew it was also something he wouldn't let go of either.

"But..." the Doc began, but Wall put a firm hand on his shoulder.

"But *nothing*." Wall said, staring at the Doc. Tom's eyes were those of a dead man's-devoid of any kind of emotion. He looked deep into the Doc's eyes and spoke carefully.

"Doc, we need to concentrate on the problem at hand, not this. Sheriff's fine as you can see. What you can't see is what's going on right now and we need to get back to that right here and now. Understand?"

The Doc nodded and moved to get away, but Wall's grip tightened.

"Understand me, Doc. Your sheriff is fine. The issue at hand and that's it."

The Doc nodded emphatically and Wall let him go. He ran to the main street. Wall looked back at Veronique, who was walking towards him.

"Let's get going, Sheriff." Wall said, waiting for her.

She smiled.

"I like how you call me Sheriff," she said.

*

"We got to bide our time, figure out when to make our move," Scar said. Spoon nodded.

"When the hell you reckon that'll be? When the rest of the goddamned dead start swarming around?" Spoon asked quietly. He didn't want anyone to hear him, even if he couldn't see anyone else around.

Scar nodded. It was a good point. Wall had kept a damn solid eye on them and even when he wasn't around, he made sure that they couldn't move anywhere. He held a chain up and threw it down in disgust.

"Next time they try and move us, we make a shot for it."

Spoon agreed.

"We could take out the sheriff easy," Spoon said. "That fat ass Doc Benson doesn't look like he has much starch to him."

"Yup. Just gotta worry about Wall," Scar said. He thought he might have an idea, but Doc Benson, Veronique and Wall had walked back into view.

"You boys behaving?" Wall yelled.

The two men said nothing.

"Figured," Wall said, looking at Veronique. "You reckon we can shove these assholes in your jail for a bit?"

Veronique nodded.

"Plenty of room," she said and walked towards the two men.

Scar nodded slightly to Spoon who tried to hide a smile.

"So you don't think you're clever," Veronique said as she approached the two men. "If you try anything, I'll kill you where you stand. And then, I'll eat you."

Wall didn't bother hiding a smile.

Scar scoffed.

"Just what the hell do you think you can-"

As Scar was speaking, Spoon made his move. He had grabbed his chain and tried to loop it around Veronique's neck.

Except, she wasn't there when he went to grab her.

The next thing that happened was Spoon was kneeling in the dirt, grabbing his throat as was Scar. Veronique stood quietly three feet away. The Doc rubbed his eyes as Tom looked on in mild amazement.

"I wasn't kidding, gentlemen." She said. "Now get up, or I'll hit you hard next time."

Wall chuckled and walked over.

"I think they get the point, right boys?"

The two coughed painfully and stood up.

"Hell," Wall said. "Her jail might be the safest place for you two. I wouldn't try nothin' else."

Scar nodded but Spoon just glared.

***

After moving the men into the jail, Wall, Veronique and Doc sat around Veronique's desk to discuss options.

"Ain't a whole lot of options here, folks." Doc said.

Wall shook his head.

"There's got to be some reason for this, and we find that, we get a lead on how to stop it before it gets worse."

Veronique looked out of her window to the street. It was empty.

"I ain't never heard of nothing like this," Wall said.

"I have." Veronique said quietly.

Doc coughed and sat up straight.

"I beg pardon?" he asked.

"What are you talking about?" Wall asked.

Veronique didn't look at the men, but began to speak.

"I was born in Slovenia, then grew up in Romania, but when I was still a little girl my father moved us to Moldavia for better work. In Moldavia, there was a legend of a thing called the strigoi. It was where the vampire legend originated, although we know those aren't real...don't we?"

Tom put his head down for a moment and let her continue.

"The original legend was that a strigoi was both human and demon. Dead yet alive. These things could be *strigoi mort*, but not exactly."

"Okay, so why would they suddenly just show up here in the middle of goddamn nowhere?" Doc asked. "You seem to know about them, but who else would?"

Veronique took a deep breath.

"Bosen," Wall said. "He from your village?"

Veronique nodded.

Bosen had run the hotel and brothel where he had met Veronique and had nearly killed Wall. Bosen had revealed to him that the town he had been in wasn't a town, but a trap for criminals. A trap where the unsuspecting victims were ultimately eaten by Bosen and the town's residents.

"Bosen makes sense," Veronique said. "He was furious after I burned the town down. We parted company after that and I did my best to vanish." Veronique said.

"You think he found you?" Wall asked.

"Again, it would make sense. He swore he'd kill me if he ever found me."

The Doc coughed and slammed a fist down on the desk.

"You want to include me in this goddamn conversation please?" Doc said, angrily.

Tom cleared his throat.

"This fella Bosen we know might be responsible for this. We find him, we got a shot of stopping what's going on."

"But, what's this about burning down a town?"

"It don't matter," Wall said. "We need to concentrate on right now, not back then."

Veronique sat up straight, still looking out the window.

"Meeting's over," she said. "We have more coming into town."

Both men looked out of the window and saw seven folks walking in the distance. Five men, one woman and a boy; all dead and walking down the street.

Wall sighed and pulled his gun to check how many rounds he had left.

Four in the chamber, and a box on his horse.

Veronique seemed to have read his mind. She walked to the gun cabinet behind the desk and unlocked it. She pulled out a double barrel shot gun and a second colt, which she tucked into her pants.

"Take what you need," she said to Wall. She regarded the Doc and said, "Take what you think you can handle."

"Just ammo," he said getting out of his chair.

"But how do you know this Bosen person? What kind of man can-"

Wall shushed him.

"Later, Doc. Trust me. You don't want to be in any kind of rush to find out what kind of man he is,"

This made Doc swallow hard. He stood up and grabbed a handgun.

"Everything here is a nightmare," the Doc said to himself.

*

Wall, Veronique and the Doc walked into the center of the street to meet the seven dead folks shambling in their direction.

"I don't think they see us," Wall said.

"How the hell do you know?" Doc said a lot louder than he intended.

At the sound of his voice, all seven heads snapped to the general direction on Doc's voice. They snarled in unison and began to shamble with purpose.

"Call it a goddamn hunch," Wall said, disgusted. He pulled his gun which was now loaded. "I'll meet them up there. You two hang back here in case there are any surprises." He looked at Veronique, who stood her ground but nodded.

Wall smiled.

"Is that alright, Sheriff? I know I'm a little out of my jurisdiction,"

Veronique smiled back.

"As as it says in your adventures, you are a Texas Ranger. Your jurisdiction is wherever you happen to be." She winked.

Wall turned and walked toward the seven ghouls, gun drawn and trying to calm himself down. His mind was racing with what was in front of him but also of what was behind him.

He walked slowly, trying to decide which of them to shoot first; he had the luxury of time as they shambled down the road, but then he noticed that each one of them had something around their necks.

Signs.

He could make the signs out the closer he got, but they must have gotten out of order.

TO THE

THE WHORE

EATEN

STABLES

BRING

BE

OR

It didn't take long to translate it, but by the time he did, they were almost on him. He drew his gun about fifteen feet out and fired.

Click.

"Aw hell," Wall said as the boy snarled at him.

***

"What in the hell is he waiting for?" Doc asked, watching the scene unfold.

Veronique cocked the shotgun and began to run to Wall, who was checking his gun and backing up.

"Sheriff, don't!" yelled Doc, who didn't have to fight hard to stay where he stood. "He said to wait here!"

She didn't answer and ran faster.

Much faster than Doc would have thought possible.

She slowed down about ten feet behind Wall just as he holstered his gun and drew a knife.

The boy, who moved faster than the other six, lunged for Wall as he pulled his arm back and stabbed the little boy in the side of his skull.

The boy made a small grunting sound and fell, sliding off of the knife, black goo spilling from the wound.

Wall gagged, but didn't retch. Still he rested his hand on his knee as the other six approached, all snarling.

The shotgun exploded behind him and he whirled around to see Veronique, gun poised. She motioned for him to turn back around.

He did and saw one of the men missing a large portion of his head. The thing dropped to its knees and feel over forward.

172

Down to five.

"Don't fire," Wall said as he launched himself at the nearest thing, stabbing it in the head with the knife.

Wall quickly dispatched the rest of the ghouls and sat down in the road. Veronique came up behind him and put a hand on his head.

They were silent for a moment until Wall said, "Did you read the signs?"

"I saw they had them, but didn't read. I wanted to stop them from attacking you."

"Well," he said. "It was a message. Words were all jumbled, but it said 'Bring the whore to the stables or be eaten.'"

Veronique stood quietly.

"Bosen," she said.

"Be damned surprised if it weren't."

She took her hand off of his head.

"I guess I shall go to the stables then," she said. "I have to protect my town."

Wall got up from the ground and stood in front of her.

"You ain't going alone."

"Yes Tom, I am. It's me he wants."

"He's gotta go through me first."

She smiled weakly.

"You're sweet, but no. This is my fight."

"Our fight." He corrected.

She grabbed him and kissed him deeply. When she pulled back she was crying.

"You were a dream, Tom."

"You're still mine, and I ain't no dream. I'm right here."

She stroked his face.

"Monsters don't get to have dreams."

"I don't see no monster in front of me."

"But there is one in front of you. That's just it. That's why you're a dream for me. A dream I won't ever get to have."

Tom cleared his throat.

"I got dreams. Dreams with you in them. We don't have to go to those stables at all. We can just go."

"Dreams don't come true," she said looking away.

"Didn't your mama ever tell you to believe in your dreams?"

Veronique laughed a bitter laugh.

"Yes, yes she did. Until we moved to Moldavia. But I believed in them. All the time. Then I became...*this*," She held out her arms. "A monster in girl's dressings. I dreamed about being normal again all the time. I thought I just didn't believe in my dreams enough. Then I thought that I wasn't trying hard enough to live up to my dreams. But now? Now I'm thinking that sometimes your dreams have a hard time believing in *you*. Maybe you don't abandon your dreams as much as they abandon you and that just...broke my heart. So, no. My dreams are dreams, nothing more."

Tom stared at her sadly. Then he grabbed her and kissed her. He pulled back smiling at her.

"Alright. No dreams. This is real life then, and I want you in mine. Monster? I don't know that. I know your heart. Whatever the hell else you are doesn't matter much to me."

"You aren't coming with me to the stables," she said.

"Damn right," he said and punched her as hard as he could in the jaw.

She fell backwards, knocked out cold.

He picked her up and walked down and met up with Doc.

"Thanks for all your help, Doc," Wall said as Doc stared blankly at him. "Open up that goddamn door. She ain't as light as she looks."

Doc didn't bother to protest and opened the door. Wall brought her in and lay her on the floor behind her desk. He stood back up, grabbed a shotgun, some shells and faced Doc.

"You listen here. I'm going to end this thing. You are not to let her out of this building, you hear me? No matter what she tells you, you keep her here."

"What about us?" Spoon yelled from the jail.

Wall ignored him.

"Why'd you hit her?" Doc asked.

"Cos she can't go where I'm going. Under any circumstances. Only way to do it."

"Well, she's a girl. She ought to just listen."

Wall smiled.

"Yeah, not this one. Keep her here."

He walked out of the door and said on his way out,

"But whatever you do, don't piss her off."

*

Wall neared the stables on the other end of the town, and heard the horses neighing restlessly.

No, not neighing...*screaming.*

He forced himself to not break into a run, but the louder the screams became, the harder it was to resist.

Resist he did, but someone else didn't need to resist.

"What in tarnation is *that?*" said an older man of about 49 running past Wall.

So much for not being seen, Wall thought.

He watched the man round the corner of the stable and then heard presumably him, scream briefly and then was silent except for the horses which now began to lessen. Thick, black smoke and a sickly sweet smell began to hit Wall's nose and he knew what it was; roasting meat.

He swallowed hard and crept up to the back of the stable and worked his way around to catch a glimpse of what was happening.

Wall's eyes began to burn from the smoke, but it didn't stop the visual he was seeing. He doubted he'd ever be able to unsee it.

In the center of the horses pen were four things; something that looked like a large metal bridge, horses, dead folks and a huge fire underneath the bridge.

The horses were being driven onto the bridge and over the fire where they were being roasted alive. Wall could see that some of the dead folk had caught on fire as well just from stumbling into it. But, the dead folk were also eating the horses that weren't on the bridge and it was taking a long time. The horses couldn't get away and the pen had been reinforced with razor wire. Several horses were strewn along the fence line either dead or dying. The coppery smell of blood and smoke choked the air around him. There didn't seem to be any purpose for this atrocity and that alone made Wall furious. He fought nausea hard and scanned the area for Bosen.

He saw no one that wasn't already dead, but he did see the man who had run ahead of him lying on his back, dead.

Then, he twitched and began to move.

Wall couldn't look anymore and turned away to walk back behind the stable to figure out what to do.

He walked two steps and saw him.

It wasn't Bosen.

"Hello Tom," Hank the bartender said.

Tom raised the shotgun, but Hank reached out lightning fast and pulled it out of his hands. Hank threw the shotgun far and away behind him.

"You ought to know better than that," Hank said, not smiling.

"Yeah, well I guess I don't learn very well. Maybe next time."

This time, Hank did smile.

"Ain't gonna be no next time, bounty hunter," Hank said. "Where's the whore?"

"Where's Bosen?" Wall asked.

"Bosen? Hell, he's dead," Hank said, laughing a little. "Took care of him after I tracked down the whore. Said he wanted to leave her be, after seeing what she was doing here."

Wall blinked.

"Doing what?"

"You remember when I last saw you? Bosen gave you all that bullshit about what we were trying to do?"

Wall nodded so Hank continued.

"How he loved this country and wanted to give back by only killin' the criminals? He convinced most of us that was the way to go, stay out of the light. Well, after everything I've been through, I say to hell with that. How do you stay quiet and hid when you used to be feared like a god?"

"So you killed him. What happened to the rest of them?"

"All of them," Hank said and gave Wall a cold look. "Every last damn one of them. They want to live like a secret, then they can buried like a damn secret too. Just one last loose end to tie."

Wall nodded and swallowed.

"Well, I guess two loose ends. You'll be the easiest one."

"The horses. Why did you do that?"

Hank smiled a sick smile.

"Know what a strigoi is, Wall?"

Wall nodded.

"No shit, really?" Hank was genuinely surprised. "Looks like you're more educated than I thought you were. Now tell me, know how to make one? Or a dozen? It's a lot more simple than you'd think."

"I reckon burning horses is a part of it," Wall said, disgusted.

"Close. It's committing an obscene act in front of the eyes of God. So obscene that they very after effect of it causes the dead to rise out of *protest*. That's what I've done here. Frankly, I'm glad you showed up cos I was running out of horses."

"You're gonna pay for that, in case you were wonderin'," Wall said looking Hank right in the eyes. The look was such that Hank physically balked and nearly stepped back. Wall was legendary for his eyes, if not his skills as a Texas Ranger and a gunslinger.

His eyes were cold, dead and terrifying.

"I seem to have you at a disadvantage, Wall. I took your gun and I'm pretty damn sure that I'm going to eat the hell out of you here shortly. A spooky set of eyes ain't gonna do spit."

Wall smiled. It was nearly as cold as his eyes.

"You ain't gotta worry about my eyes if that's where you're looking," Wall said and quickly reached around to his back holster he'd made a few years before. His arm swung back around with a 2 shot Derringer and popped a bullet into Hank's knee.

Hank howled in agony as he dropped to the ground clutching his knee.

Wall moved in closer and kicked Hank as hard as he could in the face.

Twice.

Bleeding and unconscious, Hank bled out of his knee slowly.

Just the way he wanted him.

He grabbed him by the hands and started to drag him to the other side of the stable.

His plan was to drag Hank over by the pen and hope some of the dead folk would gnaw on him for a little bit while Wall figured out how to save the rest of the horses. Then he could worry about taking care of the rest of the dead folk.

Wall got halfway to the pen when Hank suddenly came back to the land of the awake. His hands twisted and grabbed Wall's wrists tightly. Wall was then yanked forward and thrown about thirty feet and landed next to the burning corral.

He rolled and felt his ribs shift in his chest. He hissed in pain, but got to his feet as fast as he could and saw Hank start to change.

"Guess you ain't that educated after all, Wall." Hank said in a deepening voice. His skin started to crack and peel as the transformation began.

Wall had only seen the briefest part of the transformation when Veronique had begun to do so. He had only seen part of her face mid-transformation before the darkness took him and he saw no more until he woke up hours later.

This time, he was watching the whole thing.

And it was horrifying.

Hank's face turned into a rictus of fangs and his skin cracked and fell off, exposing a black hard looking exterior. His arms unhinged and nearly detached as they extended. He looked very much like a spider with four legs instead of eight. Hank's clothes ripped and fell off as the transformation went on; it lasted no more than 15 seconds, but it felt like an eternity to Wall.

The nearly ten foot tall Hank-thing reared back and screamed.

Wall nearly screamed too, but he was looking for something-anything to use to fight it off, but he was at a loss.

The thing screamed at him again.

"Shut your goddamned trap and just get on with it!" Wall yelled. "Go on and try to eat me, but give my ears a rest you ugly son of a bitch,"

Another scream bellowed out, but this time it wasn't from the Hank thing. It came from further away. As the Hank thing turned, Wall immediately knew what it was.

Veronique.

Transformed.

And Wall smiled.

The Veronique-thing was bigger than the Hank-thing and the Hank-thing shuddered visibly as she quickly filled the space between the two.

Something like a whine came out of the Hank-thing as it was lifted up by the other creature. The Veronique-thing began to twist the Hank-thing until it simply ripped in its center. The Hank-thing screamed as its insides poured out onto the ground. Where it hit the ground, it sizzled as if it were some sort of acid.

The Veronique-thing screamed something that sounded like a word, but Wall couldn't make it out. Suddenly, in the center of Wall's head he heard Veronique's voice loudly and clearly.

Move!

Grunting in pain, he staggered away from the burning corral and Veronique threw what was left of Hank into the fire. The fire exploded as if someone had dumped gallons of whisky on it. Everything in the corral was incinerated and the force of the blast knocked Wall to the ground.

***

Wall opened his eyes slowly to a half obscured blue sky and black smoke. There was a figure standing over him and he could see who it was.

He coughed. His ribs and back sang out in agony and he rolled over to cough harder. He hadn't hurt this bad in his memory. He saw two naked legs that he hoped to hell were Veronique's.

"Are you okay?" she said.

Wall tried not to laugh so he threw up instead. He saw that she was backing up.

He turned his head and looked up. She was naked, getting dressed.

"Good morning," he croaked and she laughed.

"Are you okay?" she asked again.

"Hell no I ain't okay," he said and struggled to stand. "Gotta get them horses out of that damn thing,"

"I took care of the horses," she said and helped him up.

He leaned on her and she pointed him to the stable bard, where 8 nervous looking, but still alive horses stood together looking around, wondering possibly why they were still alive.

"Thanks," Wall said and looked at her.

She smiled at him. She looked better than when he had first laid eyes on her that day.

"You look better," he said. "Not just because you're in your birthday suit."

She put her head down and said, "I have bad news about your two prisoners."

"They somehow met a fate worse than a hanging?"

"I needed to save you," she said. "I haven't fed since the last time I saw you. We can live without feeding like that, but...we aren't as strong. I couldn't take Bosen without being strong...or Hank as it turns out"

He looked at her and then turned to look at the corral. It was still burning, but it was finally dying down.

There were corpses, but thankfully no longer moving.

He looked at Veronique.

"Finally saw you," he said.

She looked up at him.

"And?"

He smiled.

"Least I didn't pass out this time," he said.

"I'm a monster," She said.

"You saved my life,"

"I'm a monster," she repeated.

"No," Wall said, putting his hand on her face. "Hank was a monster. He was killing folks to try and kill you. You were trying to do good in spite of what you think. He was raising the dead, slaughtering horses and such. *He's* the monster. You didn't ask to be what you are."

She smiled weakly.

"I was turned into this, and I don't think there's a way to turn back."

"Well, we'll just figure out how to live with it I reckon." He said and kissed her forehead. "It might come in handy."

"What do you mean, 'we?'"

He guided her away from the wreckage and began to walk away from it.

"I ain't letting you slink off this time, woman." He said through his teeth. "This seems like a halfway decent town to live...well, now that all the dead folks are dead."

"Well, I don't know Mr. Wall," she said. "I have a small issue with you hitting me a while back there,"

He coughed.

"Yeah, sorry about that. I couldn't think of what else to do."

She stopped and pulled his face to hers. She kissed him long and deep, then pulled back.

"I think I know something else we can do,"

He smiled.

"I don't know how that's gonna work with my ribs, darlin' " he said. "That's gonna hurt I think."

She smiled.

"Well, I didn't eat the Doc. He's back at his office where I sent him to wait for us. He'll take a look at you. And then we'll see how bad it's gonna hurt."

They walked away, holding each other and very decidedly not looking back at what they had seen already. They were looking at something new for the first time in a long time.

THE DINNER CONVERSATION

What's that?

Oh sure, here's the gravy. Sorry. My mind has been wandering a lot lately since Sal passed away.

Oh, thank you, but you don't have to keep offering your sympathies, Jill. I appreciate it. I also appreciate you coming to have dinner tonight. It gets awful lonely around here these days.

I know. It's been a long week hasn't it? It's been hardest at night when I'm trying to go to sleep. I reach for him, you know? Absent mindedly of course. A habit. And the reaction is still jarring. There's just a pillow there now.

No Sal. Just his *pillow.*

I've been thinking about getting a new bed. Smaller, since it's just me now, but not yet. The bed still smells like him, and it's comforting as it is depressing.

Yes, the turkey is pretty juicy isn't it? Slow roasting is the key and that turkey bag is *great.* Sal found that. He almost always made the turkey around here. About the only thing he *could* cook...

Yeah, well, he wasn't a good cook otherwise. If it was up to him, we would have starved to death!

Yes.

Yes, it was a terrible way to go...

No, I don't mind talking about it. I haven't really talked about it with anyone besides the police. It might do me some me good actually...

Yes, the police. They thought that I might have pushed him down the cellar steps. Yes I know, little me, right? Just walking up behind him and pushing him down there. I know, insane.

Oh, yes, the stuffing is an old recipe from Sal's mom. It *is* pretty tasty, but I've always preferred mashed potatoes myself. Sal hated them. I had to learn how to make the stuffing to the letter of his mom's if you can believe such a thing. And his mother, oh God. What a lousy human being! Ha!

Sure, you can have more potatoes. I have a lot, believe me.

You know, that was the last thing Sal and I argued about that night. His mother. She's been dead for almost twenty years and he *still* wouldn't admit that she was, above all else, a selfish *you-know-what*. She used to drive me crazy, especially near the end of her life, God rest her soul.

Sal had a propensity to behave a lot like her. I mean, just as *ugly* as she was sometimes if not uglier. She had a mean streak a mile wide and sometimes, mama's boy would show that side too. He sure did the night he died...

More wine? I'd love some, although I'd better slow it down a bit. I'm already a little tipsy!

Anyhoo, where was I? Ah, the night Sal died. Well, I had just cleaned up after dinner. I'd made a wonderful Irish stew which he normally loves...I mean, loved...

But that night, he just wasn't in a good mood. He was downright mean. He told this *awful* joke that really made me angry.

What was it? Do you *really* want to hear it? Okay. He said "How many potatoes does it take to kill the Irish?" He knows I don't like ethnic jokes, especially about the Irish because I am Irish. But, this time I let him do his stupid joke, so I bit and said "How many?"

"None," he said and laughed himself hoarse.

Well, you can imagine my disgust! What an *awful* thing to joke about and I told him so. He just laughed at me and said that the Irish were a 'weak people' and pushed away from the table. I finished cleaning up the kitchen, but I was furious. How *dare* he say something like that, even though I knew he was kidding, but the 'weak people' thing was *totally* his mother's influence.

Oh, Jill the things that woman would say to me because I was Irish and a ginger. She was awful.

You know, Sal *never* defended me? As affectionate as he was and could be, he never *once* stood up to her for me. I would be in tears for *hours* and he'd just shrug and say "Hey, she's an old woman. Just ignore her."

But I couldn't. Not even *once* could I just ignore her. I'd always get pulled into an argument with her and Sal would break it up, trying to smooth things over and sometimes it would work and I'd apologize to the old buzzard. But other times I wouldn't and Sal would yell at me the whole way home, saying I was being a bad wife and I should respect his mother, blah blah blah.

You remember how he was, Jill. Dog with a bone.

But he couldn't just defend me once, could he? Even after she'd been dead for so long. Just couldn't do me the courtesy.

So, he went into the living room to watch the news while I did the dishes. The more I washed, the angrier I got and decided that night, he was going to get a piece of *my* mind.

Yes, I have *plenty* of mashed potatoes! Please, help yourself. I'm so glad you like them!

Anyway, I walked into the living room and coughed to get his attention. He didn't move or say a word. I coughed again and he said "What already?"

I tore into him about his little joke. About his cracks about the Irish being weak. About how much like his mother he had become and he just sat there staring at me. I must have gone on for bout ten minutes and he just stared at me. When I got done I stood there. I had never once talked to him like that before and it felt good. Don't get me wrong, I love Sal...I mean...I *loved* Sal...you know what I mean.

What did he say?

He said after all of that ranting I had done, that I had just proved that his mother was *right!* My jaw dropped and he went back to watch the news. I couldn't believe my ears. I must have stood there for a long time because he finally said, "If you're gonna stand there, you can at least *shut your mouth.* You're breathing all heavy and I can't hear the news."

Isn't that just an awful thing to say?

What did I do?

I just...stormed off for one thing. Back into the kitchen, of course. My *place.* Where I should have stayed according to him. He would say that sometimes, that my place was there in the kitchen since I couldn't have children. Or so he liked to tell folks...

You didn't know? Oh, it was a total *scandal* according to his mother. He told everyone that the doctor said I was unable to have children. That it was a shame and all that. His mother said he never should have married me and that I should have told him that I couldn't have kids to save him trouble of marrying me.

I know awful, right?

Except it *wasn't me.*

It was *him.*

He was sterile. He was so embarrassed and didn't want anyone to know. He *begged* me to take the heat for it and I was young and naïve and a newlywed, so I agreed. But he was such a bastard about it...and he *still* never defended me when his goddamn mother...oh, my language! I'm so sorry Jill!

That's sweet, honey, but I'm still a lady! And yes, I may be a little drunk. But oh, my language...no excuse.

No no, I *shouldn't* have any more wine. It is good though...why you're just a bad influence on me! Half a glass then.

So I went into the kitchen to throw the dishes around...except I'd cleaned them all. So I started to clean. *Deep* cleaning. I started on the vegetable bin. I started taking all the veggies out and threw them on the floor. Peppers, onions and just threw them down. I had the ten pound bag of potatoes in my hands and Sal came in, hollering about the racket I was making.

By this time, I was crying and he just launched into me, saying the meanest things he could think of…oh Jill it was simply awful.

But then, he pushed it.

Too far.

I was crying at this point and sitting on the floor with my face in my hands, just taking it all in. And then he said it. The bastard…oh, there's my language again.

What's that? What did he *say*? Oh, Jill, he said he wished he'd never married me. That if he knew I would be like this, he wouldn't have and that I should have told him about *not* being able to have children. Can you believe it?

I must have snapped my last nerve. I stood up and told him he was a bas-well, you *know* what I called him. I reminded him of all those years ago, begging me not to tell his precious mother about him being sterile. He had the nerve to call me a liar!! I'd been married to him for 36 years and I know what I know. He had chosen to side with his mother *again*. Even dead, she was still ruling him. Even though she was dead, he was still a mama's boy.

I told him I shouldn't have married him after meeting the awful *thing* that he called his mother and he came at me! I was so scared.

What did I do? Well, I got out of the way. His leg was bothering him, so he was easy to avoid at first. But then, he started to catch up to me…I was scared, Jill. Damn scared.

And then I realized something. Sal was just hollering and swearing and I realized I still had a *ten pound bag* of potatoes in my hand…

He came at me and I let him. He was about five feet away and I swung that bag of potatoes as hard as I could at his head. Of dear sweet Jesus I did…knocked him clean off of his feet and sent him to the floor where he landed hard. He was still awake though and he started to swear after a few seconds. He shook his head and started after me again. I could tell he was groggy from the first hit. It looked like I'd broken his nose and he was bleeding from his forehead. I held on to the potatoes and wound up and he stopped. He said "Don't you dare hit me again, you little Mick bitch!" Then, he charged.

Well, you know where the cellar door is, Jill. It was open because I'd been doing laundry and he charged at me. I was on the right of the door and I swung left. Hit him in the same spot. He gave a little yelp.

See, I had knocked him off course and *redirected* him into the cellar.

Well, you know how long those stairs are going down to the basement… He fell for what seemed like a long time. When he hit the bottom, his neck made such an awful snap. Just awful…just…

Who else *knows*?

It's just you, Jill. It was the wine, but you can see I didn't *really* kill him. He fell. Didn't push him at all. I was just *defending* myself and….

No, I didn't tell the police. I figured folks would like to remember Sal as a good man and he *was* a good man most of the time. You knew how he was...

Well, no. I *don't* think I really should go to the police, Jill Henderson. I don't know why you're so upset. Sit down and eat, Jill. Have some more mashed potatoes..what?

Yes, from the same potatoes.

Well, I *washed them* for crying out loud! I'm not going to *waste* them am I?

Now hold on one minute, Jill...just sit down.

Oh, be careful honey. You almost fell over. You've had too much to drink. No *no*, you can't drive. I don't think you should go anywhere right now.

Nonsense, it's okay. We're still friends Jill, put that phone down. Please...let me make you some coffee...put that goddamn phone down! Oh dear, I'm sorry...my language...Jill?

Come into the kitchen with me Jill and I'll fix you...right up. I'll make you something...

Let me just move this bag of potatoes out of the way.

Why look.

It looks like I still have about seven pounds of potatoes left in here...

灯台の手紙
(THE LETTER IN THE LIGHTHOUSE)

11.19.46

To Whom It May Concern,

My name Alexi Bazhanov. I am an Engineer Major for the Red Army. I am writing this in English as it seems likely that this letter may be discovered by an English speaking explorer. There is also a shorter letter in Russian in the off chance there is a search party dispatched to retrieve me.

If you are reading this, I am already dead.

Very sad to say, you might be soon as well. There isn't anything you can do about it now. Stop looking around you; there's no one else here. But be assured, you are being watched.

I am writing this, knowing what is about to happen to me and honestly, what may possibly happen to you.

Hopefully, it will end with me. I am a Soviet officer...excuse me, a Russian officer; I no longer with to think of myself as Soviet.

I am a man.

But, sadly, it is why I am marked to die and possibly you as well.

It's not going to happen to you right now. You have time, but not a lot of it. Neither do I, so pardon me if I skip some things.

It was built by the Japanese. They blasted rock in this forsaken part of the world and built the lighthouse. For all intents and purposes, it was a good idea; a generous idea. As you have noticed, it isn't very easy to get here by boat. So many ships have wrecked, that the lighthouse was a blessing.

But that's not why they built it.

They sensed the coming war. They knew what was coming-they've always known what was coming and this was their response.

This was their weapon.

This was their revenge.

185

After the war came and went, the Japanese were defeated in a violent and severe manor as were the Germans and of course, the Italians. The world was safe again.

And, of course, Russia, carried on. We reclaimed this area and of course, the lighthouse which at the time, seemed like a fantastic idea. It was part of a string of other lighthouses on a fifty mile stretch along the coast line. The commission came down to retro fit the lighthouses with small atomic reactors to function without a full time keeper. This idea too was a good one. What kind of life could one expect manning a lighthouse for weeks, months on end?

I am laughing as I write this. The end is soon for me.

So, as a major engineer, I was sent to oversee the construction. It was quite simple, really. The lens of the light would rest in a mercury pool for ease of rotation while the reactor would ensure the light would not extinguish. Marvelous plan, really. I was, at the time proud to be a part of it.

The crewmen and I had been here a single day when it all started.

Our first order of business was to relieve the lighthouse keeper. He was an older man named Yuri Denisof. Life long bachelor with minimal family; ideal for the long stretches of solitude. There was a small boat poised to collect him and his meager belongings, bring him back to the larger ship and transport him back to Russia.

He was not here to greet us.

My crew scoured the lighthouse to search for him. And in less than an hour, we had discovered what was left of him.

At first glance, he appeared to be sleeping by the giant lens in the highest point of the tower; seated, facing the ocean. As we moved closer, we saw that he had torn open his midsection with a small knife and tossed his entrails out of the window. What was left, were being eaten by the birds that were all over the area. The look on his face was one of resolve. Almost, relief. I assigned three men to take care of Mr. Denisof and made the decision to bury him at sea. Certainly, not an ideal circumstance.

After that decidedly bad start, the crew made it possible to live in the lighthouse until the reactors were installed. The lamp was improved enough so the lighthouse would function without occupancy.

But, the lighthouse had occupants and always will I dare say.

I will jump ahead for the sake of time-my time specifically; it is running short at this point.

In a record three weeks, the reactors were installed and the mercury poured for the new swiveling lens. There isn't a reason this lighthouse shouldn't run for years unattended. It was a spectacular show of workmanship, and I am proud of the men who completed the work.

They should have fared better.

The reactors were, of course, in the lowest level of the lighthouse and, as the saying goes, out of sight, out of mind. This wasn't hard to achieve because the problems stated almost immediately upon completion. The crew had broken out vodka, wine and bread to celebrate the completion of the reactors and they had done a very good job of incapacitating themselves. The lighthouse was lit up and the men were being loud and reckless. And who could blame them? They did an amazing job as I knew they would. We were set to leave in the morning to return home, so I allowed them to relax.

The lighthouse is quiet, you see. Even with the reactors, the only sound is the ocean. It's calming and soothing even when in a storm. So when the scream came, it was more than just apparent. It was terrifying.

The scream came from everywhere at once. Someone dropped a bottle and it shattered, but not as shattered as the crew, who looked all around them.

It was a scream of pure agony and the men huddled together. No one said a word, even as the scream began to subside. The lights went dim-not out, but it was darker than it should have been. There was a gaping silence that was becoming louder than that scream. They looked to me, as I was the officer in charge. I tried to remain as calm as possible until the scraping began.

It sounded like someone raking a metal pipe against the curved wall in front of us. Huddled as we were, it was hard to move, but I was able to take one of the torches and scoured the wall for the sound source.

There was nothing, but a symbol on the wall-one that had not been there previously.

死

No one knew what that symbol meant.

No one but me, of course. It was Japanese for death. I did not tell the crew this, as they were already in a panic.

A sound of metal scraping once more began, but this time from the center where the crew were now all clutched together. One of the men screamed and the group separated quickly, making a circle. The men turned and looked as a young man howled with agony; he had a metal pipe impaling him from the top of his chest and onto the concrete floor. But it wasn't just a pipe.

It was one of the rods from the reactors.

The pipe began to move, drawing another symbol on the floor, scraping and grinding as the young crewman shrieked. No one dared move or say a word beyond gasping. When the symbol was complete, the rod dropped with the young dying man onto the floor. Blood spilled onto the symbol, covering it, but I saw it. I knew it, too.

憎む

This symbol was HATE.

Again, I said nothing about it, but instead urged the men to make haste to the outside of the lighthouse, to which they all agreed.

And of course, the door...

It wouldn't open.

Every light in the entire lighthouse snapped back on to full and the men reacted.

"Open the door!" they began to yell.

"Let us out!"

The scream returned, and the metal scraping sound began anew. He men and I turned to see the rod pulling itself out of the dead young man and hovered in the air. Then, it straightened itself horizontally and flew at the nearest crew men. It skewered three of them and lifted them up, screaming. It flipped them over quickly, and they slid off, howling until they collided into the wall on the opposite end of the room. They made a sickening sound and crumpled broken, dead and bleeding on the floor.

The men shoved me aside-I was staring in disbelief-and tried to break down the door. While they were panicking, the rod came back and repeated its previous actions twice more with similar results. The men were so obsessed with the door, they hardly noticed that they were being picked apart by an unseen force bent on killing them all.

The twenty men that had come to this forsaken lighthouse was now halved and the culling continued.

The rod claimed another two, but this time they were flung at the men trying to open the door. Three of them men were struck dead upon impact while the other three were knocked over-myself included.

The rod suddenly dropped loudly onto the floor and one of the last remaining men was lifted off from the floor and slammed into the wall with crushing force. His limp broken body was then manipulated up and down against the wall in random patterns. The two men left screamed in terror, but I did not.

I watched the message being scraped in blood on the wall. It was a larger symbol this time.

ウィジャ ボード

The body was hurled to the ground with a sickening thud and the door opened. The two remaining men bolted through the door and I quickly followed them out. The two men ran outside toward the ship, but I went to the entrance to the basement level.

The symbol was for *kokkurisan*, or *ouija*. That's when I understood. There was a small chance I could do something about it.

I ran down to the basement and opened the door. Everything worked fine and hummed perfectly. I looked at the floor...*really* looked at the hard concrete floor.

There weren't just cracks in them, there were symbols. Japanese symbols etched into the floor. I scoured the floor where I could and it was covering the entire floor; and now under the reactors as well.

The lighthouse was a giant conduit for malicious entities; a gate way to the other side.

And it was not only open, but angry.

Very angry.

I backed slowly out of the basement and climbed the stairs. I walked toward the small makeshift dock, where I assumed the two men had already left. And they had tried.

The boat was there, but in broken pieces.

As were both men; the appeared to have been torn into shreds and left in random strips on the rocks.

The birds were already feasting.

And so here I am.

You are reading this and you're likely to die, but perhaps my confession will save you. It's all that's left to do.

That's what this is now; a confession.

Although not personally involved, I am a Russian, not a Soviet and due to my lineage, I am guilty of crimes against the Japanese empire dating back to the Russo-Japanese War in 1904. I am also guilty of similar crimes during that last Great War for atrocities against the late Empire of Japan.

These crimes I am guilty of I'm ashamed to say.

I was a translator for the European forces as I endeavored to learn the language and culture in 1932 as a mere underling for the Red Army. My interceptions of transmissions led to the capture of forces in the Pacific which lead to horrible deaths in the gulags and prisons.

I don't know if this will work to break this curse for whoever travels to this godforsaken place.

The removed head of one of the young men decimated earlier has just been flung in though the open window of the lens room.

Death beckons. May it be swift.

Alexi Bazhanov
Engineer Major
November 19th, 1946

Epilogue

Dear Mike,

The curious letter left by the late Alexi Bazhanov appears to be authentic, although there is no actual evidence at this point to verify the deaths of the men or the symbols that were claimed to have been written on the walls and floors.

What is fact is that the reactors no longer work and there is the possibility of a radiation leak albeit, a low one. This lighthouse is structurally intact and the possibility that it may be brought back into service is rather exciting.

However, the idea that a "vengeful" Japanese spirit lurks in this lighthouse to exact revenge on those who have done the Empire wrong, are just simply absurd.

I will be at this installation until January, so wish me luck!

Say hi to the good old US of A!

Let's hope the little spirits aren't too mad about Hiroshima!

Yours,
Martin

THE TURBULENT FLIGHT HOME

Somewhere in Eastern Europe, approaching Germany,
October 1ˢᵗ 1968 1348 hours

Paul's head rested against the green metal wall. He'd been in the air for about three hours and the plane stank. This was made worse with the sun still beating on the plane and the 30 other grunts sitting around him. They were all laughing, talking about going home. Paul was just grateful that no one had tried to shoot him for three hours.

The thrumming of the plane's engines normally soothed his over active mind, but not today for some reason. He was going home and he should have been excited, but all he wanted was to pass out.

That, he decided, wasn't going to happen any time soon.

He picked up little bits of conversation. Some folks were talking about sleeping late for a month. Others talked about girls, jobs, friends and TV shows. The one show that kept coming up was some space bullshit called *Star Trek*, or something like that; Paul had seen a few episodes of it before he deployed out of Pittsburgh.

His brother Ben liked it just fine, but Paul had no interest in it at all. Paul was the younger of the two and although both brothers got along well, James had always been the intellectual one. He was creative and serious. Paul was far from serious; headstrong, funny and always with an eye for the ladies. He flatly told James he'd watch the show with the sound off and a joint, maybe some Hendrix while he watched that Uhura chick shake it in space.

Man, he couldn't remember the last time he got high.

James never liked pot, but Paul had been ready to make it a life avocation; he wanted to be a guitar player in a band like his hero Jimi Hendrix. That or a pot farmer in Jamaica.

And of course, James disapproved.

James wanted him to go to college like he did.

"You can be anything you want," James said. "But not if you rot your brains with that shit. That'll get you nowhere."

"Look at Hendrix," Paul would reply. "The man is a genius."

191

"You watch. He's gonna drop dead one of these days from all of that junk he does. And, news flash little brother, Hendrix was already making something of himself. He was in the Air Force. He was working as a musician when he got out, making money. You can't even play."

Paul would be damned if he was going to join the Air Force, and he said so too.

Three weeks later, the Army didn't give him a choice of where he went.

And now, two years later, he was finally going home.

He felt like a different man now. He still wanted to play guitar, but now he had a plan of how to go about things. James had said the Army would straighten him out and much to Paul's surprise, it did. Probably not in the way either of them had thought, but it did snap him into focus.

For one thing, Paul had never liked white people.

It was a huge bone of contention between the brothers and their father who had raised both boys on his own. The phrase "don't trust whitey" was used frequently. James never bought into it, much to the dissatisfaction of their father.

"They always gonna keep us down," he said. "Ain't never done nothing for us. We on our own."

James didn't buy it. Paul did.

Now, Paul understood things even his brother couldn't possibly understand. When you're in a jungle surrounded by people trying to kill you, you'd better trust the guy next to you-black or white, or you're dead.

He'd become a soldier. He learned to trust his platoon, not because there was a choice. You're stripped of your identities in basic. You're all shit, regardless of your skin color. You're all torn down. Then, you're remade. By the time he was ready to hit the jungle, he got it. He was surprised at the transformation in him and his fellow soldiers. Of course, not all of them got it. He still heard 'nigger' under people's breath, but now, he didn't care. He knew who he was. What he was.

He was a soldier.

He was a man.

That didn't mean he necessarily liked being in the middle of a conflict that most of his friends were back home protesting. He spent the war being mostly terrified. But, he was a goddamn soldier with a mission.

Kill the enemy.

And he did for two years with his brothers. His new brothers.

Now, he was going home with a plan and he couldn't wait to see his brother to tell him.

If he could only sleep.

Most of the passengers were from his unit, but there were a few guys he didn't know. Everyone was now quietly talking, a few guys sleeping, with only the engines of the C-97 to remind them they were all alive and going home. Paul rested his head against the metal hull again and tried in vain to at least pass out.

Thump.

Paul sat up and looked around. No one reacted to it.

Turbulence, thought Paul. *Must be it.*

He put his head against the hull again.

Thump. Thump.

He sat up again and looked around him. He looked to Smitty, a soldier from his unit.

"Smitt, you hear that?" he asked.

Smitty turned slowly to him, a half grin on his face.

"Yeah, a whole lotta nothing for like three hours. It's kinda nice, ain't it?"

Paul smirked.

"I guess, but it sounded like something knocking into the plane."

"You're hearin' shit, Paulie." Smitty said, chuckling.

Thump. Thumpthump.

Smitty's smug expression changed.

"Okay, that's what you heard?"

Paul nodded.

Smitty stood up.

"Anybody else hear that?"

The soldiers who were looking at each other and then, the thumping increased.

"What the hell is that?" asked Smitty.

Smitty moved himself into the long aisle and motioned for Paul to come to him, which he did.

"We should go talk to the pilot," Paul said.

"That's what I'm thinking. Ain't no turbulence I ever heard, man."

The two men walked to the cockpit carefully, and about ten feet before reaching it, one of the cockpit crew opened the door.

"Hey, you boys hear that?" asked Jessup, the navigator. "The hell are you guys doing back here?"

"That's why we were coming to see you," Smitty said. "Sounds like you're hitting potholes and shit."

"That's odd," Jessup said. "Sounds like its back here by you. No turbulence at all so far."

Thumpthumpthump.

The three men all looked toward the back of the plane. The passengers also looked toward the back when more thumps came in a flurry.

Paul looked down.

"What's in the cargo hold?"

"Hang on," Jessup said and disappeared back into the cockpit.

Smitty and Paul looked at each other.

"Why'd you ask what was in the hold?"

Paul turned and started to walk back to the back of the plane.

"Cause that's where the sound is coming from," Paul said as he walked. Smitty followed, frowning.

Paul walked past the seats to the thick metal plate covering in the floor. The noise was louder now, and seemingly concentrated.

"Smitty, it's here. Help me with this." Paul said, reaching down.

"Hold on, man," Smitty said, grabbing Paul by the shoulder. "We ought to find out what's down there first."

Turk, a big soldier who hadn't said a word to anyone since the flight took off said, "That's where the bodies are,"

They all took turns looking at the large man, who didn't even bother looking up from his book.

"Who are you big guy?" Smitty asked.

"I'm the guy mindin' his own bees wax," Turk said quietly. "Whatever the hell is down there can't be good. Y'all should just let it ride."

Jessup burst through the cockpit door and nearly ran down the aisle.

"We're carrying back the dead," he said, nearly panting. "Somebody down there might still be alive."

Paul and Smitty looked at each other.

"Well, you wanna go or shall I?" Smitty said smiling an unhappy smile.

"Damn," Paul said. "I guess I could go."

Turk chuckled.

"Sure as fuck ain't gonna be me," he said to no one. "Might as well let the boy go in."

Paul flinched, but that was all. He wasn't going to wait around to debate if Turk meant boy because of his age or otherwise. He let it go. Smitty however, had other plans.

"No one was asking you anyway, ya fuck." Smitty said and then did smile. Paul chuckled as he tried to figure out how to open the floor hatch. Turk didn't say anything.

Paul grabbed the latch, turned it and yanked it open. The smell hit him first and he nearly threw up. The other soldiers gagged and backed away from it. Grimacing, he looked down and saw nothing but darkness.

"I'm gonna need a light," he said in a shaky voice.

Jessup made his way through.

"It has lights, but they don't operate while we're in flight."

"Well that's kind of useless," Paul said quietly. "I guess I can use a zippo,"

"No," Jessup replied. "And you're not going down there. I am." He pulled a flashlight out from his camo.

"Hey, fine by me." Paul said getting up. "I wasn't really looking forward to going down there anyway."

"I'll bet, boy." Turk said, chuckling.

Paul forgot his nausea and snapped his head in Turk's direction.

"You best knock that 'boy' shit off, Private." Paul said.

"I'm a specialist," Turk replied. "I reckon I can call you boy if I feel like it."

"Nice, asshole." Smitty said smiling. "Guess they didn't tell you Corporal is kind of a higher rank, right?"

Turk actually moved in his seat to look at them.

"They making niggers corporals now?" he asked no one in particular. "Hmmm. Glad I'm getting out I guess."

Smitty went for him, but Paul held him back.

"We ain't doing this, Smitty. Fuck that asshole. We got shit to do."

Smitty was actually growling and the Turk laughed.

"We get off this plane," the Turk said. "You can try and teach me something. Listen to your boy over there."

Paul held onto him for a moment longer and Smitty began to relax.

"Sounds like a plan, asshole." Smitty said finally through gritted teeth. He looked at Paul.

"Why didn't you let me at him?"

Paul smiled.

"Ain't worth it. Trust me."

"If you guys are done," Jessup said, sounding a little relieved the situation was diffused. "I'm gonna head down there. Might be a VC in there, so you boys be ready up here."

Jessup pointed the light into the hold which revealed a thin looking staircase leading down.

"Hello?" he called out. "Anybody down here?"

Thump.

It came louder now that the latch was open and everyone flinched.

"Okay, going down." Jessup said, and he slowly descended.

"Guy's got some balls," Smitty said.

There was a general agreement among the soldiers and they waited for anything other than the Thumps, which were now increasing.

"I'm gonna go to the cockpit-see if there's any more flashlights up there," Paul said and quickly walked up the aisle. He knocked on the door and heard the pilot grunt.

He opened the door and saw the pilot and co-pilot doing what they do.

"What's up soldier?" the pilot said without looking.

"You got anymore flashlights available? In case something happens to your guy in the hold?"

The co-pilot turned to Paul.

"There's a couple in the storage box right behind us. About three of 'em in there. Don't all you boys start going in the hold, though? Just wait till Walt gets back up."

Paul nodded and closed the door.

The utility crate was where the co-pilot said it was. He opened it and grabbed two more flashlights. He headed back and that's when he heard the scream.

"Hey, what's going on?" Smitty yelled in the hold.

Another scream followed by another volley of thumps, but now there were multiple thumps.

"Paul? You find 'em?"

"Yeah," said Paul, handing one to Smitty. "Let's get down there."

The other soldiers parted like the sea and made room for the two men to go down below when they all heard another scream, this one calling out to God.

Smitty pointed his flashlight into the hatch.

"Hey, somebody's coming up! It's one of us."

They looked and a soldier, covered in dirt and gore was stumbling up the stairs slowly, as Jessup screamed in the background.

"Soldier, you okay? What the hell is going on down there?"

The soldier ignored this and continued to shamble up the stairs.

"He was probably marked as dead by accident," a soldier named Peters said. "Looks like they was wrong."

"Let's help him up here," said Smitty as Peters and Paul reached into the hatch to pull the man up. Each grabbed the man under his arms and pulled him straight up.

"Give us room!" Paul said as they went to lay the guy on the floor. The other soldiers moved back as the injured soldier struggled with Paul and Peters.

"Easy fella," Peters said. "Looks like you're gonna be alright now."

"Who else is down there?" Paul asked, but before there could be an answer, Smitty jumped into the hatch, yelling, "Holy fuck!"

Paul looked at Peters.

"Try and calm this guy down. Put your hand on his chest and keep him still." He stood up. "Someone get a blanket to cover this guy. I'm going down."

He made his way to the latch, but then saw Smitty running back up.

"Stay the fuck up there!" he yelled, staggering up the stairs. "Holy living fuck,"

Behind him, Jessup still screamed and something else…something like…moaning.

Smitty nearly fell onto the floor. He was bleeding from several wounds on his arms and his hands.

Paul bent down and helped him up.

"What the hell is going on down there?" Paul nearly yelled.

"Close the fucking hatch!" Smitty spat out. "Now!"

"What about-"a soldier started to say.

"Now!"

Someone kicked the hatch closed.

"Stand on it!" Smitty said, trying to get to his feet and failing. "A couple of you guys, fucking stand on it."

Two men did as Paul helped Smitty into a seat. Peters was still on the floor with his hand on the injured soldier's chest. The soldier was still struggling and beginning to moan.

From below, the thumps were coming from seemingly everywhere, and the screams of the Jessup were getting quieter.

The thumps were moving to the hatch.

"Smitty, what the hell-" Paul started.

"All of 'em," Smitty gasped. "Every fucking soldier down there. They attacked the Jessup."

"But why would they do that?" Paul asked.

"They fucking attacked *me*, Paulie. They're crazy or something. Moaning and shit. Like they're...I don't know, dazed? High? But man..." He started to sob.

"Calm down, Smitt" Paul said. "What the hell are these wounds?"

"Bites," he replied. "They were biting me. They were...*eating* that guy."

"Eating him?" Paul said, and then everyone looked at the injured soldier that Peters was attending.

No one looked harder than Peters himself.

He looked down at the soldier, who was still struggling, but now was snarling.

It all happened quickly for Peters. The soldier grabbed Peters' arm and pulled him off balance. Peters fell across the soldier's midsection, which is where the soldier hooked his arm over Peters' head and his other arm across his back. He pulled Peters towards his face and the soldier bit into the side of his chest.

Peters screamed as the soldier pulled back with a mouth full of uniform and flesh; it pulled off surprisingly easy as the soldier began to chew. Peters struggled to get away, but was held firm by the soldier, who went and took another bite. Peters screamed again.

The surrounding soldiers were stunned. With all of the violence they had seen during the war, nothing compared to the scene before them. As Peters screamed, Martinez, a small soldier, snapped out of his daze and pushed forward to help. He grabbed Peters and tried to pull him off of the other soldier, whose face was now covered in blood.

"Come on, man help me out!" Martinez yelled, struggling to the now screaming and squirming Peters. Paul jumped over and tried to pry the death grip the soldier had on Peters" neck. The soldier snarled and tried to bite Paul. Paul put his boot on the soldier's neck and pulled.

The soldier's arm came off, tearing a chuck of Peters' neck with it.

Someone yelled, "Aw, fuck!" as a stunned Paul threw the arm toward the cockpit.

The soldier was unfazed, but Martinez managed to get Peters up and off of the soldier. The other soldiers moved in and began to kick the soldier on the ground, who still seemed unfazed by all of this. He just gnashed his teeth and snarled.

"What the hell happened to that guy?" asked Martinez, trying to stop the bleeding coming from Peters neck, and failing.

Paul was trying to get Smitty to lie down on the seats when he heard three very loud thumps. The two soldiers on the hatch made startled noises. Paul stood up and looked at the hatch. With two men on it, it was still opening. The two men wavered on it and the hatch opened just enough that a hand shot through. The hatch came down on it and the hand struggled. One of the men jumped on the hatch and it cut into the hand. No screams came from below, just more moans and grunts. He jumped again and the hand came completely off.

Turk stood up and moved into the aisle. He pulled his service revolver.

"Maybe we should let 'em up." He said.

A few of the soldiers nodded in agreement, One of the soldiers kicking the injured soldier on the ground pulled his Colt and aimed it at him.

"Watch the windows!" someone yelled.

"Back away," the soldier said and when it was clear, he shot three times into the downed soldier's chest.

Two things happened at once.

Three black holes appeared in the man's chest and absolutely nothing else. The shots didn't seem to do anything to the man except renew his resolve to stand up. The other soldiers backed away as he did, stand up clumsily. He hauled himself up and turned to face the shooter, who was now stunned. He held the gun up.

"Back off!" he yelled and fired another shot into the snarling soldier now advancing toward him. The shot has no effect as the shambling soldier grabbed the shooter and toppled onto him, knocking them both down.

"What the hell!" Paul nearly screamed as the skin of the shooter's face was grabbed by the cheek and torn off in a solid piece. A thick, gurgling scream erupted from the unfortunate soldier's mouth as Paul chose to help the downed soldier and nearly ran towards them. He grabbed the snarling soldier by his hair and pulled. He had hoped the pain and the snapping back of his head would be both distracting and successful. It was neither. He came back with two fistfuls of hair and scalp. He gagged and threw the chunks onto the floor.

"Somebody help Paul!" Smitty said, sitting up and watching in horror.

Turk, revolver still in hand walked into the aisle behind Paul, who had no idea what to do next. He pushed Paul roughly aside and put the butt of the gun directly against the temple of the ghoulish soldier, who was eating the chunk of flesh ripped from the screaming, struggling man underneath him.

The gun exploded and the bullet tore through the man's head, travelling violently through the other side of his head, spraying three soldiers with bone, blood and brain matter. The three soldiers now covered didn't have time to react as the plane violently pitched forward.

The bullet had gone through the cockpit door.

For twenty seconds, the plane was in a freefall and the bulk of the soldiers both alive and not slid and crashed against the cockpit. Smitty managed to hold onto the seat in front of him that he was thrown into. The two soldiers standing on the hatch collided and slid violently down the aisle, desperately trying to grab onto to something to prevent their descent.

Twenty seconds later, the plane slowly began to correct and level out. The battered men slowly and unsurely got to their feet. After a minute Paul asked "Everybody okay?"

Peters mercifully had passed out and the poor bastard that Turk has saved was unconscious as well.

That left the biter.

He lay still and unmoving at last; his blood all over the floor, but he wasn't biting or trying to do anything anymore.

He was decidedly dead.

Paul made a break for the cockpit to check on the pilots. He hoped they had just been startled by the gunshot. When he opened the door, the co-pilot, Hennessey was barking into the radio. The plane's captain had a valley in the back of his head as he sat slumped to one side, dripping blood. Blood was all over the left side of the interior windshield.

Paul gagged a little and asked the co-pilot, "Are you okay?"

Hennessey jerked his head around.

"Do I goddamn look okay?" he said. "Hell no I ain't okay. Which one of you assholes shot the Captain?"

"It was an accident. One of the soldiers below..." Paul's voice trailed off.

"Below?" Hennessey said. "There's nothing down there but dead soldiers."

"They ain't all dead, but they are pretty fucked up."

"Ain't dead? Explain that."

"I can't," Paul said. "Let me see what's going on back there. I just wanted to make sure someone was flying this thing."

"Yeah, yeah…we're okay. He's not though…" Hennessey said, nodding to the dead Captain. "Keep me posted about what's going on back there, you got me?"

"Yeah," Paul said and left the cockpit.

Paul closed the door behind him and looked around in the cabin into a sea of expectant eyes.

"What's up Paul?" Smitty asked through gritted teeth. He looked bad, but so did everyone else.

"Turk shot the captain, but the co-pilot has it under control."

Turk, who had gone back to sitting down as if nothing had happened, jerked his head up.

"Shot the captain?"

"Yeah," Paul said trying not to glare at Turk. "Right in the head."

"Humph," Turk said, dismissing it all and he went about reading his book.

"Unbelievable," Paul said walking to Smitty.

"Hey, you alright?" Paul asked. Smitty looked up at Paul with bloodshot eyes.

"Man, I feel like I have the goddamn flu now and these bites hurt like a bitch. So yeah, it's like, Tuesday in Da Nang.

Paul smiled and looked away for a moment. Something wasn't right and he noticed it too late.

Not only was the hatch open, but three bodies were half out of it.

The bodies were moving out slowly and onto the floor. It was happening slowly and Paul took a quick look around to see if anyone else had noticed.

They hadn't.

"Smitt can you get up?"

"Man, I ain't movin'"

Paul grabbed the big man and hauled him up onto his feet.

"Get the fuck off of me, Paul. Jesus-"and then he saw them too.

"Guys, we got problems!" Paul yelled as he moved Smitty towards the front of the plane.

Heads whirled around and the soldiers got up or turned and drew their side arms.

"What the fucking-"

Shots rang out as three of the soldiers fired into the three shambling soldiers who had somehow managed to not only stand, but advance.

"Stop firing!" Paul yelled. "That shit don't work!"

Turk moved his big self into the aisle, gun drawn and walked toward the advancing soldiers.

"It does if you head shoot 'em, *boy*." He said and raised his gun, taking his time to aim. A smile broke out across his face as he fired into the forehead of the nearest one. The soldier's head snapped back and he collapsed to the knees before falling forward, down and unmoving.

Turk turned around and faced his audience.

"See? That simple. This will be easy."

The other soldiers motioned for Turk to turn back around, but it was too late. A fourth biter on the floor that no one had managed to notice and was missing his lower torso grabbed Turk by his legs. He pulled himself up slightly and bit into Turk's calf. Turk screamed and fell over backward.

"Holy shit," Smitty said. "It's Jessup."

Paul looked and indeed, it was the flight navigator, biting and chewing on Turk's leg like a ravenous dog.

"What happened to his legs?" Someone else asked.

"Fuck you, what about my legs??" Turk screamed. He was punching Jessup in the head having dropped his gun.

Paul looked at Smitty.

"I don't wanna shoot Jessup in the head," he said quietly.

"Paulie," Smitty said. "That ain't Jessup anymore I don't think."

That fixed it and Paul walked to Jessup's head and shot him, point blank in the head.

Jessup stopped moving, but Turk didn't. He began to crawl backwards away from the thing that had tried to eat him.

He backed into the two remaining ghouls that he had targeted originally. They fell on him and began to tear him to pieces.

Paul slowly backed away. He looked behind the grisly feast in front of him and saw more soldiers with the same glazed look coming through the hatch.

"Alright men," Paul said, raising his Colt. "Take your time, fire at the head. They ain't in no rush and neither are we, but be careful. No way we know how many is down there."

Paul carefully aimed at one still eating Turk's face and decided to shoot the one chewing into his mid section. He found it difficult and missed the first two shots. It was hard to break the training of being trained to shoot for center mass and switch to head shots, but improvising was Paul's best trait. He took a deep breath and shot the next one.

"Don't need everybody right now," Paul said lowering his gun. "Let's not empty it all into them. Take your time."

Paul holstered his gun as two soldiers took his place. He went to talk to Smitty, who was sitting at an odd angle and looking dazed.

"You alright?" Paul asked.

"No," Smitty croaked. "But I would like to tell you that I'm not as bad as those two motherfuckers over there." With a shaky arm, Smitty pointed at Peters and the soldier with the half torn face. "You may consider a pre-emptive bullet or two in their skulls." He laughed. "And, mine."

Paul looked and shuddered.

"Yeah, I ain't popping you." Paul said.

"Right, I can do it."

Paul looked at him.

"The fuck you can, you can't shoot nothing." Paul said flatly. "Hell, only reason I shot VC was because they were laughing at your bad shooting ass."

Smitty coughed a laugh and then it turned into just a thick, choking cough.

"No one shoots you, not even you." Paul said and stood up.

"Anybody on here got any fucking idea what the hell this shit is?"

No one said a word. They just looked at Paul, or just shot into the heads of the folks coming through the hatch.

"And how about some of you guys moving ahead and closing the fucking hatch?" Paul walked and looked at the two unconscious men. He grabbed the nearest soldier and said, "If either of these two move and start doing that shit," he pointed down the aisle. "Give a bullet in the head."

The soldier shrugged and looked at him.

"You ain't my fucking CO," the kid said, but Paul's return look told him otherwise.

"Before you shit your pants kid," Paul said. "Right now, I *am* your CO. Me and that guy." He pointed to Smitty. "Don't shoot him."

Paul went into the cockpit once again.

He closed the door behind him.

"How we doing back there?" Hennessey asked.

"Not fucking good," Paul said.

"Well, we ain't doing much better up here either. I was getting static on the radio and just started getting really weird radio updates."

"How weird?"

"Fucking weird. Tell me what's going on back there."

Paul described what was going on in the back. Hennessey shook his head and every now and then would swear under his breath.

When Paul was done, Hennessey simply turned on the radio.

"You turned off the radio?" Paul said

"Listen," Hennessey replied.

The broadcast was from the US Military. It was a looped repeating message. It was brief and to the point.

"This is Oberschleissheim Army Airfield. The base is currently quarantined. Please coordinate your flight with one of the other airfields."

"Quarantined?" Paul said.

"Right. And I checked the other airfields. Same message."

"Well, we can't land there. Where then?"

Hennessey shook his head.

"I'm going to start hitting up the UK, but we'll be making it on fumes. Can't get any response from anyone just yet."

"You think..." Paul began but stopped.

"Think what?" Hennessey asked. "And what's all the shooting back there?"

Paul shook his head.

"I think we're quarantined too. Maybe what's going on here isn't just here."

Hennessey visibly shuddered. He turned and looked at Paul, almost pleading.

"Can you get the captain out of that seat?" he asked. "It's making this hard to do."

Paul nodded.

Ten minutes later, the soldiers in the cabin had managed to close the hatch and pile the bodies on top of it. It was a grim scene Paul walked back into from the cockpit. He had taken the captain's body and moved it from the pilot's seat to the navigator's chair and threw a spare utility blanket over him.

Paul looked at Smitty, now lying down across two seats and twitching slightly. He looked at Peters and the young faceless soldier who didn't move at all.

The soldier he had told to watch them came over to him.

"I think they're dead," he told Paul.

Paul nodded.

"Well, I guess we know what we gotta do," he said.

The soldier nodded back and drew his gun, but Paul put a hand on his shoulder.

"Use a knife or something. I think we're all goddamn sick of gunshots."

The soldier nodded and holstered his gun.

Thump

Paul sighed and looked down the aisle. There were at least ten bodies on the hatch, so no one was coming back up unless the plane started to pitch like that again. He took the chair in from of Smitty and leaned over to take a look.

He looked bad. *Really* bad. He was breathing short, shallow breaths and his skin color was going from pale to gray. He wasn't gonna make it. If the plane couldn't land, none of them were gonna make it.

He was going to have to take care of Smitty sooner or later.

He turned around and sat hard in the seat. He looked down at his boots, caked with blood and gore. He looked at his hands. He wished he had a guitar.

He wished his brother was there for the first time. Not to tell him he was sorry for how they left things, but to see his brother. Give him a hug. Tell him he was right. See that big ass grin on his face.

Thump Thump.

Paul started to laugh.

What would Hendrix be doing right now?

Thump

Thump

Moan

That came from directly behind him and he knew what it was.

Paul swallowed hard and drew his knife to say goodbye.

WHERE THE APPLE SHINE WON'T REACH

For SM—no offense...

Brenda lay on her bed, three pages to go in her book. Her face was moist with tears and she was biting her lip. Seven books in, this was to be the last book for the *Dark Gift* romantic vampire series. The absolute last, according to the publisher; in spite of the two previous sequels that were also to have been the last. But this was to be the absolute last one. It was even called, "Last Rites."

Brenda had waited patiently for this one book for nearly three years and she had gone to the midnight sale date. Midnight, Halloween night at Holmes and Bernard's Bookseller and Music Superstore invitation through lottery only please, thanks so much. She stood in the small line that had begun to form the night before Halloween (*but she was third in line thank goodness!*) and ran to the display and grabbed her book-$34.99-no sale price for the early birds. She paid for it and bolted for her car so she could begin the long night, day and night of "Last Rites" in her apartment, all alone with the curtains closed tight and not stop reading until she was done.

Then she would take a shower.

The book itself was mammoth; nearly fifteen hundred pages long, not counting the 45-page author's introduction. (*"I love each and every single sick one of you!" the grateful author concludes.*)   The other books for *Dark Gift* ran from 300 to 675 pages throughout the run of the series. This one, though... Brenda was very intimidated by its sheer size, but was also delighted because she knew it would be worth the wait to read it. She knew that there was so much to get out of this book. And how could it be anything other than huge?

Nearly twenty-four hours later, here she was, weeping and nearly done with the entire series. It was beautiful. It was a dream how wonderful the words were so well crafted. Helen, the story's heroine, had spent the bulk of the Dark Gift series madly in love with Kirk, a young looking vampire she met in high school. They have adventures and high romance with other vampires and human friends as well. But then there came werewolves, ghouls, (*one tried to kill, then eat Helen!*) mummies, (*it was awesome-they went to Egypt for a class trip*) and finally, Count Dracula *himself* in this, the final book.

Dracula, who was actually Kirk's uncle, tried to get between him and Helen. And Dracula nearly succeeded, but Kirk, ever resourceful, stopped a very bad union just in the nick of time. But then, Kirk was nearly destroyed by the ancestor of Van Helsing, Dracula's old enemy, but Helen, and her latent psychic powers (*found in book three, "Head Trauma,"*) came to the rescue.

And that was only up to page 750!

There was more-a lot more, leading up to the last three pages in this sprawling series, where Helen and Kirk marry and where Helen agrees to finally accept Kirk's "Dark Gift."   As she turned the last page, Brenda's eyes went wide. She let out a very tiny 'squeak.'

She quietly closed the book and sat on her bed for several minutes. She felt…fulfilled somehow. She shuddered slightly and sat up. She wiped her face and sighed. She was hugging the book as if it were a small child. A thousand thoughts ran through her mind; she wanted to cry, she wanted to kiss, she wanted…

She wanted. Most of all, she *wanted.*

She stood up and went into her bathroom. Resting the book gently on the toilet tank, she stepped into the shower and turned the cold water on strong.

Oh yes, she wanted.

Ten minutes later, she stepped from the shower and toweled off. She grabbed the book and padded into her bedroom. Tossing the book oh so carefully on the bed, she opened her vast closet and chose what she'd wear tonight. It was nearly Midnight, and still Halloween. There was always a little fun to be had and she had so much pent up energy from the book, she couldn't contain herself.

Wouldn't contain herself.

She wanted to explode and giggled.

She felt naïve and older than her years; she knew love like Helen and Kirk's couldn't exist, but oh, she wanted it so bad. It was so beautiful to her. The stories had touched her in ways she couldn't have ever imagined.

And now she would go out, and hope in her heart of hearts that maybe, just maybe…

There would be something in the world for her.

She smiled and went out of her front door to find something.

Something she wanted very much.

Anything.

Four and a half hours later, Brenda sat on her bed, crying. Her face was buried in her hands and she sobbed hard. No, there wasn't a love like Helen and Kirk's. There wasn't anything close to it. No instant attraction, no doe-eyed romance, or romantic adventure. No pale skinned beautiful waif and certainly no glittering supernatural hero. There was what there always was; anger. And hate. And emptiness. Just a void that could never be filled by anyone or anything. She was alone. All alone.

She stood up angrily and walked across her room. She kicked the young man lying crumpled in a heap and unconscious on the floor. He gave a small muffled yelp. He slowly came too, and began to weep.

"Where…where…where…"

She kicked him again.

"Shut up!" Brenda snarled. "Just shut up!"

She began to pace, glaring at the young man. He was looking up at her now, petrified.

"Please…look, what did I…"

Brenda stopped and knelt down to him. She grabbed his neck and pulled him closer. His eyes went wide as her face turned into a snarling rictus of sharp teeth that extended from ear to ear.

"What did you *do*? You didn't do anything! Absolutely *nothing*!"

The young man started to scream and Brenda sank her teeth quickly into the lower half of his face. He struggled briefly, but then was quiet again. She fed and fed well, but cried the entire time. When she was done, she pulled herself up off of the floor and went into the bathroom.

She looked at her face.

Vampires weren't heroes. They weren't romantic. They didn't sparkle in the sun, they didn't fall in love, they didn't have fabulous adventures and although they could see themselves in the mirror, they were not beautiful.

They were most often covered in blood and left a trail of corpses behind them.

She hit the mirror as hard as she could. It shattered and she nearly screamed, but held it.

The books.

She wanted to destroy them.

She ran into her room and picked "Last Rites" up off of her bed. She was going to tear it in half. Brenda looked at the cover.

She looked at it carefully.

And she wanted to cry.

She sat down for a long time until finally, she opened the book and began to read.

Vampires weren't a lot of things; nothing like how they were in the "Last Rites" books.

But, they could still dream.

THE MOON SEES YOU

The boy lay in bed, crying. The tears wouldn't stop, but he was quiet. A pillow in his teeth as he tried to keep from breathing too heavily. He needed to calm down, had to calm down, but the calm he sought wouldn't come at all. He looked up and saw the moon through his transom-like window; he could see the bright round thing through the thin, Star Wars curtains and the light was very *very* bright tonight. The old rhyme rang through his ears.

You see the moon and the moon sees you.

Except in his mind, another verse added itself.

And the moon saw what happened.

Not that it would matter what the moon saw. He had a better shot of the moon actually *doing* something about it than anyone else. Not his sister, who was in the same situation and not his mommy who worked the night shift and looked the other way.

The moon saw what happened, but so what?

So did everyone else and the moon still had a better shot of saving him.

But, he didn't think the moon would. It wasn't the moons fault; it was just the moon after all. What could the moon do?

He finally stopped crying, thinking of what the moon could do.

***

His dream was lush and colorful. He wasn't him, but something else.

He was a wolf. A big and beautiful wolf, running through the neighborhood. A wolf, but not a wolf; he still felt like himself, a quiet 8 year old boy, but now, he was running fast and he felt so powerful. He ran harder and faster. He ran up the hill, past the apartments where he lived, past his grandparents' house, past his friends and his school and ran and ran.

He ran all the way to the town park, where the very beginning of the Appalachian Trail began and ran further still, straight to the highest point and then, he stopped.

He saw the moon.

And the moon, saw him too.

The boy wolf howled.

And the moon heard him.

"I saw what happened," the moon said. The moon had a lovely voice; a voice like a mother should have and the boy wolf howled again.

"I know," she said, sadly. "It is heartbreaking, my little son in spirit. But, you must not dismay, for I have heard you."

The boy wolfs ears shot up, or at least that's how it felt.

"There is nothing that I do not see, little one." she said. "And there is nothing I do not hear, especially on nights such as this. The moon sees you, and hears you."

The boy wolf, who could speak no words, bayed sadly at the moon.

"Shhhh, little one." said the moon. "You asked what possibly the moon could do. I will make you safe. Would you like that, little one?"

The boy wolf felt something move behind him.

It was his tail.

He yelped and looked up at the moon.

"Be ready," the moon said and everything disappeared.

***

The next night, after dinner, the boy finished his homework and decided to put himself to bed. There were no arguments from his father, already into a bottle of cheap gin. His mother was at work and wouldn't be home until five in the morning. He started to walk up the stairs when he heard his father snap his fingers at him.

"C'mere boy," the man slurred. He was already really good and drunk. "Give daddy a kiss."

The boy's stomach rolled, but he did as he was told. He was a good boy, as he had been told on so many occasions.

Except when he wasn't a good boy. Then, he was a great number of things, including the latest one, a word he'd never heard before.

Cum stain.

He didn't know what that was, but apparently he was one, so like a good little cum stain, he obeyed and climbed back down the stairs.

His father was a tall man, but small looking while sprawled on the couch, watching a movie of the week.

The boy leaned over him and gave his a kiss on his cheek.

"Good night, Daddy," the boy said and forced himself to give a little smile.

Daddy smiled back.

"Not feelin' too good?"

"No, Daddy."

"You ain't missing no more school," he growled.

The boy nodded.

Daddy frowned.

"This ain't about last night is it?"

The tone and manner in which those words were uttered sent a jolt through the boy. It was usually the tone of voice before things got a whole lot worse, but the boy tried to remain calm and just stood there, looking at the floor. He was careful to not look Daddy in the eye.

"No, Daddy, I'm just really tired," yhe boy said quietly.

His sister, who was ten and sitting in a chair with her homework, looked up. Normally, her main job was to give the boy as much grief as possible, but the last few weeks, she had unexpectedly given up that hobby.

"He didn't look too good in school today, Dad." His sister blurted out. She tried to sound casual, but failed.

Daddy's eyes narrowed and he shot a look at her.

"I didn't ask," he started, sounding flat. "For your goddamned opinion."

Her eyes went wide and she pulled her book up to her face.

"Right," Daddy said, shaking his head. "So, maybe you are coming down with something. You go on to bed and I'll..." He stopped and looked his son in the eyes.

"I'll check you over later,"

The boy swallowed hard and turned to go to up the stairs. On his way up he looked at his sister, who was looking back at him, like he was a condemned man.

***

The moon was brighter than ever and the boy just stared up at it. His wish was to fall asleep soon and be the wolf again in his dreams. Then he could visit the moon and talk to her.

She felt safe.

She felt like home.

She felt like love.

It was unlikely that it would happen, but it gave him something to think about and that would help him fall asleep.

But he remained awake, looking at the moon.

And the moon was looking at him.

***

The boy was beginning to doze off finally when he heard the door rattle. He snapped instantly awake, opening his eyes. The moon was still there, although in a different position in the sky. It's light was poking through the thin curtains brighter than ever and he made a silent plea for her to do anything to help him.

"You up boy?" his Daddy said, sounding like he was trying to be quiet and failing. He was slurring and staggering, knocking over things on the boy's dresser that was right near the door. The boy swallowed hard and got ready for the worst.

Don't be afraid, little son. The boy heard the voice. She was here! His heart pounded harder and for the first time not out of fear, but out of hope.

"Thank you!" he said aloud.

He said it aloud, but that isn't what he heard himself say.

***

"What the hell is that?" Daddy asked, sounding confused. "Boy, you got something in here?"

Daddy couldn't see very well even though the room was bathed in moonlight. He had never seen the moon so bright, but he could only make out the dark shape of his son on his little bed. The boy was moving, almost writhing in the dark.

"C'mon, get up boy. I know you're up." Daddy said, moving unsteadily towards the bed. "Don't wake up your sister,"

Although his daughter slept in the next room, the walls were thin and there wasn't any need for them both to be awake. The Daddy was careful, but not that he thought he needed to be. It was his home that he paid for. King of his castle, even though it was a cheap apartment. Still his, goddamnit.

"Get up," he said flatly, hovering over the young boy. He grabbed the flimsy blanket (the only thing he could see in the moonlight) and pulled it off the boy. Daddy's excitement was growing, but just what the hell were the sounds coming out of this boy?

He thought it was snoring at first, but it was more…guttural. As the blanket was pulled off of him, the snore became a growl.

Then a snarl.

A very loud snarl that sounded like a large angry dog.

Daddy backed away from the bed. That wasn't his boy. He was drunk, but he wasn't entirely stupid. He knew a dog when he heard one.

"Boy? Where'd this goddamn dog come from?" He yelled, no longer trying to be quiet.

The snarling thing on the bed moved and the boy's bed creaked from the weight.

Daddy found that he still couldn't see, but the one thing he *could* see was a pair of yellow eyes.

"*Do you see the moon?*" the thing on the bed asked. It's voice had a rasping eagerness to it.

"What?" Daddy asked, now for the first time in a long time afraid.

"*Do. You. See. The. Moon.*" It asked again.

Daddy staggered back away from the bed and the yellow eyes that seemed to narrow.

"Yeah, I see it," he said. "Where's my boy?"

"*The moon sees you too.*" it responded, ignoring the question.

Daddy stumbled over a small sneaker on the floor of the room that seemed to be shrinking as he watched the yellow eyes follow him.

"*The moon sees everything.*"

The thing on the bed stood up and finally, Daddy could see it, at least in silhouette.

It was a large dog looking thing, up on its haunches. It was also in tattered clothes that vaguely resembled...trucks?

"*The moon knows,*" it said, though a mouth of jagged teeth. The moonlight caught one side of the thing's mouth and the teeth seemed to glow.

"This...this ain't real," Daddy said, nearly whimpering. "You back off now, this ain't happening!"

The thing snarled at him and he yelped.

"Girl!" Daddy called out. "Call the goddamn police!"

He called to her a few more times and the thing on the bed growled.

"*The moon protects,*" it said and snapped its jaws at him.

There came no sound from his sister's room.

Daddy went to open his mouth again, but the thing suddenly moved off of the bed and right into Daddy's face.

"Is that...*you* boy?" Daddy nearly whispered. "Please, don't...I'm...sorry,"

The thing snarled and drooled on Daddy.

"*The moon does not agree,*" it said before Daddy began screaming.

***

The official police report claimed that a wild dog running loose in the neighborhood had somehow gotten into the apartment and tried to attack the boy, while his father perished trying to protect him. The boy was not injured in spite of the tattered pj's he was found wearing.

The boy's father died as a result of severe lacerations to the neck, face and groin. The boy's sister claims to have heard nothing and had been sleeping peacefully when her mother came home to find her husband mauled to death, but her son, although slightly shaken up, otherwise unharmed.

212

The boy was briefly questioned. Because of his age and the severity of the trauma, he was sent for evaluation to the hospital's psychiatric division. The boy's only recollection of the incident was to say that "Blood looks black in moonlight."

The boy, however, opened up about a great many *other* things that had nothing to do with what the police had termed an 'animal attack.' The things described by the boy and later, confirmed by his sister had caused a major upheaval in the small New Jersey community.

The animal attack was quickly forgotten in the light of the things the boy had claimed.

*

The boy, who was now a man, sat on the side of the tiny bed. A small girl lay there, looking up at him in the moonlight, smiling.

"Daddy," she said. "The moon is really bright tonight. Can you close my curtains?"

The boy who was now a man nodded, but said,

"Just a little bit, okay?"

"Why?"

"You see the moon, right?"

The little girl nodded.

"Well, the moon sees you too." He smiled at her.

She smiled back.

"Just close it a little bit then," she said and yawned.

And the boy who was now a man did just that very thing.

STORY NOTES/AFTERWORD

These notes are not really in any kind of order. I know a few people who read collections by story title and not story order. These notes have been assembled much in the same way.
Enjoy!
NWP

A Box of Candy
(Originally Published in FEAR THE ABYSS by Post Mortem Press, 2013)

My writing process is usually pretty simple—I get up and just start writing and whatever comes out that grabs me right away, gets written. This story was different in that there was a theme to the anthology for which it was written. Up until this point, I had been writing stories just randomly and finding the market for which it seemed best suited. The fine folks over at Post Mortem Press had invited me to be part of the anthology called Fear the Abyss, which boasted some pretty big named authors, including one of my favorites, Harlan Ellison. The guidelines were simple; they wanted something otherworldly, not necessarily horror, in the vein of *The Twilight Zone* and the like. A bit more 'sci fi' if you will.

I don't write science fiction really, but I was willing to write it because, Harlan Ellison.

The concept was pretty simple. A widower on a cruise with the ash remains of his wife with the full intent to dump them overboard. I did want to write a sweet story where the guy gets to talk to his wife again, but once she started talking in the story…well, it all kind of went to hell.

That's the fun part about writing, at least for me; when the characters take over to drive. You, as the writer, make these folks up in your head, but when they show up on paper…well, they can kind of take over for you and the Candy in the story was no exception. By the time it rounds the corner so to speak, I couldn't think of a better fate for her.

Buzz
(previously unpublished)

This story was written for an anthology that never happened, as sometimes happens. The original raw version had a lot of issues, mainly that I was still pretty raw myself. It was rejected by a few publications and it's just sat around in a box for a while. When I was compiling stories for this collection, I kept thinking about this one in particular. I read it with the eyes of someone who writes a lot better than he used to (I can only hope) and figured out where the clunky bits were in addition to the really great notes on the rejection letters. (Yes, I keep those. Every single one of them.)

I liked the story a lot, but upon re-reading the notes, I adjusted here, removed there and added some all over. The story is pretty good now, I think. Good writing, as they say, is rewriting and there is a whole lot of truth to that statement.

I wanted to hint at something Lovecraftian with this story and I sorta/kinda got there. If you aren't into Cthultu Mythos or that sort of thing, don't feel bad if you missed it. This story *(with burning bus full of children and all)* was an attempt as 'subtlety."

Decorations
(Originally Published in THE BIG BOOK OF BIZARRO by Burning Bulb Publishing, 2011)

This story appears to be a revenge tale but is actually (what I thought at the time) a female empowering revenge tale. I get a little tired of guys always being either the hero or the villain of the stories I read and was the second such story I had written with a female protagonist. I didn't want her to be a cliché and thus began a series of what I hope to be consistent strong female protagonists in my fiction if for no other reason than I don't know any cliché women in my life. Most of the friends I have are women and none of them are cliché. The strong characters I create are in some way or another, reflections of them all.

That being said, I don't know any who would do what Riley does in this story. (Well, maybe two of them.) The idea for the Burl Ives song at the end actually came from a CD copy of the song skipping in the exact same spot and it was creepy to actually hear it. It's probably why it stuck so hard in my head.

When I sent this one to Gary Vincent, he wrote me back in the most vivid and gleeful acceptance letter I have ever received to date. Considering the content of the story and where it ends up, I knew right there we were going to be cohorts and pals.

Fishing Hole
(Previous Unpublished)

Two of my favorite authors are Mark Twain and Joe R Lansdale. I believe if there is a successor to the late Twain, it is Lansdale, hands down. Both of their writings tell the truth; which is something bold to think because we are dealing with fiction. Stephen King once said "Fiction is the truth inside the lie," and he remains correct. There is something very distinct and honest in their works, and because of the heart they put into their writings, I wanted to write something akin to it, or as least get as close as I could. "Fishing Hole" is the product of that attempt. I've sent it out multiple times, and was summarily rejected each time, although additional notes in the rejections claimed they liked the story a lot.

I took all of the recommended changes for the work save one-the beginning. The key to short fiction essentially is to hit your mark true from the get go; grab the reader right away and don't let go. For horror fiction, that is sometimes, if not more often than not, vital.

I think my mistake in this one was thinking it was a horror tale and it really isn't at its heart. And the heart, is where the truth inside the lie lives. The beginning for me is key, because it sets the tone. It remains the most descriptive into to any story I've written and it was important to me that you get to know a character that isn't even really in the story except in flashbacks.

I don't know where this story came from to be honest. I had no such relationship with my father they way Jeb and his did. It was something so clear in my head, I really can't pinpoint where it came from, but I'm glad that it was there if only to write this one. It may never see the light of day outside of this collection, but I'm really glad it exists.

Just Enough Rope
(Originally Published in WESTWARD HOES by
Burning Bulb Publishing, 2013)

I am a rather big fan of Larry McMurtry; in particular his LONESOME DOVE novels. I like western novels a lot more than I ever thought I would admit, and honestly, I didn't think I'd like writing them as much as I have found that I do. "Just Enough Rope" was my first attempt at writing a 'straight' western. 'Straight' in that it wasn't going to be supernatural at all.

I failed.

Before I knew what the hell was happening, monsters showed up and made the story...well, a western with monsters. I became rather attached to the main characters as well, which shouldn't have come as a surprise; when you write enough, your stories breathe because on some level, your characters are alive.

The mighty Burning Bulb folks (Gary and Rich) contacted me about doing a Western Bizarro story probably about ten minutes after writing "Just Enough Rope." It was so great because I literally just replied and attached the story to it, which almost never happens.

But I guess I can't say that anymore, can I?

Monk's Run "Pilot"
(Unproduced Teleplay, 2007)

While I was working on what would become DEMONS DOLLS AND MILKSHAKES, I wanted to write something different, so I thought about a TV show. It was one of those things where in about an hour of coming up with the basic idea, I came up with EVERYTHING at once. The characters, the bad guys, absolutely everything and I wrote a one hour pilot in about a week. I changed a thing or two but the cold open remains intact. I had five years of stories for "Monk's Run" and I have decided that this will eventually be the third book in a series of novels about Kat and Bruce from DD&M.

Maybe.

Just gotta write that second one though…sigh…

My favorite part of the script is the villain, Hirsch. I've no idea where he came from, other than my little head, but he popped up out of nowhere. I want to write this guy for a very long time.

Additionally, his counterpart in the story Ahmo is based on actress/model Ahmo Hight whom I became good friends with *after* writing her in this script. I had her in mind for the character from the start and thought the name was cool enough to just use it. I eventually sent her the script and she dug her character a lot; which is good if we ever wind up doing this thing, the part's already cast!

On a side note, I sent this to a guy I knew from a mutual acquaintance who wrote and directed films. (*He probably still does for all I know. I'd ask him, but he's been a douchebag the last few times I've seen him and frankly, I don't have the patience. I will say that he isn't bad at either filmmaking or writing. He's just not as good as he thinks he is…*) He confirmed he got the script and said he'd get to it asap. After two months I inquired if he'd gotten a chance to read it. He said he hadn't and oh, could I send it again please.

Sure.

And I didn't see or hear from him for *years*.

When I did actually see him again, it was when folks were buying my first novel. He said hi and then started hitting up my publisher for stuff.

Spiritus Ex Machina
(Originally Published in FROM BEYOND THE GRAVE: A COLLECTION OF 19 GHOSTLY TALES by Grinning Skull Press, 2013)

This story originally appeared in an anthology called FROM BEYOND THE GRAVE. The submission ad called for interesting ghost stories. It occurred to me that I had actually never actually written a ghost story, much less an *interesting* one...

This was one of the few stories that I did research on before actually writing the story; I write fiction, so research isn't really a huge thing I do. But, research this I did and I wound up writing a very odd ghost story and possibly the one story I believed to be the scariest story I had written at the time. In a way, I still think it might still be, but I am biased.

The location of Penkridge, UK is in fact, a very real place. My older sister Adina lives there with her husband Clive as does my friend Dave. The next town (or village, rather) has the great name of Wolverhampton. I did my very best to make all of the dialogue as genuine as possible and had Dave check it for authenticity. His response was, typical for him, brief.

"It's alright," he said. What a pal.

When I decided on the type of ghost I was going to use, it begged the question of "Why the hell would a Japanese spirit occupy an English racecar?"

To which I replied, "Because I say so, that's why."

There is reference to a car that crashed in the 1955 at Le Mans. That was real and ultimately inspired this story. I remember reading that story a few days before the call for the anthology came out and by the time it did, I had worked out all kinds of things in my head about this one.

By the way, if you are ever in Penkridge, there is an Indian Restaurant called Flame which serves the absolute best curry in the universe as far as I am concerned. Really.

Spring in New York
(Originally Published by Hacker's Source Magazine, Issue 9, 2005)

This story is my first published work and one that I am very proud of, but man, it's like looking at a picture of yourself when you're an awkward little kid. I wrote it between lives, so to speak. I was living in a really cool but tiny apartment in Dover, New Jersey and had finally gotten a beat to shit PC on the total cheap, but it had a copy of Windows Dinosaur with Office 1876 (I'm exaggerating a little) but it goddamned worked, and that's all that counts. I started "Spring" in January of 2001 and worked on and off in a very infuriating manner for about three months.

In May of that year, I moved to Pittsburgh and packed up everything I wanted to take with me-including this story.

It sat on a floppy disc until September.

September 11th, 2001.

Yeah.

I don't know why it sat there for so long; I had moved into an apartment with my fiancé, and was enjoying the change of scene and the utter lack of anyone I knew well, but I could not get the images of that day out of my head. I was able to see the Twin Towers from the steps of my grade school on a bright clear day. As a performing musician, I played a ton of shows in the Village and we'd always pass the Towers on the way back home. They were a huge part of my skyline since I was a child. To see them fall in such brutality was simply awful.

Before the evening fell that night and before going to bed, exhausted from calling back home to make sure the folks I knew that worked in New York were okay, I opened up this story and started to write it again.

Now, as dour as all of that sounds, the story itself really isn't. The elevator pitch for this story (*as Jon Towers would be likely to ask*) is this; One day, Lucifer decides to go to Manhattan to look for a girl he likes. It happens to be the first day of spring. Mayhem ensues…

The Date
(Written Exclusively for The Wicked Library Podcast, 2015)

This story was written with a pile of stories right after I had finished "Spring…" and has been heavily rewritten for a special episode of The Wicked Library that featured stories from Dan Foytik and Neil Gaiman.

Yeah, that Neil Gaiman.

The original version (*which I hadn't read in about 13 years*) was very clunky as that was before a real solid sense of style had been developed on my end. I changed the genders of the main characters and made it a lot tighter. My friend Maria always loved the suicide hotline sentence and thus, it remains intact for all of its tactlessness.

Everything Here is a Nightmare
(Previously Unpublished)

This was always going to be the title of this collection, and when author Sydney Leigh had told me that the collection should have a story with the title, I sank a bit because I didn't have one.

At the same time, I was writing the sequel to "Just Enough Rope" because as I mentioned earlier, I really kinda loved the characters of Tom and Veronique. As I wrote it, it occurred to me that the title of the story (which at the time was "Monsters Don't Dream") could in fact be "Everything here is a Nightmare" if I really wanted it.

And holy cow, I did.

The title came from a drive by conversation with my friend, Becky Anderson. (*For the record, not Rebecca, but Becky. There is a difference!*) I asked how she was and she said smiling,

"Nelson, everything here is a nightmare."

I told her that was true and also the most awesome title for a book. She agreed and said I should get to work on it, so…here it is. Thanks Becky!

About the story; I wanted to make up for the sad ending of "Rope" somehow, and "Nightmare" was my chance. I think I have one more short work with those two crazy kids and then I'm going to have to give them a whole novel.

My favorite part of the story is how genuinely angry people got at the corral scene. Please let me know if you get angry too! Authors love it when readers get angry at stuff.

The Dinner Conversation
(Previously Unpublished)

My friend Evan told a really awful Irish joke to my good friend Tom. Tom was offended by the joke, declaring, "Hey, I'm Irish and that's really offensive."

We all laughed, except my friend Bill who, who without even looking at Tom stated in his clear and booming voice,

"The Irish are a weak people."

We could not stop laughing, as horrible as a thing that was for him to say.

Now, I have to clarify that neither Bill, nor anyone else involved in that little exchange was out to offend someone. Bill isn't a PC kind of guy, but that doesn't make him insensitive. (Although saying he is sensitive is a reach too, frankly.) We all told mean spirited jokes on a regular basis, because, assholes.

This story came from that joke, mean as it is.

灯台の手紙
(The Letter in the Lighthouse)
(Previously Unpublished)

I will be the first one to admit that this story is really fucked up.

I was involved with a project where authors would be assigned a location and a fictional account would be written about the location. The location I was assigned was the Aniva lighthouse that rests abandoned between Russia and Japan. It is a wacky story-the real story. Mine is wackier. It might possibly be the most gruesome story I've written as of yet. The story was accepted for the publication, but I pulled it out for reasons I won't get into here. I do wish that publication all the luck in the world and the authors who contributed to it.

The Turbulent Flight Home
(Originally Published in RISE OF THE DEAD by Burning Bulb Publishing, 2014)

This story came about in a really fun way, and it sort of helps bring this collection together.

I met Jon Towers and David Fairhead at a small bookstore now called Rickert and Beagle. There was a book signing-the very first one I had ever attended and exciting as hell because, holy shit, I was going to be signing books! Also in attendance was my good friend, author Jesse Saxon, authors Kimberly Bennet, Rich Bottles Jr and Gary Lee Vincent.

It was with delight that Jon, Dave and myself all kind of huddled together and talked about old horror movies, wrestling and pretty everything you could talk about before a book signing.

Great time to be had by all in other words.

Since that point, Jon invited me to join his podcast network, Red Horse Radio. Dave had a show there too and hey, wouldn't it be cool if I had a show as well? *(The answer was a severe fuck yes from me.)* Jon and I created "Storytime at the Wicked Library." The first season consisted mostly of stories in anthologies I had appeared in *(Which at the time, was two. Since then, The Society 13 Pod Cast Network was created where The Wicked Library, Dave's Kettle Whistle Radio, Jon's Red Horse Radio, Dan Foytik's 9th Story Podcast, TBA with Mr Pink, Mouthing Off with Chris Westrick and Tony Rowsick's ProgWatch all have a home.)*

But I'm getting off topic...

I ran into Gary Vincent and the legendary John Russo at a convention. Now the thing about running into John Russo is this; he's awesome. He's kind, funny, sincere and will talk to you for hours about nearly anything at all. He's a really nice guy and hey, he co-authored the original "Night of the Living Dead." That is a hell of a resume bullet point!

David Fairhead had told me a few days earlier he had been invited to contribute a story to an anthology of tales centering on the world of NOTLD. About five minutes into seeing Gary and John, Gary had invited me to contribute as well and I would have been jumping around, but I had my daughters with me and there isn't a force on Earth to keep two excited nerdy ladies still in a convention that also boasted having a fucking life sized TARDIS on display.

I did all of my jumping around on the inside.

The caveat is that that the story needed to take place in the time frame of the original NOTLD.

Even cooler.

So, for my story, I wanted to use the hero of NOTLD, Ben as a passing reference of an unintroduced younger brother. I had the whole thing charted out that even set up how Ben would wind up at that cemetery in Evans City while the newly created 'brother' would be flying home from Vietnam with a stronghold of corpses that suddenly spring to life.

The original title was "Flight of the Living Dead."

So, I did research of all sorts of things, including racial tensions, planes, army stuff, what have you and kicked out a cool ass zombie story and with the exception of the 'zombie' in DEMONS DOLLS AND MILKSHAKES, this was my very first living dead story.

I sent it in and waited to see if it made the grade.

I heard from Gary and the story made it, but with two adjustments.

First, the title. Gary, the ever vigilant editor, found a bunch of other works with the same title, so that was fine. The title it wears now I actually like a lot more.

The second one stung; I couldn't use the character Ben from the original movie of any references to it.

Balls.

The story as it stands still works I think. I'd never written anything like this and I never tackled the subject of racism in any of my work. I think I did okay, but I'm sure if I got stuff wrong, I'll hear about it soon enough. I tried to not make anyone out to be a cliché or stereotype-even the racists.

However, the zombies were totally stereotyped.

Where the Apple Shine Won't Reach
*(Originally Published in MON COEUR MORT by
Post Mortem Press, 2011)*

This wasn't my first published work, but it's the one that actually started me taking writing a lot more seriously. The story of a young girl and her fascination with a series of novels pretty obviously based on the TWILIGHT series of novels by Stephanie Meyers (the original version included a small dedication—"To SM-No offense") was not a terribly long story, but it had a nice punch. I had written it as a sort of exercise and put it away. At the time, I hadn't had much of an inclination to submit it anywhere until I met Stephanie Beebe. My friend Dave was in from the UK and I took him to a comic book convention in Pittsburgh. He had a great time, looking at all the cosplayers and just geeking out like a young lad should when we came upon the Post Mortem Press table. Stephanie was hanging out while her erstwhile husband Eric was away doing something quite Eric-like. There was a sign that read something akin to "Writers Wanted" so I inquired. I got the low down from Stephanie, who said they were looking for stories that were "Anti-Twilight" for an anthology to be named at a later date. I took a card, got the info and knew that by later that afternoon, I'd have my little story in their hands.

And they did.

Stephanie to this day says that she 'discovered' me and I'm not going to be the one who argues with her. In all fairness, ten minutes later, I ran into Gary and Rich from Burning Bulb with a similar sign for THE BIG BOOK OF BIZARRO and did almost the exact same thing with "Decorations" (which had been written around the same time.)

I had gotten acceptances from both publishers pretty much right on top of each other.

The story of Brenda was a fun one and only had two characters. This did not deter comic artist Crystal Ash from adding more when she asked to make a comic version of it; we went on to do two issues of the expanded story which was/is called "Forever After." A third and final chapter awaits…

The Moon Sees You
(Previously Unpublished)

This story is as close to autobiographic as I have ever intend to get, minus the supernatural element.

There are a lot of questions over this story, even by the handful of folks who have read it mainly because of the content. I would refer you to the

Stephen King quote I gave earlier…"Fiction is the truth inside the lie" and this story is no different.

I have come a long way as a writer and as a human being, the latter I think being more important since I'm a husband and father. It was scary to write this one for me. I allude to my childhood a lot, but kind of keep the details to myself. Some of them popped out in this one unintentionally and the temptation to pull them back was countered by my inner child insisting that they stay right where they are. This story took some weight off of my shoulders; weight I didn't need to be hauling around. I'm grateful for this story. Sometimes, writing is also an exorcism.

And sometimes, it works.

ACKNOWLEDGEMENTS

Thanks to all who have helped with this collection. You're help was appreciated and to attempt to name you all here would be feeble. So, I have created this space for you to write your name!

Special thanks to _____ for your help! It was you specifically, _____ that helped the most! Really!

A few special mentions must include Sydney Leigh for your insight, Paul Anderson for your always reasonable advice, counsel and over use of the word "fuck," Bret Bouriseau for all this extra energy and infectious inspiration, Daniel Knauf for being a badass, Dan Foytik for taking over The Wicked Library podcast at the *exact right time*, Gary Vincent for reasons obvious...and thanks for taking another shot on me, Dr. Jon Towers for always being the inspiration for pushing new ideas, and TREMENDOUS thanks to my new favorite super editor, Jessica Pacelli!

Much thanks to Heidi Halbig, Rochelle Delgado, Justi Hillberry, Nick Wang, Chelsea Cefalu, David Fairhead, Linda Nagel, Ken Cain, James Gunn, THE Becky Anderson, Mike Miles, Tom Pecosh, Bill Owings, Jesse J Saxon, Tabatha Nase, Mae March, Brady Allen, Lindsey Goddard, Ahmo K Hight, Tony Rowsick, Tobiah Hale, Valerie Guidi, Joe R Lansdale, John Russo, Rich Bottles Jr, Stephanie Yager Eric and Stephanie Beebe, Sherri and Doug Campbell, Maddie "Sista from anotha Mista!" Holiday Von Stark, Hannah Storey, Dan and Michele Storey, Rosemarie Klisiewecz, Deb, Annabelle and Sammi.

Big shout outs to all at Society 13.

I know I've left folks off and it was a pure mistake. Your help was not. Thank you thank you thank you!

ABOUT THE AUTHOR

Nelson W Pyles is an author currently living in Pittsburgh, PA. His first novel DEMONS DOLLS AND MILKSHAKES was released to critical acclaim in 2013. He is currently working on two novels. He created the popular podcast The Wicked Library (www.thewickedlibrary.com) and remains the executive producer. He runs the Society 13 Podcast Network (www.society-13.com) with David Fairhead. For more information please visit   www.nelsonwpyles.com,   www.facebook.com/nelson.pyles   and @nelsonwpyles on Twitter.

OTHER GREAT TITLES FROM

WWW.BURNINGBULBPUBLISHING.COM

WOL-VRIEY
BIZARRO AND TRANSGRESSIVE FICTION

BOSTON POSH (BUD MALONE #1)

In 2028 AD, the USA is a nation ravaged by hungry dragons and dinosaurs. In Boston, Massachusetts, private eye Bud Malone is hired to rescue a kidnapped heiress. But nothing is as it seems.

Malone works to unravel a tangled web involving Boston Chinatown, a 200-year-old woman with a 9-year-old body, white robots, a human-liver-eating psychopath, a golem, a porcelain dragon, and a snake goddess with a crush on him. There's also a woman obsessed with chicken sex. Then Malone meets Posh Lane, a gorgeous call girl who's desperate to quit her pimp.

Romantic sparks ignite between Posh and Malone, but Posh's past suddenly catches up with her in a BIG way. To save Posh, Malone agrees to run a quest for Earth's new rulers, the Forks. But, Malone has no idea that agreeing to the Fork's odd request will send him on the weirdest trip he's ever been on in his life.

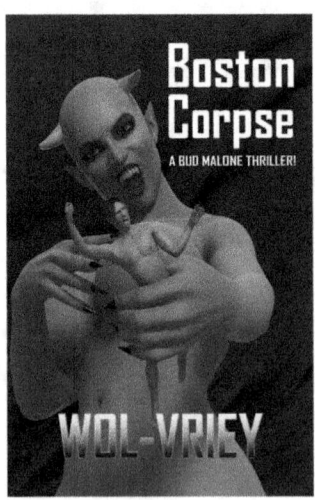

BOSTON CORPSE (BUD MALONE #2)

MAGIC CAN BE MURDER! - Drag queen Lucy Tang is back in Boston, and is hell-bent on settling her vindetta against casino owner Sookie Ling. And suddenly, Bud Malone, PI, has the case of his life to resolve.

When Boston's robot police force are baffled by a mind transfer case, they come to Malone for help. The one person who can likely help Malone out here is the witch Soledad Bathory. But Soledad seems to know a lot more than she's telling him. It's a case not made easier when Malone meets Soledad's beautiful cousin, Josephine 'Slave' Bailey. Slave has her own plans for Malone, most of which involve teaching him BDSM and making him her new Master.

Oh, and Rick Rogers owes Sookie Ling a whole lot of money, a gambling debt that's going to be literally Hell to pay!

BOSTON CORPSE - Not your average detective novel!

Burning Bulb
PUBLISHING

WOL-VRIEY
BIZARRO AND TRANSGRESSIVE FICTION

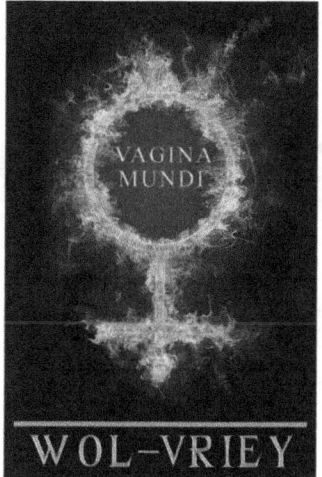

VAGINA MUNDI

Rachel Risk is a professional thief with super-strong hair that can stretch like tentacles to manipulate objects. Ashley Status has both a digitally augmented brain, and 'muscle-purses' in her arms and legs in which she stores inflatable objects—cars, guns, rocket launchers, etc.

When Raye is framed as the fall girl in a jewel robbery, the pair flee Chicago's vengeful robot gangsters and take refuge in the Hotel Bizarre, where the gorgeous 'vagina singer,' Femina, is performing for a week.

But the Hotel Bizarre is even stranger than its name suggests, and very soon Raye and Ash are involved in an deadly adventure, a struggle for survival the likes of which they'd never imagined possible—with loads of deviant sex, drugs, music, and violence at every turn. And just what is the old woman in the skin desert really doing with all those cats glued to her walls?

VAGINA MUNDI—a Bizarro Hymn in praise of WOMAN!

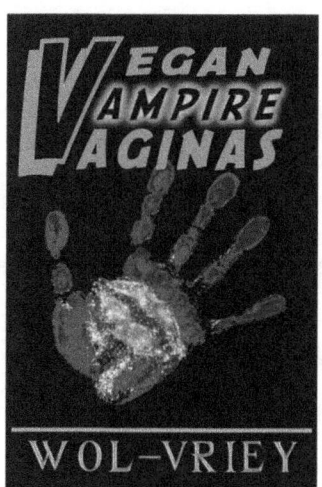

VEGAN VAMPIRE VAGINAS

The biggest bank heist in US history. And Tom Palmer can't remember pulling it off. And no, this isn't your standard case of amnesia. After a one-night-stand gone horribly wrong, Boston salesman Tom Palmer wakes up with a vagina implanted in his left hand. Then his day gets worse.

Tom is transported across space-time to a nightmare version of Boston, one where the Bizarro virus has transformed half the population into cannibals. Worst of all, Tom discovers that in this new Boston, he's the infamous gangster Pussypalm, wanted for robbing the Federal Reserve Bank of Boston a year ago. He also learns that the vagina in his hand is prophetic, i.e. it talks . . . after sex.

With 130 people left dead during his bank heist and six billion dollars missing, Tom knows he's living on borrowed time. It is in his best interests not to remember anything. Because once he does . . .

Burning Bulb
PUBLISHING

WOL-VRIEY
BIZARRO AND TRANSGRESSIVE FICTION

VEGAN ZOMBIE APOCALYPSE

In the post-apocalypse worlderness, zombies rule the earth. They're allergic to meat, and brains literally make them explode. Zombies now eat blood potatoes, parasitic tubers grown in the flesh of humancows corralled in maximum security farms. Two fugitives meet in the ancient ruins of Texas. The first is Soil 15-f, a womancow who's escaped her farm a week before she's due to be killed and her blood potato crop harvested. The second fugitive is Able Kane, former head necros food technician, now sentenced to death for heresy. But Soil is no ordinary humancow.

Unknown to herself, she's the vegan zombie agricultural revolution, and the zombies desperately want her back. And the necros equally desperately want Able Kane dead. He's fled with a forbidden discovery which will reshape the world for the worse if used. And Able is just hardheaded/misguided enough to use it.

MELANIE NEMESIS CATCHPOLE

In Springfield, Massachusetts, Melanie Catchpole is hired to fetch back a magic teddy bear worth millions of dollars from a warehouse across town. Problem is, the warehouse is down in Springfield's O-Zone-that totally weird sector of the city where Bizarro fell to Earth. The 'O' is a fairytale land, a place where dreams and nightmares literally live and breathe.

Worse still, the gingers—mutant cannibals—prowl the O. The gingers have already eaten everyone else Melanie's employers sent to get back the magic teddy bear.

Accompanied by the handsome but ruthless Doug Fisher (who she finds sexy but doesn't dare entrust her heart to), Melanie enters the O-Zone. Melanie and Doug are instantly caught up in an adventure they'd never have believed credible even if written as fiction . . . and Melanie's used to experiencing the very weird as the norm.

And now, additionally, there's a mystery to unravel: What does the dark, freezing-cold being called The Fixer want with Mary, the barkeep's daughter?

Burning Bulb
PUBLISHING

WOL-VRIEY
BIZARRO AND TRANSGRESSIVE FICTION

BIG TROUBLE IN LITTLE ASS

From Bizarro master storyteller Wol-vriey comes a truly weird western tale that will leave you awe-struck and on the edge of your seat...

In the town named Little Ass, tight-assed prostitute Rosa over-hears a gunslinger's plans to assassinate rancher Edison Bennett. Once the badass Bennett learns of the plot, he ensures there'll be hell to pay for any attempt on his life!

Yes, it's going to take all of gunslinger Jude's shooting prowess, his eclectic collection of strange firearms, a trusty horse that requires an owners' manual, and the help of the lovely and invigorating Nell (who's EXTREMELY odd when the going gets weird), to survive the Bizarro hell that Edison Bennett unleashes in order to hold onto the land that he'd stolen from Madam Zizi.

BIZARRO 101 (A BASIC PRIMER)

Welcome to the strange place:

A collection of 37 flash fiction stories designed to introduce one to the Bizarro/New Weird Genre.

Weird, dreamy, nightmarish, absurd, sad, surreal, humorous . . . this collection of tales is all this and more.

***

"This primer is the very essence of any and all styles and types of Bizarro writing. Wol-vriey collects, distills, and bottles up these 37 tiny stories for your sensory enjoyment. This is an absolute must-read for anyone new to the genre, because it demonstrates the scope of what Bizarro is, and what it can be."
— Teresa Pollack, Bizarro commentator and blogger

Burning Bulb
PUBLISHING

BELLY TIMBER

From the writers of Darkened Hills, Detour to Armageddon and Night of the Living Dead comes a novel unlike any other...

In the 1800's, ordinary people learned the secret of the Kala and undertook extraordinary measures to rid the earth of this evil. This is their story.

For John McCormick, life on the Indiana frontier held nothing but promise. His settlement along the White River would soon become the crossroads of America. Friends and family from back in Ohio and other points east were all making plans to see what all the fuss was about in the newly-formed city of Indianapolis. Yes, things were good. John had his general store and his friend George Pogue had his blacksmith business. Claims were being staked and relations with the native Indians were amicable. The town was growing and nothing could be better... or so he thought.

In Ohio, an evil was brewing. The Lecky Family, a group of ruthless Mongolian nomads, had made their way to America and were practicing their cannibalistic religion of Kala with reckless abandon. No one was safe, not even John McCormick's family.

Burning Bulb
PUBLISHING

EVERYTHING HERE IS A NIGHTMARE
Collected Works Vol 1.

"Pyles makes it look easy. His characters come instantly alive with the cocksure verve and swagger of rock stars."
- Daniel Knauf, creator of HBO's "Carnivale,"
Executive Producer/Writer, ABC's "The Blacklist."

The critically acclaimed author of Demons, Dolls and Milkshakes returns with fifteen tales of horror and suspense with Everything Here is a Nightmare.

From zombies in the old west, to a young boy tempted by the Devil. From vampires with romantic longing, to an abandoned lighthouse haunted by vengeful spirits. From a serial killer getting unholy justice, to a haunted English race car, Nelson W Pyles invites you to explore a landscape of fear, suspense and horror.

Take his hand and hold on tight. Remember that whatever you find here, whatever you see, no matter what you might think it could be... know this: Everything Here is a Nightmare.

Burning Bulb
PUBLISHING

ANTHOLOGIES
BIZARRO AND TRANSGRESSIVE FICTION

THE BIG BOOK OF BIZARRO SPECIAL KINDLE EDITIONS

OTHER AWESOME COLLECTIONS

 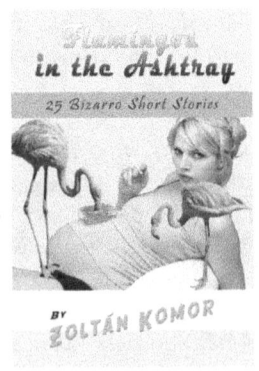 

Burning Bulb
PUBLISHING

ANTHOLOGIES
BIZARRO AND TRANSGRESSIVE FICTION

THE BIG BOOK OF BIZARRO

The Big Book of Bizarro brings together the peculiar prose of an international cast of the most grotesquely-gonzo, genre-grinding modern writers who ever put pen to paper (or mouse to pad), including:

NIGHT OF THE LIVING DEAD horror writers John Russo & George Kosana; HUSTLER MAGAZINE erotica contributors Eva Hore, Andrée Lachapelle, & J. Troy Seate and established Bizarro genre authors D. Harlan Wilson, William Pauley III, Wol-vriey, Laird Long, Richard Godwin and so many more!

From Alien abductions to Zombie sex, The Big Book of Bizarro contains OVER FIFTY STORIES of the most outrélandish transgressive fiction that you'll ever lay your capricious and curious hands upon!

WESTWARD HOES

Nine outlaw writers rode into town from obscurity to pen nine tantalizing tales of horror and fantasy, and leaving once they branded their own personal marks on the weird western genre and became living legends of the American Frontier experience.

Like drunken Indian scouts, the writers fervidly tracked down and captured the Western genre, tore off its fashionable veneer and ravished its exposed essence.

So belly up to the bar with your favorite soiled dove and enjoy perusing these thrilling tales of Old West debauchery, danger and desire; compiled by the publisher of The Big Book of Bizarro and featuring the bizarro novella *Big Trouble in Little Ass* by Wol-vriey.

Burning Bulb
PUBLISHING

GARY LEE VINCENT'S
DARKENED
THE WEST VIRGINIA VAMPIRE SERIES

DARKENED HILLS

When evil descends on a small West Virginia town, who will survive?

Jonathan did not start out his life to become a rambler, it just worked out that way. William was a troubled youth with something to hide. Both were from Melas, a small town tucked away in the West Virginia hills... a town where disappearances are happening more and more frequently.

After the suicide of a wanted serial killer, the townsfolk thought the nightmare was over. But when a centuries-old vampire is discovered they find out the hard way it's just getting started. Dark secrets can only stay hidden for so long and when the devil comes to collect, there will be hell to pay. Can Jonathan and William find a way to stop the vampire before it's too late? Find out in *Darkened Hills!*

DARKENED HOLLOWS

In the heart-stopping sequel to the award-winning *Darkened Hills*, Jonathan and William must return to West Virginia to face possible criminal charges stemming from their last visit to the damned town of Melas, where both had narrowly escaped the clutches of a vampire seethe.

And as livestock start mysteriously getting murdered with all of their blood drained, worried farmers are searching for answers - leaving the local Sheriff and his deputy racing against time to learn the cause before a more violent crime is committed.

Burning Bulb
PUBLISHING

WWW.DARKENEDHILLS.COM

GARY LEE VINCENT'S
DARKENED
THE WEST VIRGINIA VAMPIRE SERIES

DARKENED WATERS

When the world goes to hell, the chosen must arise!

As Talman Cane orchestrates a flood of epic proportions in this third installment of the *Darkened* series the towns of Melas and Tarklin are caught completely off guard by the deluge. Hell-bent on finishing what they started, the evil brothers return to the lunatic asylum to take care of the witnesses and add to the ever-growing army of the undead.

Aided by Lucifer himself and the insane vampire demon Legion, the stage is set to channel all of the forces of hell to come forth. In an all-out race to survive, Jonathan, William, and Amanda soon discover they are up against impossible odds as Lucifer opens the Gateway to Hell, ushering in the zombie apocalypse and the End Times.

Find out who will survive this cosmic battle of the ages in *Darkened Waters!*

DARKENED SOULS

Melas and the Madison House are about to be rebuilt.
True evil is about to be reborne!

Young ex-priest and vampire-killer William is drawn back to the West Virginian town that almost killed him, where his vampire arch-enemy Victor Rothenstein still stalks the earth.

The town of Melas lies destroyed after the battle of the End of Days. But why is wealthy Jackie Nixon so eager to rebuild it using the bone dust of murdered souls?

Terrible evil has visited before, but the Gateway to Hell is about to be reopened in a horrific climax. And this time – it's personal.

WWW.DARKENEDHILLS.COM

Burning Bulb
PUBLISHING

DAVID J. FAIRHEAD

"David Fairhead writes compelling stories that offer very human characters and very inhuman monsters. There is no subtlety in Fairhead's imagination - he is simply dying to scare the hell out of you." - Nelson W Pyles author of DEMONS, DOLLS AND MILKSHAKES

THE FALL

Hopelessness... How do you protect your loved ones when Hell itself opens its insidious mouth?
Horror... Nightmarish Creatures invade your world and there is nowhere to hide.
Blood... How long can you hold out before they come for you?
Pain... Where do you run to avoid being eaten alive by monsters with a voracious appetite for your flesh?
Screams... While you selfishly run for your own life.
Questions... Who is to blame? Where did they come from? How many people survived...and how does the human race find the means to fight back?

THE FALL OF TOMORROW is man's last tale of desperation told by those that are striving to salvage some hope against a ravenous bastion of evil beasts bent on ruling our world.

DWELLING IN THE DARK

From David J. Fairhead, author of the FALL OF TOMORROW, comes DWELLING IN THE DARK- A soulful anthology of creeping terror to keep you up in the small hours with horror set in the past, present and future. Overlapping bits of puzzle fitting each other, before and after The Fall of Tomorrow.

A place where three children facing a monstrous foe can only pray that their bloody summer would just come to an end. Go back to the 1960's- THE COMMUNE where overindulging hippies use a mage's diary to control the end of the world, only to see first-hand that their drug induced visions have horrific ramifications. Where a young boy's visit to a haunted house becomes a lesson in RESIDUAL morality. The story, DEEPER- plunges two brothers into a sinkhole only to find they were being hunted by an insidious creature from its depths. Visit the old west as hero Dekker Collins battles evil gunslingers in DEMONEYE.

And so much more...!

Burning Bulb
PUBLISHING

www.FairlyDarkProductions.com

ZAKARY MCGAHA
BIZARRO AND TRANSGRESSIVE FICTION

SEA OF MEDIUM-TO-HIGH PITCHED NOISES

The zombie apocalypse is changing; the world is coming to an odd demise; and a serial killer tries to change his ways and redeem himself before it all goes away. Now, Crabby has entered the world he left behind; the world of the undead. And things are changing. Everything will come to an end. In this new wave of the apocalypse, everything changes every five minutes. And death would be an absolute luxury. Psychological torment meets physical bloodletting in Sea of Medium-to-High Pitched Noises.

PARK MASTERS

Bad breakups, Bigfoot costumes, ghost bears, and more. Park Masters is a wacky, intelligent, quirky comedy about the power relationships have on people, good or bad. Also, it's just plain fun!

Burning Bulb
PUBLISHING

WEST VIRGINIA - THEMED
HUMORROROTICA

BY RICH BOTTLES JR.

HELLHOLE WEST VIRGINIA

From the heights of Mothman's perch high atop the Silver Bridge in Point Pleasant to the depths of Hellhole Cavern in Pendleton County, evil lurks within the shadows as the sun sets upon the haunted hills and hollows of West Virginia.

Bizarro author Rich Bottles Jr. blows the coffin lid off horror genre clichés with this tour de force cast of Eco-friendly vampires, beach-yearning zombies and sex-starved she-devils.

LUMBERJACKED

If you are easily offended or do not possess a truly depraved sense of humor, this story may not be the light summer reading fare you desire. As for the four feisty female freshmen stranded on top of West Virginia's third highest mountain, they have no choice but to experience the sick, twisted debauchery and perverted mayhem described deep inside the tight unbroken bindings of this horrific missive.

Lumberjacked takes the reader to a nightmarish world where character development and aesthetic integrity are prematurely cut short by the swinging axes of maniacal lumberjacks, who are hell bent on death and destruction in the remote forests of Appalachia. And at the climax, when paranoia crosses over to the paranormal, Lumberjacked makes Deliverance look like a family raft trip down the Lower Gauley.

THE MANACLED

What happens when twin brothers lease out the former West Virginia State Penitentiary with the false purpose of filming a documentary on supernatural phenomena, but their true intention is to make a pornographic movie?

Chaos ensues as the disturbed spirits of murdered convicts, along with the reanimated dead from the neighboring Indian Burial Mound, take their vengeance on the unwary and undressed trespassers.

Zombies, ghosts, mobsters and porn collide in this bizarro tale from horror author Rich Bottles Jr.

Burning Bulb
PUBLISHING

![RISE OF THE DEAD — AN EARTH-SHATTERING ANTHOLOGY OF ZOMBIE TERROR]

Featuring Stories By:

John A. Russo   Tyson Blue   E.L. Stice   Nelson W. Pyles
Andy Rausch   Stephen Spignesi   R.D. Riley   Zakary McGaha
David J. Fairhead   Gary Lee Vincent   David C. Hayes   Rachel Montgomery
Paul Victor Wargelin   David F. Walker   William Vitka
Rich Bottles Jr.   Douglas Brode

RISE OF THE DEAD - a collection of seventeen tales of unspeakable zombie terror. Featuring a foreword and short story by John A. Russo!

www.TheJohnRusso.com

Burning Bulb
PUBLISHING

NIGHT OF THE LIVING DEAD

Why does Night of the Living Dead hit with such chilling impact?

Is it because everyday people in a commonplace house are suddenly the victims of a monstrous invasion? Or is it because the ghouls who surround the house with grasping claws were once ordinary people, too?

Decide for yourself as you read, and the horror grips you.

All the cannibalism, suspense and frenzy of the smash-hit move are here in the novel.

www.TheJohnRusso.com

"THE BLAZING SADDLES OF SEX SATIRES!" - GEORGINA SPELVIN

THE BOOBY HATCH

It's a Zany Love Lab where
Looney Professors Measure Pleasure!

From Legendary Horror Writer
JOHN A. RUSSO

THE BOOBY HATCH

With NIGHT OF THE LIVING DEAD, John Russo helped
blaze a path in the horror genre that has never been equalled.
In this hillarious erotic novel, he blazes a path through the
wild, zany Sex Revolution of the 1970s.

Sweet, innocent Cherry Jankowski works for Joyful Novelties,
where she tests sex toys ranging from the ridiculous to the
sublime. But she can't find love or peace of mind and her
efforts are hampered by a Peeping Tom, an exhibitionist, a
cross-dressing boyfriend, a quack psychiatrist, and even her
own product-testing partner, Marcello Fettucini, who can't
get it up anymore and is scared of losing his job!

www.TheJohnRusso.com

Burning Bulb
PUBLISHING

THE ACADEMY

The Academy. It's every parent's dream, turning their little darlings into geniuses, superachievers, perfect little children.

And if there's a problem, the Academy fixes that too. It's a simple operation. Just a little device. Then a teeny pink scar on a tender little skull . . .

One boy knows the secret. Now he wants his mind back. But it's much, much too late. Too late for anything but the ugly feelings. The bad feelings. The messy sexy feelings. The knife-cold hatred, the murderous rage, for total, screaming, blood-drenching revenge . . .

www.TheJohnRusso.com

Burning Bulb
PUBLISHING

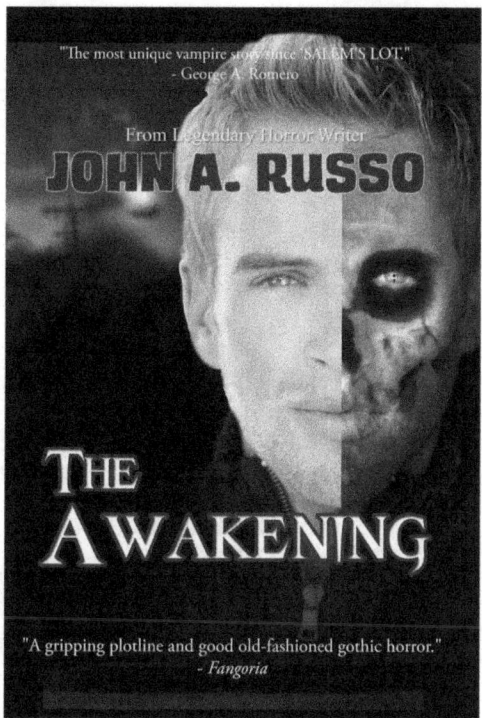

"The most unique vampire story since 'SALEM'S LOT."
- George A. Romero

From Legendary Horror Writer
JOHN A. RUSSO

THE
AWAKENING

"A gripping plotline and good old-fashioned gothic horror."
- *Fangoria*

THE AWAKENING

For two hundred years, he has rested. Now he rises. Now he will be satisfied. Nothing can stop him. No one can resist him.

Benjamin Latham is young and handsome, his eighteenth-century mind wakened to a bizarre twentieth-century world. And there is the need deep within . . . an animal need, frightening, murderous, unholy . . . a vital need that must be fed.

And with his need comes a power over men and women to do his bidding, to quiet his dark craving . . .

Until the murders begin. And the inquiries. All suggesting the same hideous truth.

Now Benjamin must find a sanctuary: a lover, a partner, a friend. Someone who can share his darkness. Someone he can lead to . . . The Awakening.

www.TheJohnRusso.com

Burning Bulb
PUBLISHING

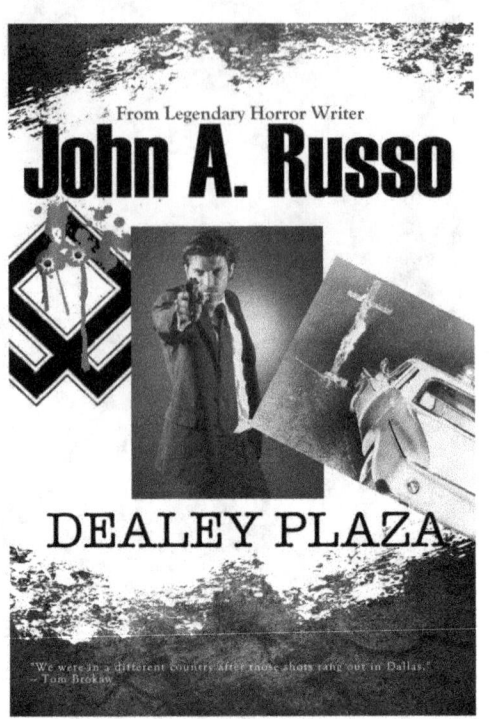

DEALEY PLAZA

From legendary horror and suspense writer JOHN RUSSO comes a harrowing tale where no one is safe!

Dealey Plaza is one of the most notorious places in America, and when youthful conspiracy buffs go there in 1964 to stage their own reenactment of the Kennedy Assassination, four of them are brutally murdered ~ the first victims of a hate-filled legacy that continues for four more decades.

The survivors of that long-ago Dallas trip, each of them now icons of the American way of life, are about to be honored ~ or killed.

Who will live and who will die? Will it be country-western star Lori McCoy? Her loving husband? Her scheming ex-husband? Or the case-hardened FBI agent and longtime friend who risks his life trying to protect them?

www.DealeyPlazaBook.com

Burning Bulb
PUBLISHING

"A sense of infectious fun, straight from the author's pen."
– Nightmare Library

From Legendary Horror Writer
JOHN A. RUSSO

LIVING THINGS

"Russo carries his talent for the horrific neatly over into the novel form."
– West Coast Review of Books

LIVING THINGS

Beneath the shimmering Miami sun sprawls one of the Mafia's biggest empires, a glittering worldof lavish beachfront mansions, neon-painted nightclubs, beautiful women, expensive cars—and absolute control over the state's billion-dollar drug trade. But, one by one, its ganglords and henchmen are falling prey to a new rival. His powers are fueled by monstrous ancient rituals; his hellish undead legions slaughter mobsters and innocent citizens alike, his unholylust for power is virtually unstoppable.

Now a burned-out ex-detective and a brilliant anthropologist must enter a gruesome, nightmare world to fight this master of malevolence and illusion. Their time is short, their weapons few, and they face an ultimate, terrifying choice - annihilation or the loss of their souls to the eternal torment of those who never die. . .

www.TheJohnRusso.com

Burning Bulb
PUBLISHING

ELVIS PRESLEY, CIA ASSASSIN BY ANDY RAUSCH

"I can guarantee you. Read this book and you'll never look at Elvis the same way again!"
~ Douglas Brode, author of ELVIS CINEMA AND POPULAR CULTURE

SOON TO BE A MAJOR MOTION PICTURE

In 1970, singer Elvis Presley secretly met with President Richard Nixon. This new comedic novel imagines that Presley became a Central Intelligence Agency operative, eventually moving up through the ranks to become a skilled assassin.

Presented in an oral history fashion, the book tells us about Presley's secret transformation by the people who knew him best.

Did he fake his death in 1977? Was Presley involved with the Watergate scandal? The Iran hostage crisis? Communicating with aliens?

Read this book to find out the answers to these and many more questions.

Burning Bulb
PUBLISHING

MAD WORLD BY ANDY RAUSCH

"*Mad World* is dark, twisted, no-holds-barred fun."
—Jason Starr, author of *Bust*, *Slide*, and *The Max*

EVERYONE'S PLAYING AN ANGLE IN THE CITY OF ANGELS

Mad World tells the stories of a black hitman who doubles as a university professor, a Catholic priest who longs to be a gangster, a would-be author from Kansas, a gay phone sex operator who claims he's straight, a group of rich twentysomethings playing a deadly game of life and death, a vicious Mafia boss, and a sleazy Hollywood movie director. As each of their stories intersect, the body count piles up and the action comes nonstop in this tense, white-knuckle thriller by first-time author Andy Rausch.

"A wild ride. If you like it gangster, *Mad World* delivers."
—Daniel Birch, author of *Get Some*

Burning Bulb
PUBLISHING

BLOODLETTING: A TALE OF REVENGE BY ANDY RAUSCH

"Relentless… Addictive… The kind of nightmare you don't want
to wake up from."
—Heywood Gould, screenwriter of *Rolling Thunder*

He was just an average Joe. But when he finds his family held at
gunpoint by merciless thugs, he's told he must murder a Mafia
chieftain if he ever wishes to see his loved ones again.

Against all odds, Joe keeps his end of the bargain, but the criminals
don't. Now at his wits end, Joe is pushed beyond his breaking point
and forced to exact bloody revenge against those who've done him
and his family wrong in this powerful and violent novella by author
Andy Rausch (*Mad World*).

"Andy Rausch has a tight noir style that combines gritty, realistic drama
with a cinematic flair that makes for a powerful, compelling (somewhat
Stephen Kingesque), authentically visual reading experience."
—Stephen Spignesi, author of *Dialogues*

Burning Bulb
PUBLISHING

THE TAILSMAN

From the creators of *The Big Book of Bizarro* and *Westward Hoes* comes a new comic unlike anything you have ever seen!

He's hot on the trail, looking for some *tail...*

Sly Franko was a man of the West, a forger of the wild frontier. Like the Country Western song that would be written years after he died, the words, "Faster horses, younger women, and more money," seemed to be the anthem of this horn dog cowboy.

Franko would ride into town on a blazing saddle, find the closest saloon to wet the whistle, belly up to a good card game, and find him a hot-loving hussy to get his cowpoke on with.

However, Sly might have met his match when a visit to bathroom leads to terror and death. Can Sly and his poker buddies solve the mystery before more of the townsfolk are murdered? Find out in this exciting premier issue of *The Tailsman*!

WWW.BURNINGBULBCOMICS.COM

THE HAGS OF BLACK COUNTY

by Michelle Bowser

Ruled by a committee of Hags, and fueled by toothless rivalries, Black County lurks just far enough out of the way to be completely unnoticed by the rest of civilization. Its inhabitants have been mentally warped for generations and the land itself seems to have the power to drive anyone unlucky enough to visit into ridiculous hillbilly madness. When a construction Company needs to bury a pipeline through its ludicrous hills and valleys, a twisted charm goes to work and every aspect of already bizarre Black County life takes a gory turn for the hysterical. Take a preposterous trip along with its citizens, both native and new, through escapades such as the Hag parade, the grand opening of Madame Skunk's House of Ill Repute, the demolition derby riot and the rabid, zombie clown apocalypse.

THE ABANDONED SOUL

by Daniel Sellers

After spending most of his 20s in a drug and alcohol fueled daze, a young man finally hits rock bottom. Having used up his friends and their good graces, he ends up squatting in an abandoned house. Forcibly sobering he begins to realize that he is not alone in this abandoned house. Left with one last friend and a mountain of regrets, he must decide if this presence is a guilty conscience, or a malicious hunter.

WE WISH YOU A HAPPY KILLDAY

by Jason Heroux

"We Wish You a Happy Killday" is the story of an international b eloved holiday called "Killday" where one day a year everyone over the age of fifteen is permitted to register for a license allowing them to kill one other person. But this year Chad Ovenstock doesn't feel like killing anyone. His friends and family urge him to participate in the festivities, but he can't seem to get into the holiday spirit. On the day before Killday Chad comes in contact with Ambrose, an old friend who suffered a nervous breakdown and is now part of The One Ant Army, a mysterious cult dedicated to making the future disappear. When the holiday finally arrives Chad refuses to participate and tries to survive on his own, surrounded by constant gunfire, countless corpses, and the nagging suspicion that Ambrose may have secretly brainwashed him into becoming a member of The One Ant Army cult.

Burning Bulb
PUBLISHING